Sign up for our newsletter to hear about new and upcoming releases.

www.ylva-publishing.com

Emily Waters

Honey in the Marrow

honey in the marrow,
buzzing at the bone
if the grief cannot consume you, dig the stinger out
this grief is not your home

ACKNOWLEDGMENTS

Thank you to Astrid, Lee Winter, and the Ylva team for coming to my little corner of the internet and scooping me up. This has been a very exciting journey. Thank you to Alissa McGowan and the other editors who helped whip this story into shape. Thank you to my partner Jacob for supporting me by giving me the time, space, encouragement, and furniture I needed to work on this book. And thank you, especially, to Charity and Zowie, who both said, rather emphatically, "DO IT!" when I told them about publishing this book. I did it.

CHAPTER 1

Stella Carter wakes up and reaches for her phone. For the first time in weeks, it feels like something is going to happen today that actually matters. The sunlight slants across her bed, and she rolls over, sweaty and uncomfortable. She has trouble sleeping at night, and when she does finally fall asleep, she sleeps half the day away, rising only when hunger insists.

It's almost noon. She has one missed text from Addie.

See you in a few hours!

Maybe fifty-one is a little long in the tooth to be taking on a roommate, but when her niece called three months after Ron's funeral, saying she wanted to move to California and asking if she might stay with Stella for a while, it made sense to invite her to move into the spare bedroom. Stella's husband is dead and buried, so she's always alone in the house.

Maybe that's what Addie was angling for all along. Stella offered to fly out to Nashville and make the drive with her, but that was met with protest. Stella didn't force the issue because she didn't really want to do it, and besides, Addie is twenty-three and perfectly able to make a trip like that alone.

Now that her niece's arrival is imminent, Stella looks around her little bungalow with new eyes and mounting dismay. She's been here a month and a half, but it looks like she moved in yesterday. Not wanting anything to do with the duplex she lived in with Ron, after he died, she used the money from his life insurance to buy a two-bedroom house in her old neighborhood, thinking maybe she could start her life over again, as if she just moved to LA.

As if she could undo the last eight years.

The past few months have been unsettling. One day, she's a high-powered prosecutor, a special assistant deputy district attorney for Los Angeles County, married to a deputy chief of the LAPD, and the next, she's a widow on indefinite leave, haunting the five rooms of her new house.

She had meant to get things more ready for Addie, but the days had slipped away from her, each day bleeding out and quickly away while she did nothing. She took a month of bereavement leave from the district attorney's office and then decided on a whim not to go back. Part of her restart on life. She wants to be the old Stella Carter, a different Stella Carter. The one she was before she got married, before she threw away a thriving law career and left Nashville for sun-soaked Southern California, desperate for distance from her family.

It was the boldest and most daring thing she ever did. But when she arrived in LA, she was paired with a team of homicide detectives who showed her the worst parts of the city: the rapes, the murders, the seedy underbelly of the entertainment industry—people with money who thought themselves untouchable.

What she really is searching for is life before that damn woman, Captain Murphy.

She closes her eyes, shakes her head. She's not going to think about any of that anymore.

Every room in this 1930s house is small, and though she got rid of most of her stuff when she moved, it still feels cluttered. Addie's room is the smaller bedroom, and while the coffee brews, Stella looks around at the stacked boxes and trash bags. She should unpack, clear the room, but the task seems insurmountable, like she couldn't possibly do it alone.

Nothing seems to work like it used to.

Addie arrives in the early afternoon, looking fresh and happy despite four days of driving cross-country. Her dyed blonde hair is growing out to its original light brown color, and she wears it just above her shoulders. Stella shows her around and listens to her happy chatter. Addie's sedan is packed to the brim, but it takes her less than an hour to drag her luggage and boxes into the house. Stella feels exhausted just watching her.

"I might go lie down for a while," Stella says.

Addie nods. "Sure. I've got this."

Within the first week, Addie has shelved all of Stella's books, including from the boxes she left unpacked. Addie organizes them by color, and the rainbow spines detract from the scuffed paint on the built-in shelves.

Addie photographs the books from several different angles. "For Instagram," she explains.

As if that means anything to Stella.

Then Addie moves some of the furniture from the garage into the living room. In no time at all, the house feels lived in.

Within three weeks, Addie has a bartending job and instructs Stella to tell her parents, if they ask, that Addie has a serving job. Stella doesn't care if Addie bartends—the money is better—but she also doesn't want her out-of-state niece working in a dive bar where people are more likely to commit crimes, people Stella spent years putting in jail.

But Addie tells her it's at the Irish pub, Casey's.

"That's a cop bar," Stella says.

"Is it?" Addie asks innocently.

Casey's is within walking distance from both the police administration building and the district attorney's office. Over the years, Stella had more than her fair share of wine there. It's not exactly her style, but the homicide detectives she worked with liked it well enough.

"What could go wrong in a bar full of cops?" Addie asks.

Stella stares her down. "Maybe I'll get a job there too." Stella's joking, but it comes out sour. She needs to figure out what she wants to do. She's waiting for something to fall into her lap, for someone to come rescue her.

"Let's go to Target," Addie suggests, changing the subject.

Retail therapy. "Okay."

She lets Addie drive the hybrid she bought a year into her promotion to special assistant. Ron's newer SUV sits in her one-car garage, untouched.

They're pulling into the Target parking lot when Stella says, "Hey, do you want Uncle Ron's car?"

Addie glances over at her. "What?"

"It's only a few years old," she says. "Real good condition. It's just sitting there."

"I have a car."

"You could sell yours." Stella glances out at the glowing red bullseye on the front of the store. "I could sell Ron's car, I guess, but it makes more sense to keep the one with fewer miles." She looks back at Addie. "I don't know anything about cars, really, besides that."

"Maybe. I'll think about it."

Inside the store, Stella grabs a cart and trails behind her niece. Addie checks the list on her phone but tosses seemingly random things into the cart too: a candle that smells like piña colada, a pink mug that says *Hello Gorgeous* in a curly rose gold font, and a set of three wooden cutting boards. She also buys a pack of twenty-five velvet hangers and a plastic laundry basket.

Stella has been undressing in the laundry room and using the washing machine as her hamper. It might be pathetic, but it's efficient.

They go through the clothes section on the way to the registers. Addie buys three pairs of black jeans and several black tank tops.

"Jesus, who died?" Stella blurts out.

Then she feels stupid and sad.

Addie wore a dark green dress to Ron's funeral, a tiny bit of color in an otherwise gray day. Stella remembers the green dress, the yellow flowers on the casket, Captain Murphy's long red hair, pinned up because she was in uniform. The cap came off one of Stella's lipsticks, staining the lining of her purse, and she'd had to throw the purse away. Then she started throwing other things away, and then she decided to move.

"It's my uniform for the bar," Addie mumbles. "Let's go."

Back in the car, Stella calls for a pizza. When she hangs up, she asks, "How did you even know about Casey's?"

"How does anyone know about anything?"

"Is that supposed to be rhetorical?" Stella snaps.

"I found it on the internet," Addie says. "If it bugs you so much, I don't have to work there."

"It doesn't bug me. I just momentarily forgot that this is the world's tiniest town."

Later, Stella eats pizza standing in the kitchen while Addie's on the phone in her bedroom. There aren't a lot of secrets in this house. The insulation isn't great, and Addie's door is open anyway.

"I don't know. I haven't started yet," Addie is saying as she rustles her shopping bags. A pause. "It's fine. The house is really cute, and we're getting settled."

Stella strains to hear what her sister-in-law—Addie's mama—is saying on the other end, but of course she can't.

"Yeah," Addie says. "I mean, super depressed, but wouldn't you be?"

Stella dunks her crust into the container of ranch dressing, and it drips on her shirt on the way to her mouth.

"She just isn't doing anything. I think if I can get her doing something, anything at all, she'll feel better… I don't know. I haven't been here that long."

Stella realizes that Addie is probably talking about her. Is she depressed? She looks down at the ranch on her shirt, the dirty kitchen, today's half-empty pizza box sitting on the empty pizza box from two days ago.

She's just lazy. She's always been lazy, and now Ron isn't here to snap her out of it. Ron isn't here because someone got into the police administration building and randomly shot him. Now he's dead. That's all.

She isn't depressed. She's fifty-one, still a mess, just like she was at forty, just like she was at thirty-three, just like she was at seventeen. But she's doing fine, and she can start her life over.

Stella wipes her mouth with the back of her hand, wipes her hand on the hem of her shirt, then takes it off to dump into the washing machine.

She falls asleep in her bra and sweatpants, the fan in her bedroom squeaking as it spins.

Addie is home during the day a lot, though often she's sleeping. Often Stella is too. She tries to leave the house at least once a day, however sometimes all she can manage is a walk around the block or a drive to the nearby CVS to buy shampoo or razor blades or chocolate. Mostly chocolate. The checkout people there are starting to recognize her.

She comes into the house with a bag of mini chocolate bars and an avocado face mask. Addie is watching the coffeepot. She's wearing a pair of cotton shorts and a gray tank top. Her hair is in a messy bun on top of her head.

"Hey, sugar," Stella says, pushing up her sunglasses.

"Hey." Addie yawns and pulls a mug out of the dishwasher.

"How was work?"

"Kinda slow. They still have me on the taps. It'll be a while before I can work up to a cocktail shift." Addie's the newest, so mostly she pours beer and wine and buses tables. "You could come see it, you know."

"I've seen it," Stella reminds her.

"Not with me behind the bar," Addie says. "I've come to see you at work before."

Stella remembers the visit well. A sixteen-year-old Addie spent a week in California, sitting in courtrooms or hanging out either in Stella's office or with Ron, who showed her a few tourist attractions before Addie lost interest in sightseeing. Stella has always loved her niece, but she prefers this grown-up and independent version of Addie over the sulky teen from before whose eyes were ringed in black and arms in rubber bracelets practically up to her elbows.

"You could come tonight," Addie continues. "It's Thursday, so it won't be too crazy."

"Honey…" Stella is suddenly tired and desperate to get out of doing anything ever again that doesn't involve eating snacks while wearing soft pants.

"Drinks on the house," Addie says. "We have that wine you like from Markham Vineyards." The coffee machine beeps, and Addie turns to fix her cup, stirring in a little almond milk and a packet of sweetener. She takes a sip and says, "Oh, my God, that's amazing."

"I guess I could stop by," Stella concedes. "What time does your shift start?"

"Four thirty."

"Good." Stella nibbles at the ragged skin around her thumbnail. "Before the shift turnover. Maybe I won't see anyone who knows me."

"Would that be so bad?" Addie wraps both hands around her mug. Her green nail polish is so dark, it's nearly black, and it's chipped on both thumbnails. When Stella's nail polish chips, it looks awful. On Addie, it's effortlessly cool.

"I just don't need it right now," Stella says.

"I mean, it seems like you could use… And wouldn't they understand about Uncle Ron?"

"About Ron?" Stella says. "Sure. But I'm not one of them anymore." She shakes her head. "It doesn't matter." She doesn't expect her young niece to understand the inner workings of the criminal justice community.

Addie drinks her coffee, changes into workout clothes, and goes out for a run. She comes back, showers, and dresses for work. She wears all black—usually skinny jeans and a black tank top or T-shirt. Today she has on a black V-neck, the fabric so thin that Stella can see the straps of her sports bra through it.

Stella used to be that young once. Pretty and soft.

But when Stella was that age, she was in law school being recruited to one of the bigger private firms in Nashville. She spent nearly ten grueling years there before deciding she hated working for a private firm. So she went to work for the State of Tennessee for a number of years, thinking she might help people, and then, desperate for a change, moved to Los Angeles County.

Looking back now, she wishes she'd stuck it out with the private firm. She'd have a lot more money, and there would have been no Ron. A life without the sudden shock of heartbreak.

Addie sits on the floor at the base of her floor-length mirror, surrounded by makeup. Stella perches on the edge of her bed and watches her buff foundation over her already perfect skin, then concealer, then powder and bronzer and blush. She manages to wing out her black eyeliner evenly with a few, quick flicks. Stella doesn't tell Addie all that makeup isn't necessary because she used to hate people telling her that when she was younger.

"What are you going to wear?" Addie asks, digging out a pink tube of mascara from the bin of makeup at her knee.

"I dunno."

"You're going to shower?" Addie asks hesitantly.

"I guess."

"And wear real clothes?"

"Okay. Hint taken."

"I just think it'll do you some good to leave the house," Addie says. "Talk to someone who isn't me."

"You never said anything about talking to people." Stella means it as a joke, but it comes out somber.

"You'll be fine." Addie finishes her lashes and drops the mascara back into the bin on the hardwood floor. "Okay. I gotta go. I'll see you there."

On her way out, she leans over and pecks her aunt on the cheek. Then she grabs her hoodie and her purse and heads for the door, calling back, "And don't forget to brush your hair!"

Stella stands in the shower, staring at the water swirling around her feet and down the drain of the porcelain tub. She loses track of time, and it's nearly five by the time she manages to wash her hair and bathe. She lies on the bed, wrapped in a towel for another fifteen minutes before putting on underwear. She dons a pair of jeans and a soft pink sweater. She skips drying her hair, instead running some mousse through it to let it dry up into golden waves. She can't bring herself to put on makeup and simply rubs some moisturizer into her face.

Her car is filthy inside, so she decides to take Ron's SUV. A police administration parking pass hangs from the mirror. The inside of the car still smells a little like him, but she drives through her tears. She is determined not to let Addie down, not to promise her something and then let it drop.

When she arrives in the parking garage, she looks in the rearview mirror. There is no hiding her red, swollen eyes. She wipes her cheeks with her sleeve, her nose with the back of her hand, and decides she won't care about any of it. No one will notice in the dark bar anyway.

It's been years since she was in this bar, since before she married Ron, but everything looks exactly the same. All the high-top tables are occupied, so she plants herself on a stool at the end of the bar, up against the wall that separates the bar from the restrooms. Her back is to the entrance.

"Can I get you something?" a man's voice asks.

"Glass of merlot. Whatever the house is will be fine," she says without looking up.

He looks at her, tilts his head. "Are you Addie's aunt?"

She snaps her head up to look at him. He's tall, handsome, young. "Yeah."

He grins, revealing a row of perfect white teeth. "I'll tell her you're here."

"How'd you know?" Stella asks.

"You look like her," he says. "Merlot coming up."

Addie arrives before the wine. She smiles at Stella, a real smile that lights up her whole face. But when she gets closer, the smile falters.

"You're here. I was in the back, cutting lemons and limes. Are you okay?"

"I'm fine," Stella says. She nods in the general direction of the bar. "Place looks the same."

"Are you sure you're okay?"

"Yes, I swear. Just tired."

"Do you want some food? The kitchen just opened. There's happy hour stuff."

The handsome young bartender comes back, sets a glass of wine in front of her on the polished bar, then turns to another customer.

Stella sips the wine, and it's good, definitely not the house wine. There are worse things than sitting in a bar drinking a decent glass of wine, and Addie looks so hopeful that Stella can't cut and run now. She's made it this far, and there's no harm in eating something. "Maybe some nachos." There's nothing Irish about nachos, but it is LA, after all.

Addie nods. "I can make that happen."

Alone once more, Stella fishes around for her phone before realizing she left it in the SUV. Her purse is full of wrappers and crumpled receipts. She used to always keep a paperback with her, even if it was a trashy novel, but she hasn't been that person since before moving to Los Angeles. Maybe she should get a library card. Read something again. Hide out in someone else's problems for a while.

The bar is starting to fill up now that shifts are ending. No one who comes in is in uniform, but Stella can tell who the cops are and even recognizes a few of them, though she's hard-pressed to come up with names. There are probably a few lawyers too, but they rarely socialize with their assigned squads.

By the time her nachos come—a huge plate heaped high with chips and beans and melted cheese and sour cream and *pico de gallo*—the place has almost filled up. Other than the stool right next to her, the bar top is fully occupied.

The cute bartender brings her a refill.

She feels less edgy after she eats something. The wine helps too. And she doesn't want to admit that Addie was right, but it feels good to be out of the house and somewhere other than the drug store or the grocery store.

Addie stops by again with a little bowl of maraschino cherries. "Having fun?"

The bar is louder now. People have been feeding the digital jukebox. Stella has to read Addie's lips to understand what she's saying. "The nachos are good," she says. "Maybe it was good to get out."

"Make any friends?" Addie asks, glancing across the room at the entrance.

"Too old for all that." Stella knows exactly how haggard she looks. Who would find that attractive? "How about my bill?" She pops a sweet cherry into her mouth. It soothes the burn of the jalapenos that were in the nachos.

"Oh, please," Addie says. "No charge." She waves her hand in the air, then glances back at the front door again.

Stella looks over her shoulder to follow her gaze, but no one is there.

"I'll get you a box for the rest of the nachos," Addie offers.

"I don't need it."

"You have half a plate left." Addie pulls a small white towel out of her apron and wipes at the bar top. "You can take it home."

"I may not want it later."

"So I'll eat it," Addie says. "Stay right there."

Stella is hit with a familiar ping, and she realizes that something isn't quite right. In the courtroom, she was relentless and exacting, asking a defendant or a witness question after question until she asked just the right one to catch them in their made-up story. That's the feeling she's getting now, the desire to ferret out the truth, but she's out of practice and the itch has to claw its way up through the fog, through the weave of apathy and sorrow that she lives in. It takes her a few minutes to work out that Addie is the one lying.

She's not sure about what—Addie is on the other side of the room getting the to-go box, but she keeps looking at the door.

When Addie comes back, she slides the box across the bar and glances back again. And in that moment, her shoulders relax.

Stella looks up to see what Addie's been waiting for. Not a what, but a who.

Heat crawls up the back of Stella's neck as she looks back at her niece.

"Addison, what did you *do*?" Her voice is a furious hiss.

Addie shakes her head, says, "It's…it's a cop bar."

Stella wants to slink off the stool and slither out the back door, but it's too late. Captain Elizabeth Murphy is already walking toward her in a black pencil skirt, pale peach silk blouse, and black heels, a purse hanging off her shoulder. Her shoulder-length auburn hair is brushed back behind her ears.

Stella hasn't seen her since the funeral, and before that, not since Stella took a promotion and left Captain Murphy's homicide squad. But she remembers her clearly enough. Elizabeth, even out of full uniform, is hard to forget. With her high cheekbones and striking green eyes, she looks like a young Greer Garson, despite being ten years older than Stella.

At the funeral, Elizabeth placed her hand on Stella's arm, told her she was sorry for her loss, for the loss to the force. And then Lieutenant Sam Warren led her away.

Elizabeth stops at the bar where Addie is watching her and says, "You didn't tell her I was coming?"

"I thought… I… She wasn't going to—"

"Addie!" someone calls from across the bar.

"Sorry," she says and dashes away.

"Well," Elizabeth says, looking at Stella, "how are you doing?"

"I…" Panic washes over her. "I have to go."

She grabs her coat and heads for the door, abandoning her nachos and the rest of her wine.

"Wait a minute," Elizabeth calls out, but Stella is already pushing through the door and out into the chilly night air. By the time she gets back to the SUV, she's feeling light-headed.

The inside still smells like Ron, and she starts to cry again.

CHAPTER 2

Stella cried in the car all the way home. Cried in the bathroom brushing her teeth. And she cried herself to sleep. She wakes up a little hungover from crying, and she feels numb and weird and out of sorts. She can tell her face is swollen; the skin under her eyes is tender.

She blinks at the late morning light coming through the window—curtains are still on her list, especially now that spring is coming and the days are longer. Birds are squawking outside, and there's the sound of pans and plates clanging in the kitchen. She smells bacon.

Stella throws the covers off and tiptoes into the bathroom. But the pipes are old in this house. The toilet flushes loudly. The faucet squeaks when she turns it on to wash her hands and brush her teeth.

She looks up at her reflection. Her face *is* swollen. The attributes she once considered attractive—fair skin, curly blonde hair, dark brown eyes—now give her a hollow and washed-out appearance. How she feels on the inside is starting to seep out into her skin.

In the kitchen, Addie is stirring gravy at the stove. Fresh biscuits are on the counter. The bacon is set aside. Scrambled eggs are in the pan, ready to be served. Carters always apologize with food.

Addie's hair is pinned back out of her eyes, and she's wearing a pair of cotton shorts and a hooded sweatshirt. She looks like Stella's brother, Thom, but her coloring is Joyce's, her mama's.

Addie glances at Stella over her shoulder, then looks back at the gravy. "I hope you're hungry."

Stella looks at her niece and the spread and the late-morning light. "I'm always hungry," she says. Her voice is raspy from last night's tears.

Addie relaxes her shoulders.

Stella can't stay mad at her forever. She'll just have to...explain.

Addie has pushed aside the mail and other stuff on the kitchen table and set out plates and flatware. The food is good, but then Addie was always a good cook, always good at whatever she tried. Everyone was concerned when she graduated college without a solid career plan, but Stella doesn't worry about her. She'll be a good bartender, and if she finds another job later, she'll do well at that too. And if she decides to find someone to marry and pumps out a couple of kids, she'll no doubt be a great mom.

"Listen—" Stella begins once they've eaten.

"No," Addie interrupts. "I'm sorry. I forced you to do too much too fast."

Stella draws her fork through what's left of the gravy on her plate, watches it separate and come back together. "Honey, you don't understand."

"I mean, it was my idea, so I take full responsibility. And I get it. People grieve in their own way and take the time they need, and I should just stay out of it." Addie looks down at the hands in her lap. "So I'm really sorry."

Stella doesn't speak as she slowly processes what Addie said. By the time she has thought it through, Addie is stacking dishes in the sink.

"Addie," she says, "what do you mean it was your idea?"

"What?" She turns around.

"You said it was your idea. What did you mean?"

"To come out," Addie says.

"And to see Captain Murphy?"

"I mean, it's...it's a cop bar." Addie folds her arms in front of her chest. "You could have run into any number of people you know, right?"

"But you were watching the door," Stella says. "You were waiting for Elizabeth Murphy, weren't you?"

Addie turns away to pour the remainder of the gravy in the pan into a plastic container.

"How do you even know her?" Stella asks.

"Aunt Stella, we met at the funeral. You know that." Addie pulls open a drawer and digs through it. "Does a lid for this even exist?"

"That funeral was months ago."

Addie digs some more and then pushes the drawer closed. Opens the one above it and pulls out a roll of foil.

"Addie!" Stella says again.

Addie rips off some foil and covers the gravy. "We traded numbers at the funeral. Like, just in case, I guess."

"In case of *what*?"

"I don't know!" Addie says. "I didn't think about it, really. Everyone was so sad and confused. Anyway, I forgot about it, and then when you didn't go back to work, she heard about it and texted me to see if you were okay."

"Jesus." Stella drops her face into her hands.

"And then, you know how it goes. You just, like…keep talking or whatever. She's nice."

Stella scoffs. "Captain Murphy is not nice."

Elizabeth Murphy is a very talented cop, but she's also a rule-obsessed ice queen who spent more time arguing with Stella than working with her. Cops and lawyers have to work together, but the district attorney doesn't take personality clashes into consideration when assigning staff to LAPD personnel. Stella could never decide if she and Captain Murphy clashed because they were too different or too much the same. Stella found the woman to be stubborn, uptight, and unyielding. Captain Murphy considered Stella to be manipulative, and Stella thought Captain Murphy was unimaginative.

The main difference is—or was—that Elizabeth Murphy works well within the structure the law provides, and Stella makes the law work for her. They could never get past the difference in methodology. So the two of them were always at odds, always snipping at one another, never friends.

Eventually, after Stella spent five years in Homicide, they figured out how to coexist. They became *almost* friendly—until she learned that Captain Murphy, the most by-the-book woman she ever met, was sleeping with Lieutenant Warren. Feeling baffled and even betrayed, she put in for a promotion rather than think about *why* she felt that way.

"She seems to worry about you a lot," Addie says. "Very nicely, I might add."

"You can't talk to her, Addison. It isn't right." Stella has worked hard to keep her family and her career separate. With her family, she's simply a daughter, an aunt, a sister. In the courtroom, her colleagues, opposing counsel, and judges considered her to be tenacious, even aggressive. Addie isn't aware of her aunt's reputation in the courtroom, and she prefers to keep that part of her life separate, especially now that it's likely over. If Addie and Captain Murphy start spending time together, Stella won't be able to stop the lines from blurring.

"Aunt Stella, I don't understand what you have against her."

"I don't want to talk about it," Stella says. It's way too complicated to explain what she doesn't understand herself. She runs through last night's interaction again: the wine, the food, the familiar setting, the usual crowd. The feeling of being lied to. "Casey's is a cop bar..."

Addie bites her lip.

"Did she help you get that job?" Stella asks, suddenly understanding.

Addie nods.

With that, Stella goes back to bed.

Stella wishes she had somewhere else to sulk—an office, a vacation house—where someone would make her a cup of hot chocolate and let her complain for an hour.

The irony is not lost on her—she needs a friend, and that's why she invited Addie to stay with her. But Elizabeth was never her friend. Their relationship got less frosty toward the end, but they never moved beyond work colleagues. Anyway, Stella can't be friends with her because there is something about her that makes her feel totally and completely unchained. Not herself. Not in control of her feelings. If Stella is a pile of dynamite, Elizabeth is a brightly burning match.

And Stella is in no position to catch fire.

She spends the whole afternoon in bed sulking, looking at her phone, and napping. She's always tired, no matter how much rest she gets. When she hears Addie shower and then leave for work, she emerges from her room to take a bath, lighting a candle and turning the overhead light off. She soaks in the hot water for a long time. By the time she yanks out the plug, it's nearly dark out, and the flickering candle illuminates the steam surrounding her. She wraps her hair up in one towel and tucks a second around her, rubs the mirror enough to see a dim and watery reflection of herself.

It occurs to her only then that she could call Elizabeth. Tell her a thing or two.

"Stay away from Addie," she rehearses in the mirror. Then says it again, trying to sound more serious, sterner: "Stay *away* from Addie."

She brushes her teeth and her hair. Puts on real clothes—a bra, clean underwear, and a soft knee-length blush-colored dress with little cap sleeves; it's got enough shape to not look like a sack on her. She sits down at the vanity in her room and smooths moisturizer into her skin, pats concealer under her eyes, darkens her lashes with mascara, puts on a nude lipstick, and brushes some blush into her cheeks. She twists the front pieces of her hair and pins them back. Her work complete, she examines the results. She looks more like herself than she's felt in some time.

Finally feeling ready, she digs her phone out of her bag, only to find that it's dead. She unplugs the toaster—apparently people in the 1930s did not have much need for outlets—and plugs the charger in.

When the phone charges up enough to turn on, she scrolls through to check what she's missed. Her eldest brother, Brick, left a voicemail, scolding her for screening calls. There's a text from Thom asking about Addie's birthday in May. Maybe the family could come to LA? And one from Addie from the night before, asking her to come back to the bar.

She opens her contacts and finds Elizabeth. There's no picture, but there's a cell number and even an address. Someone—Warren or Esposito—must have sent her the whole contact record and all the information came with it. They'd both known her for a long time, after all.

Stella is screwing up the courage to touch the number and make the call when the screen changes and starts flashing Elizabeth's name. Had she hit something without realizing it? But then it clicks that Elizabeth is calling her. Coincidentally.

Which freaks Stella out, throwing her off her game.

She answers with a terse "Hello?"

"Stella." Elizabeth's voice is low and soft, and Stella sags against the counter.

"Hi," she says inanely. Where is her rage? Her indignation? Elizabeth has taken her out at the knees by calling first. Which is so typically her.

"I just wanted to reach out to you," Elizabeth says. "I hope you didn't feel put on the spot last night."

"Actually," Stella says, "I was about to call you."

"Oh?"

Stella sees the neighbor's headlights across the street through the kitchen window as they pull into their driveway. "I don't understand, Captain, why you've been talking to my niece."

"Ah." Elizabeth uses her softest, kindest voice, the one she reserves for victims, for family members grieving someone who has been murdered. "You know, Stella, she was very concerned about you after your husband passed. We all were. I only offered myself as support, should she need it."

Stella scoffs, taps her nails on the tile counter. "You have no right to suck her into your world of murder and death and the worst people. She's just a girl."

Elizabeth sucks in her breath, then says, "I can see how that's a valid concern, but my only intention was to be helpful. To her and to you."

"Fine," Stella says. "Sure."

"It was nice to see you, you know." Elizabeth offers an olive branch. "Maybe we could get dinner or a cup of coffee. Catch up."

Stella rests the warm skin of her forehead onto the cold tile of the counter. "I don't think that's a very good idea, Captain."

"I see," Elizabeth says.

"Just…be careful with Addie."

"Stella…"

"Bye now." Stella ends the call. Sets the phone down. Opens the back door, sticks her head out into the night air, and takes a few deep breaths. That woman is no good for her. No good at all.

She dreams about Ron. They're in the Homicide squad room. He's in his LAPD uniform, and she's still assigned to Captain Murphy. They're talking when he grabs his stomach, looks at her in horror.

He pulls his hands away. They're covered in blood.

"Why?" he asks.

She looks down at the gun she's holding and screams.

"It's okay. You're okay." Addie is shaking her awake. Stella is confused for a minute because it's dark and only the hall light is on, backlighting Addie's shape in the darkness. "It was just a bad dream."

Stella is sweaty and nauseous, and one of her legs is tangled in the quilt. She sits up a little, pushing her hair back. "I'm okay. Sorry."

Addie shakes her head. "You want to talk about it?"

"No." Stella draws her knees up and wraps her arms around them. "I don't, uh, remember."

"Okay."

"What time is it?"

"Three," Addie says.

Stella realizes Addie still has her coat on and her makeup is smudged. Her purse is on the floor by the bed. "You just get home?"

"Yeah. I closed," Addie says. "I was just gonna… You want to put on a movie or something?"

"Yeah," Stella says. "Sure." Anything is better than going back to sleep.

Stella brings her quilt to the couch. Addie makes popcorn in the microwave, salty and sweet, just how Stella likes it. They put the big bowl between them and cozy up under the quilt. Addie scrolls through the cable channels until she finds a rom-com. The movie is at a commercial break.

Stella looks over at Addie. She looks tired and washed out in the light of the television. The skin under her eyes is dark.

"You doing okay?" Stella asks. "Do you like it out here?"

Addie looks at her. "Yeah, I like it. It's different. I needed different."

"You don't get homesick?"

"No. I think if I were alone, maybe, but I have you." Addie smiles. "I wish I could help you more, though."

"I'm just gonna be sad for a while, I think. That's just the way it goes. I know it's not much fun for you."

"It's okay," Addie says. "I have Monday off. Maybe we could do something fun. Go to the beach or something."

"It's a date."

Addie turns back to watch the movie for a few minutes and then says, "Did you talk to Elizabeth?"

"What?"

"She said she'd call you to apologize."

"We spoke," Stella says. "But we were never friends, you know. And I don't need her to be my friend now just because my husband is dead and she feels bad about it."

Addie presses her lips together, tucks her chin to her chest. "I really like Elizabeth. And I don't know anyone out here. Not really."

"You know me. You know your friends from work—"

Addie looks up at Stella abruptly. "It's fine if you don't like her, but it's not your place to decide whether or not I can see her."

"Fine," Stella says. "Just leave me out of it."

They turn back to the movie until Addie excuses herself and goes to bed.

Stella stays up watching TV until the sun rises. Then she gets dressed and drives to The Coffee Bean. She waits in line with people who are on their way to work and orders a sugary drink that's more chocolate than coffee. She drinks most of it sitting in the car, then drives around until she finds the place where she used to go with Ron for breakfast on his rare day off, back when they were courting, before they got married. She'd forgotten about it until now.

Full of caffeine and French toast, she next goes to the library. She lies to the woman at the counter, says the address on her license is current, and walks away with a library card for her sin. She wanders through the stacks, looks at the new books. She picks up one about a CIA spy, but the premise is ridiculous, so she sets it down again and leaves without checking anything out.

Next, she stops at the grocery store and buys milk and creamer and butter and bread, and eggs. The things normal people always have in their refrigerator. And she keeps going until the cart is full.

Addie is awake when she gets home and watches her carry in the first bag of groceries. "Where were you?"

"Just out running some errands," Stella says. "You can help me carry some bags."

"You went grocery shopping?" Addie sounds surprised.

"Yes." Stella's voice is tinged with irritation, but she tries to cover it up. "I figured if you were going to cook for me, we should probably have food."

Addie doesn't seem to notice her tone. "That's awesome," she says, and her words sound genuine. She goes outside and brings back a couple of bags.

When all that's left is a twelve-pack of Coca-Cola, Stella grabs it and closes the back of the SUV. She's been driving it more and more. Stella can actually drive it now without weeping. In fact, the more she drives it, the more the smell of Ron fades. And she likes riding up high—she feels safe, like she's driving around in a huge black tank. It makes leaving the house a little easier.

She never used to be scared to face the world.

Addie helps her unpack the groceries. There are so many boxes of cereal and canned goods that they have to turn one of the cupboards into pantry overflow.

The sleepless night has caught up to her, so Stella excuses herself and goes to lie down. When she wakes up again, the sun is setting and Addie is gone.

She pours a glass of wine and goes to the backyard and watches the sky turn orange to purple and then shift into darkness, into the starless expanse that passes for night in this city.

On Monday, they drive to Santa Monica for fish tacos at Wahoo's and then go to the pier. They people watch and dip into shops, though they don't buy anything. Stella offers to ride the carousel or the Ferris wheel, but Addie says "no, thank you" to both.

She says yes to the aquarium, though, and Stella forks over the ten dollars for admission.

It's a small and quaint attraction. Addie seems bored by the whole thing until they get to the jellyfish. They stand and watch them for a long time, Addie's pretty face awash in the watery blue light. She even sticks her hands into the touch tank, though Stella skips that; slimy and cold is not her style.

"How far is it to the one in Monterey?" Addie asks as they head back outside. "That's supposed to be the best one, right?"

Stella thinks about it. "Five or six hours, I think."

"Really? I guess I didn't realize how big this state is."

"We could go up for a couple days," Stella says. "No problem."

They stop to lean against the railing of the pier, looking out over the water. Addie is wearing denim shorts, a blue hoodie, and white sneakers, and she shivers a little in the cool breeze. "I do like it here."

"Good," Stella says. "I'd be sad if you left."

"Daddy says that in a year, I should go back to school." Addie yanks on the dangling strings of her hoodie and then holds them hard, her fist resting over her heart. "He says by then, I'll have been here long enough that I won't have to pay out-of-state tuition."

"For what degree?"

"I have no idea!" Addie rolls her eyes. "But I have time to decide, I guess. My degree is in sociology. I'm going to have to get some sort of graduate degree if I ever want to stop working in food service."

"What made you pick sociology in the first place?"

"Honestly, I took random classes trying to figure out what I wanted to do until eventually I had to declare a major." Addie tucks her hair under her hoodie. "I looked at all my credits, and sociology was what I had the most hours in."

Stella laughs.

"I don't even know, Aunt Stella. Everyone always…maybe because I look like you, everyone in the family compares me to you. Because you were the only girl, and so am I, but you were always off doing something amazing. You always had a plan. I've never had a plan."

"Oh, honey," Stella says. "I fly by the seat of my pants all the time. Believe me."

"Really?"

"Really. And I don't have a plan now, do I?"

"That's different. You're grieving."

"And I know it can't last forever, but it's just so hard to move forward." She puts an arm around Addie's shoulders. "We're just going to have to help each other."

"Yeah," Addie says. "Just start over. That's why I came here. To start over."

That's why anyone comes to Los Angeles, Stella thinks, and she wonders what was so bad that Addie felt she had to leave it behind. But now the wind is picking up and it's getting colder. Addie's bare legs are covered in goosebumps.

"Let's go get something warm to drink," Stella says. "I think I saw a café back there."

After the trip to Santa Monica, Stella slides into her grief again, and she sleeps through the day, getting up when it's dark to scavenge the kitchen for leftover pasta, cold pizza, a half-empty box of cheese crackers. She sniffs the carton of leftover Chinese and then eats it cold, standing at the sink.

She looks at her pathetic reflection, distorted by the old glass in the window. Her real estate agent called this place an original gem, pointing out the wooden floors, the crown molding, the brick patio in the backyard. But original charm had come with a low price tag for a reason. The windows need to be replaced. The roof is patched in several places. The wiring is all single circuit. The plumbing is still on septic. She purchased it anyway, desperate to get back into the neighborhood she lived in before she got married. Like she could go back in time. Like an address change would be the balm to ease her pain.

She's four days into this low mood when for some reason, at one in the morning, she feels compelled to go out. She pulls on dirty sweats and Addie's black hoodie. Slides her feet into pink flip-flops and grabs her keys. She drives two blocks and parks outside of her old house. She studies the white Hyundai sedan and the old beat-up Toyota pickup in the driveway. She can't remember who they sold the house to, and, anyway, there could be different people here now. Ron handled things like that. She was always busy, tied up at the courthouse and unwilling to rearrange her schedule for something as mundane as real estate.

She closes her eyes, trying to picture the interior of the house as it used to be. Does a mental walk-through. The house was perfect for two people, but Ron considered it hers, not theirs, so he convinced her to sell it. Then the housing market collapsed, and they landed in the little duplex, planning to cool their heels for a year to see if the market improved. Then it was two years, and then, well, Ron died.

She meanders around the neighborhood, looking at the houses, some dark, some with lights, some with only the flickering illumination of a television. When she circles back around, Stella realizes she's been creeping through her own neighborhood in her dead husband's car for over an hour. She parks in her driveway and sits in the dark car, the engine still ticking. She should go inside before Addie gets home, but she can't move just yet.

She's still zoning out when a car that looks like something from the LAPD motor pool—boxy and unmarked, covered with antennas—pulls up to the curb. Stella looks at it in the rearview mirror. The lights go off and the engine cuts.

Addie gets out of the passenger's side.

Stella throws open her door and climbs out. "Addie?"

Addie jumps. "Jesus! What are you doing out here?"

Elizabeth Murphy emerges from the driver's side.

"Where's your car?" Stella asks.

"Liz gave me a ride home." Addie's voice cracks, like she's been crying.

"Why didn't you call me?"

"I *did*," Addie hisses, then storms past her and goes inside, slamming the front door.

Stella reaches for her phone, but these sweats don't have pockets. She tries to remember where she left it or when she even saw it last. *Shit.*

Elizabeth walks toward Stella, stopping a few feet away. "A brawl broke out at Casey's. Someone shot off a round and hit one of the light fixtures above the bar. The bartending staff was showered with glass."

"What?" Stella asks, stunned.

"Addie is fine, but she's shaken up. They gave everyone a day off while they repair the damage." Elizabeth tries to smile. "She'll be fine, Stella."

"Why did you report at two in the morning?"

Elizabeth looks perplexed for a moment. "Addie called me when you didn't answer," she says gently. "I didn't work the… It wasn't a homicide. I wouldn't report for a bar brawl."

Stella nods, flustered and embarrassed. "Of course. Yes, I know that, Captain."

"It's very late," Elizabeth says in the same gentle voice. "I'm going to check on both of you tomorrow, okay?"

It's a question, but Stella doesn't feel like she has a say in the matter. "I've never seen you in jeans before," she manages to say, apropos of nothing.

"Stella, what were you doing out here in the driveway?" Elizabeth asks, a tone of concern emerging through the gentleness.

"I was just..." Stella looks over at the SUV, her mind blank. "I should go check on her."

Elizabeth waits until Stella is inside the house. Stella watches at the window, waiting for the car to start, the lights to come on, and the sound of the engine to fade into the night.

Addie's bedroom door is closed, and the space between the door and the wooden floor is dark.

In the night, when Stella gets up to use the toilet, she finds three pieces of broken glass on the edge of the sink, reflecting the moonlight.

CHAPTER 3

Elizabeth is sitting at the kitchen table with Addie when Stella stumbles down the hall, drawn by the scent of coffee. Addie always makes a full pot.

Another Carter trait. Never let the coffeepot run cold or dry.

Stella is wearing the same clothes from the night before, minus a bra, and her hair is pulled up into a ratty bun on the top of her head.

Addie and Elizabeth look up at her.

Stella turns right back around.

When she emerges the second time, she's wearing a fresh T-shirt, clean underwear, and black yoga pants. Her hair is her hair. They will simply have to live with that deficiency. She smiles half-heartedly. "Well, don't you two make a pretty picture."

"Did you get some rest?" Elizabeth asks.

Stella says nothing and makes for the coffee. She knows they're watching her, and when she turns around, holding her mug in both hands, Addie is staring at Stella, her mouth a thin line. Elizabeth is studying her thoughtfully.

"Sit down," Addie says.

Stella sits, Elizabeth on one side and Addie on the other. She swallows a mouthful of coffee and sets the mug down. Her mug—teal with gold around the rim and down the handle—matches theirs because Addie bought a set of four at HomeGoods.

Addie speaks. "I'm not quitting my job."

"No one asked you to," Stella says. "Certainly not me."

Addie tilts her head. "Oh, really?"

"Do you want to quit?"

"No."

"Well, then, case closed. You're a grown woman, and I'm not your mama."

Elizabeth leans back, sips her coffee.

"People commit crimes all the time." Stella gestures to Elizabeth. "She knows it too. At least you were somewhere help could come fast."

"The dude who fired the gun was drunk," Addie says. "I'd already cut him off."

"Did he get arrested?" Stella asks Elizabeth, who nods.

Addie relaxes, and she curls her hands around her mug. "I guess I thought you'd want me to quit."

"I trust you to make good choices," Stella says.

"Well, you both seem substantially better by morning light." Elizabeth smiles at them and pushes her mug away. "I wish I could stay longer, but I've got to get to work."

"See you for dinner tomorrow?" Addie asks.

Elizabeth nods. "You're invited too, Stella. Josh is down from Santa Cruz. He'd love to see you." Elizabeth has three kids, all grown. Josh is the youngest and the only one Stella has met.

Stella doesn't respond.

After Elizabeth lets herself out, Addie rinses her mug and says, "I'd like you to come with me. You spend too much time alone."

Stella wants to say that she can make her own friends, but that's never been true. Every friend Stella ever had has made her. So she sighs and says, "Fine."

She tries to weasel out of it, but Addie orders her into the shower and picks out a button-up dress with tiny flowers on it for her to wear, then leads her to a chair in the kitchen and spends twenty minutes brushing, braiding, and pinning her long blonde hair up into milkmaid braids. Stella gazes admiringly at the result, even if they are a little youthful for her.

When Addie offers to do her makeup, Stella shakes her head and crosses her arms. She can do her own makeup, for heaven's sake. She applies mascara, puts on lip gloss, and dusts on some blush while Addie watches.

"You ready?" Addie asks.

"I guess. Into the belly of the beast."

"Oh, my God, calm down." Addie shakes her head. "Elizabeth is nice, and I'm starting to think the reason you two couldn't get along is because of you."

That does more than graze, so Stella says nothing.

It's simply that Stella is so good at some things, people don't understand how she's not good at everything. As if winning court cases and making friends are the exact same skill set. As if the very thing that makes her good at cornering criminals isn't what makes her fail in her personal relationships.

Addie drives. She's been to Elizabeth's home before, apparently. Stella never has, never had occasion to visit before now. Before Stella left the homicide division, the only time Elizabeth came to the duplex was when Stella shot a murderer named Arthur Sullivan—one of the rare cases she lost. Despite what the jury decided, Stella was sure that Sullivan was guilty, and he wasn't one to forget a grudge. He showed up at her house one night, armed, and she shot him with Ron's personal sidearm in self-defense.

Elizabeth came with her squad to work the scene. Stella was happy to see her and, frankly, grateful. She was shaken up, and Elizabeth's presence was familiar and calming.

She'd never killed anyone before, and the district attorney had made her pass a psychological evaluation before she came back to work, but it wasn't like she ran over some innocent pedestrian with her car. She'd killed a disgruntled murderer who had come to kill her, and she could live with that just fine. Lieutenant Esposito told her she should have been a cop, not a lawyer.

"Stella?"

Stella looks over at Addie, who is staring at her. They are parked in a residential neighborhood.

"We're here?" Stella asks.

"Where'd you go?" Addie asks.

"Sorry, I was just… It didn't take long to get here," Stella says, opening the door.

Elizabeth lives on the eleventh floor of a condominium building. Addie calls up on the intercom, and they get buzzed in. This kind of communal living isn't Stella's style, but she understands the benefits: the security, a pool, a gym.

In the elevator, Stella starts to feel nauseous and tries to calm down, push her feelings aside. By the time they reach Elizabeth's door, she feels nothing at all, so much so that she watches herself walk into the beautiful condo, shake Josh's hand, greet Elizabeth, decline an offer to hang up her sweater. She'll keep it on for now, thanks.

Dinner is a taco bar, each item lined up on the kitchen counter. They make their tacos and carry their plates to the dining table. Addie and Josh met before, and they're chatty and friendly. Stella eats her two tacos—one beef, one chicken—and answers questions directed at her. She listens to everyone else's conversation, watches Elizabeth prompt Josh into talking about himself. He's majoring in science communication, which Stella works out to be journalism or what journalism has morphed into in the age of instant news and social media.

Addie asks Josh about UC–Santa Cruz. What's it like? How far is it from here? Does he like the campus? Why did he choose it?

"I wanted UCLA," Elizabeth says, "but I was overruled."

"I've lived in LA my whole life," Josh says. "I wanted to try someplace new."

"A different California beach town," Stella says before she can stop herself.

Josh stares at her, and Addie looks down at her plate. Stella deflects by standing up and taking her plate into the kitchen. Elizabeth follows her in with more dishes.

"Can I help clean up?" Stella asks.

"Sure." Elizabeth opens a cupboard with neat stacks of nesting storage containers and matching lids. Nothing like Stella's jumbled drawer of recycled cream cheese containers and empty yogurt tubs.

They work together to put away leftovers, then Stella rinses the dishes and Elizabeth loads them into the dishwasher.

"I'm glad you came tonight," Elizabeth says as she closes the dishwasher and rehangs the dish towel on the handle.

Stella nods, then turns to look at the items on the refrigerator: Josh's senior picture, a ticket stub from a Marvel movie, a few spare magnets.

Stella's fridge displays nothing. She doesn't even know where her old refrigerator magnets are. Maybe they were thrown away in her great purge.

Elizabeth touches her arm, and Stella nearly leaps out of her skin.

"What?" She rubs her arm where Elizabeth touched her.

"I said, do you want dessert?" Elizabeth frowns, deepening the small line between her eyebrows behind the bridge of her glasses. "I didn't mean to startle you."

"Dessert. Sure. Can I use your bathroom?"

"Down the hall." Elizabeth nods toward the hallway.

When Stella comes out of the tastefully decorated restroom—white tile, marble countertops, beige towels, and the woman in the mirror a total stranger—she hears the kids talking in the living room. She pauses out of sight of everyone and takes several deep breaths, stopping when she becomes woozy. Elizabeth is waiting for her in the kitchen.

"There's peach pie," Elizabeth says.

It's not exactly the season for peaches, but the pie isn't homemade either; there's a fancy box on the counter. It tastes good, no matter what season it is.

In the living room, the kids are talking about music—Josh has a guitar but doesn't know how to play, and Addie can play but left her guitar back in Tennessee. Josh brings out his guitar, and Addie tunes it while Elizabeth cleans up the dessert dishes and Stella walks around the living area. Table lamps, throw blankets, a dusty fake plant—apparently the only place dust has managed to flourish. She's inspecting Elizabeth's dark red accent wall of ballet-themed art, listening to Addie strum chords and hum a tune when Elizabeth comes over to her.

"This wasn't so bad," Elizabeth says.

"I guess not."

"You know, Stella, your husband's benefits entitle you to grief counseling," Elizabeth says matter-of-factly while staring up at a retro print of ballet shoes. She turns to look at Stella, who is staring at Elizabeth, slack-jawed with surprise. "I think you should take advantage of that."

"I'm not… It's only been—"

"I'm not passing judgment." Elizabeth's hand reaches out but doesn't make contact. "I'm a great fan of therapy myself, whether it's for a traumatic incident or general maintenance."

Stella was admiring the art with her arms behind her. Now she crosses them in front, tucks them tight against herself.

"I know it's only been six months." Elizabeth's voice is gentler now. "You deserve to take as much time as you need, but if the LAPD is willing to pay for something, you ought not to let it go to waste. Think of it as wringing the chief of police for every penny he wants to keep in his deep, dusty pockets."

Stella nods at the sales pitch.

"You probably already have the paperwork, but I'm going to have it sent to you again, okay?"

"Okay."

"Then I'll have someone follow up," Elizabeth promises. "Now, you've had a long night, and if you want to leave, I won't be offended."

"Are you kicking us out?" Stella is relieved and offended at the same time. "You're like a drive-by shooting, Elizabeth."

"No, you can stay as long as you'd like, for all I care. But I'm setting you free." Elizabeth winks and then calls over her shoulder, "Addie, I think your aunt is fading."

"Yeah, we should probably get going." Addie stands, setting the guitar down gently on the sofa. "Thanks. This was fun."

"We'll do it again," Elizabeth assures her, and gives Addie a hug.

In the car, Stella asks Addie, "Do you think I need therapy?"

Addie turns down the music. A long, black cord connects her phone to the car speakers. "I absolutely think you need therapy. Especially if it's free."

"Tell me what you really think. Jesus."

"Do you think you're doing particularly well?" Addie asks. "Sleeping all day, eating like crap, not working?"

Addie is right, but her words slam up hard against Stella, knocking any reply right out of her, and she endures the pain that always accompanies the brutal truth.

"As long as I've known you, you've been a workaholic." Addie's voice softens a bit. "And yet something that used to be a huge part of your life now seems to hold no interest for you."

"I hated the DA's office," Stella says churlishly. That's not even true, but she feels exposed, tender, like a fresh bruise. She'll never go back to that life, never be that ruthless attorney again. Never again be the woman who passed the bar in two states on her first try, the woman who could make anyone on the stand spill the truth.

"Okay. So do something else," Addie says.

"What? What would I do?"

"You know who would be great at helping you figure it out?"

"Don't say Elizabeth."

"Elizabeth," Addie says anyway. "The woman who has been trying to be your friend for, like, six years."

"Why?" Stella demands. "What's in it for her?"

Addie shakes her head. "That's not the point."

"When we first met—"

"When you first met, she surely reacted to the way *you* treated *her*," Addie says. "Let it go. Get to know her now."

Stella slumps in her seat, mutters under her breath, "Who made you president of her fan club?"

Addie turns the music back up.

Stella knows she needs something to help her move out of this childish rut, so when she gets a big white envelope in the mail with the LAPD return address, she opens it, flipping through quickly. She is looking for a note from Elizabeth, but there's only a form letter, a page with some legalese, and a glossy brochure.

She fills out the form and the insurance paperwork, but calling to set up the initial appointment seems daunting and insurmountable, and she paces for three days trying to drum up the courage. When she finally does, she's sitting on an area rug in a warm patch of afternoon sunlight, watching the clock tick closer and closer to five. At 4:56, she makes the call. Her heart is racing and her hands are clammy. When someone answers, she gives her name and tells them she wants to book a grief counseling session.

The receptionist is kind and gentle. Stella makes a list on the back of the envelope of everything she's supposed to bring. They set an appointment for two weeks out, which feels like an eternity and at the same time way too close. After she hangs up, she lies back on the rug and takes a deep breath.

She gazes out the window at the fading sunlight. While down there, she notices the trim underneath it. Whoever repainted it didn't bother to do the underside of the windowsill. The baseboards are scuffed too, and the floor is filthy. Maybe when therapy magically fixes her and she gets a job, she can hire painters and cleaners.

"Ha," she says into the empty room.

She stays on the rug until her hips start to ache and the sun gets so low that she loses her warm patch of light. She gets up, her joints creaking, brushes herself off, and wanders off to run a bath.

She would wear work clothes to her appointment if she hadn't gotten rid of all her suits, though she doesn't know what that would prove, exactly. Maybe that she's not grieving—or that she's not grieving too much or incorrectly. That she's functioning. She wears something clean, something of Addie's because Addie does her laundry more often.

She sits in the parking lot outside the building getting hot and nauseous. Starts to cry. Realizes she can't go in.

She calls Addie, but it goes to voicemail, so having no friends or family who might come close to understanding, she calls the only other person she can think of.

"Stella?" Elizabeth answers right away. She sounds worried.

"I-I-I can't." She's crying so hard that she can barely breathe.

"What's wrong? What's happened?"

"I can't d-do it," she manages to choke out. "I can't go in there. I can't."

"Go in where?"

Stella presses the heel of her hand into her left eye. She pulls her hand away. It's wet and streaked with mascara.

"Can't go in to see the grief counselor?" Elizabeth guesses after a pause.

Stella nods, then realizes Elizabeth can't see her moving her head. "I'm not ready."

"I don't think anyone is. It's always hard. It's fine to be scared."

"You don't understand. I can't move."

"Okay," Elizabeth says. "Where are you?"

"What?"

"Which office are you at? Which doctor?"

"Elizabeth…"

"Come on, which one?"

"Veronica Barrett."

"I'll be there in ten minutes," Elizabeth says.

"I'm going to be late."

"I'll put sirens on. Stay there. You're going to be okay. I'm on my way."

"Okay," Stella says, feeling small and dumb and helpless.

When Elizabeth arrives minutes later, Stella is still crying, only now it's because she's anxious about being late and feels guilty for calling Elizabeth and feels stupid because she can't seem to do anything by herself anymore.

Someone else is driving, because the lights cut off as they pull into the parking lot and Elizabeth gets out of the passenger seat while the car is practically still moving. It looks like the driver is a woman, but Stella can't be sure through her tears. Not that she would know her; she's been away from Homicide so long that she doesn't know everyone in the division anymore, and that makes her feel strange and sad too.

Elizabeth opens the passenger door of the SUV and gets in, setting Stella's purse on the floorboard.

"Hi," she says, then adds, "Oh dear."

"I'm so stupid." Stella brings her hands up to her face again. Her makeup by now is wrecked.

"You're not. You are, infuriatingly, one of the most intelligent people I have ever met."

"I can't even…do this one thing," Stella says between sobs.

"Yes, you can," Elizabeth says. "The hardest part is going inside, and so we're going to do that together."

"You don't have to—"

"I'm going to walk in with you, I'm going to wait with you, and if you want, I'll even do the session with you," Elizabeth says softly, putting a hand on her arm. "You aren't alone."

"Okay," Stella says. "Okay. Okay." She pulls the keys out of the ignition with shaking hands.

"Let's go." Elizabeth picks up Stella's purse and slings it over her shoulder, then walks around the car and opens Stella's door.

The car that Elizabeth arrived in pulls into a parking spot. The driver cuts the engine. She feels foolish, but Elizabeth's presence is weirdly fortifying. The receptionist looks up and smiles when they step inside the door. The cool air of the office dries Stella's damp cheeks.

"I'm so late," Stella says meekly.

"That's just fine, sweetheart," the receptionist says.

Elizabeth presses gently on Stella's back, and she moves to the counter. "I'm Stella Carter."

"I just need your insurance information." The woman pushes a clipboard through the space in the window.

While Stella rummages for her insurance card, Elizabeth sits down with the clipboard and starts filling in the information. She's half done by the time Stella sits next to her.

"Are you feeling better?" Elizabeth glances over at her.

"Um…"

Elizabeth pushes her glasses up to the top of her head and looks at Stella like a mother checking for fever. "Your face isn't so red, and your breathing is better." Stella shrinks down into her seat at the scrutiny. If she were in an interrogation room and saw Elizabeth's piercing green eyes, what wouldn't she confess to?

"I guess," she says finally.

Elizabeth hands her the clipboard. The only blanks are for her social security number and some other questions. Elizabeth filled in her address and even her birthday. Stella has no earthly idea when Elizabeth's birthday is.

She picks up the pen and fills in her social security number, then squints at the questions.

"Where are your glasses?" Elizabeth asks.

"I don't know," Stella admits. "Couldn't find them this morning."

Elizabeth looks over at the clipboard. "Number one, do you find your grief is interfering with your life?"

Stella snorts and writes *yes*.

"Do you feel cut off from other people?"

Stella waves off the question.

Elizabeth continues to the third. "Are there things you used to like to do that you now avoid?"

"This is stupid," Stella says. She writes *DEAD HUSBAND* across the last two questions and hands the clipboard back to Elizabeth, who smirks and returns it to the receptionist.

The door to an inner office opens, and someone says, "Stella?"

"Do you want me to come in with you?" Elizabeth asks.

"No," Stella says, though a tiny bit of her does. It's best if she does this on her own. She wouldn't be honest with Elizabeth there. She would try to impress her or say what Elizabeth might want to hear. Anyway, the hard part was getting here, and now that she is, it's hard to remember why she panicked. "You should go back to work. I mean, thank you, but you've done...more than enough. Jesus, I can't believe I called you."

Elizabeth regards her with an arched brow but says, "You're welcome."

Stella stands and follows the waiting woman into the other room. They sit in comfortable armchairs, facing each other.

Dr. Barrett reviews the paperwork. "It says here you recently lost your husband," she says.

"Six months ago. Well...almost seven now, I guess," she says. "He was a police officer. He died at work."

"I see."

"He was murdered," Stella says. "Right in the middle of headquarters."

"That must have been devastating. I'm sorry for your loss." Dr. Barrett says sympathetically. She writes something down on her notepad.

"I worked with cops too, so I understood the dangers of the job. At least I thought I did." Stella shrugs.

Stella talks about Addie, about leaving her job, about the little house and how she mostly haunts it full time now. About how she doesn't have any hobbies, any goals, or even any friends anymore.

"Who was with you in the waiting room?" Dr. Barrett asks.

"Elizabeth?" Stella asks. "Oh, we aren't friends."

"No?"

"No. We used to work together." Stella shifts uneasily in her chair, then slips her fingers under her thighs as if her hands might betray her discomfort. "Our professional relationship was somewhat strained at the start, then about the time it started getting better, I left that job."

"So what's stopping you from being friends now?" Dr. Barrett asks. "You're two females in law enforcement of a similar age. That seems like a pretty good place to start a friendship."

"She's Addie's friend now," Stella says, barely keeping the resentment out of her voice.

"Your niece?"

"Yeah. They made friends at the funeral. Weird, right?"

Dr. Barrett considers for a moment. "Unusual, maybe, but not weird. Well, if she's not your friend, then why did she come with you today? Was it in an official capacity?"

"No," Stella says. "I just… I wasn't sure who to call, and I was having some…trouble in the parking lot."

"What sort of trouble?"

"Just coming in seemed impossible. Everything seems to be so hard these days."

Dr. Barrett writes something down again. "So you called Elizabeth, who is definitely not your friend, and she came in the middle of the workday?"

"I don't expect you to understand," Stella says.

Dr. Barrett smiles. "I'd like to see you again, Stella, if you're okay with that. Kathy will schedule another appointment on your way out."

"Sure. Okay." It feels like they barely had time to talk about anything, barely touched on Ron, but according to the clock on the wall, it's been forty-five minutes.

She leaves through another door and finds herself on the opposite side of the reception window. Kathy looks up and smiles.

"Dr. Barrett wants me to schedule another appointment."

"Great! What day and time work for you? When are you free?"

"I'm literally always free," Stella says with a self-deprecating laugh. She looks out at the waiting room but doesn't see Elizabeth. Good. She shouldn't hang around on Stella's behalf.

She rebooks and opens the door to the parking lot. The sun is bright and she squints, bringing her hand up to her face to shield her eyes.

"How'd it go?" asks a voice out of nowhere that makes Stella jump. Elizabeth is sitting on the small retaining wall by the door. She stands, dusting off the seat of her slacks. She pushes her hair off one shoulder.

"I thought you *left*," Stella says crossly. Her heart is still pounding.

"I told you I wouldn't," Elizabeth says reasonably. "Also, I sent Maria back to work, so I need a ride."

Stella slings her purse onto her shoulder. She feels put out, even though she's the one who called Elizabeth. It had seemed the only reasonable thing to do, though now it seems ridiculous.

"You want to talk about it?" Elizabeth asks as they walk to the SUV.

"I'm going back in two weeks," Stella says, "so it went okay, I guess."

"Did you like her? Therapy is a two-way street. You get to screen her too."

Stella shrugs. "I don't feel anything about anything anymore." She glances at Elizabeth. "Unless I'm having a panic attack."

"Right," Elizabeth says dryly. She looks at her watch. "Let's stop at Starbucks."

"I've already eaten up so much of your day."

"I'm the boss," Elizabeth says. "What are they going to do, fire me?"

Stella snorts. "I thought you liked Homicide. Thought you were getting on well there. It's been, what, seven years?"

"I do like my division. But I don't feel as warmly toward the LAPD as a whole."

There's a Starbucks just down the street. They go through the drive-through. Stella lets Elizabeth pay.

"Thank you," Stella says as the car idles at a light near the police administration building. "You didn't have to do any of this."

"Stella," Elizabeth says, "I think about our time working together, and there's so much I should've done differently. I feel like we were just starting to figure things out, and then you took that new job, and I didn't see you anymore. You don't always get a second chance with people, and I'd like to be friends. Josh is gone now, and I work *all* the time. It's hard for me too, you know, to meet people I can stand and have them understand about my schedule, and—"

"Jesus, Elizabeth. Fine! You win!"

The light changes, and Stella drives through the intersection.

"Addie likes me," Elizabeth says softly. "Isn't that worth anything?"

"Yes." Addie's opinion is worth a lot, and Elizabeth has been nothing but kind. Stella has no good reason to keep pushing her away. "It's fine. Let's be friends. Best friends."

Elizabeth snorts, and they both laugh.

It feels okay, actually. Laughter.

Stella pulls up to the curb. Elizabeth opens the door, looks back, and says, "I'll call you," then disappears into the building where Stella used to spend many of her workdays. A building she has no reason to enter anymore.

She heads home.

CHAPTER 4

Dr. Barrett asked Stella to plan something for every day, just one thing. Maybe do the dishes. Maybe remember to drag the garbage to the curb. Maybe go grocery shopping or see a movie.

Today, she decides, is library day. The one closest to her house is two intimidating stories. But there's another smaller branch that's right by the turnoff for Ron's old condo. She checks her purse twice to make sure she still has her library card.

She gets there ten minutes before the library opens. She parks, kills the engine, and digs her phone out of her purse. Brings up the text thread she has going with Elizabeth. Stella still needs to figure out how to spend time with Elizabeth without getting distracted by her hair, her pretty clothes, her perfect skin.

It's weird how she can miss Ron and yet think about Elizabeth and the way she made Stella feel from the very first moment they met. Being around Elizabeth makes Stella's skin buzz. At first, she thought it was annoyance, and it was, a little. Annoyance and insecurity and resentment. But once those feelings faded away, there was still that buzzing, that heat, like her bones were swarming with angry bees. It made her fingers itch, made her sweat, made her vision swim a bit.

Stella wants to be Elizabeth's friend the same way she's always wanted anything, and historically, the things Stella wants always come back to bite her in the ass. She wanted to get away from her parents, so she got married just out of high school, a comically short-lived first attempt at marriage. She wanted to get out of her private law firm, so she took a lower salary for a more fulfilling job, only to find she was still restless, unchallenged, and bored. Then she landed in Los Angeles because an ex-boyfriend from law school recommended her for the assistant district attorney job. She wanted to feel anchored in LA, so she married Ron, even though it made her work life all the more complicated. And while she had affection for him, she always felt like something was missing, something was off.

She's determined not to float from place to place anymore. Ron had been an anchor in both good and bad ways. She's been in Los Angeles nearly nine years. She has a house, one car too many, Addie, and now, a friend.

She texts Elizabeth, asking if she has any reading recommendations for someone who hasn't read fiction for the last ten years.

Elizabeth quickly responds.

You think I have time to read?

Stella is not surprised, but she knows that if anyone could spin free time out of nothing, it'd be Elizabeth Murphy.

When the double doors of the library swish open, Stella heads inside with a group of waiting patrons. Half of them move toward a bank of computers. Women with strollers go toward a big room in the other direction. Stella looks around, already overwhelmed.

Her assignment was to do something, and technically, she's done it. No one said she had to check out a book or anything.

A bright orange sign catches her eye.

New Books.

It's a much smaller collection than the one at the first library she visited, and it feels more manageable. She picks up something that looks not too girly but not too grisly. It turns out to be historical fiction. Good enough.

The machines where she can check the book out herself look complex, so she approaches a live human at the desk, who looks to be about the same age as Addie. She's staring at a computer screen.

The young woman looks up and says, "Checking out?"

"Yes." Stella slides the book across.

The young woman, whose nametag reads *Julia*, pecks at her keyboard a moment and then looks up at Stella expectantly.

"Oh! You probably want my library card."

"It does help to move things along." Julia smiles.

Stella sets down her purse to dig for her card.

Julia scans it, squints at the screen, then takes the book and waves it over a dark square on the desk. A receipt pops out.

"Due in three weeks on the fourteenth," Julia says. "And you can return it to another branch closer to home, if you like."

Stella smiles, says nervously, "I haven't used a public library in years."

"That's okay. Welcome back."

Stella relaxes a little as she takes her book and exits, stepping into the bright sun. Even if she doesn't read it, she feels like she did a good thing. She interacted with a real person. Left the house. Didn't give up, didn't cry in the car.

In the SUV, she takes a picture of the book and sends it to Elizabeth.

When Elizabeth doesn't respond right away, Stella drives home.

Addie has a date, a friend of someone she works with.

"It's not a big deal."

"I think it's great." Stella smiles at her niece. Addie is young and beautiful, and she should be going out and having fun.

"I can cancel." Addie holds her phone, thumbs hovering.

"Don't you dare," Stella says. "I'm fine, and you've done nothing but work and look after me. You deserve to go out. Where are you going?"

"A movie, I think." Addie shrugs. "Food too, I guess."

Stella suspects Addie is more excited than she lets on, that she's playing it down to save Stella's feelings, but Addie's happiness is important to her, and Stella doesn't want her to give up on LA.

Addie wears the dress that Stella wore to Elizabeth's condo—they swap clothes all the time now, washing everything in tangled loads and pulling from the basket of clean things that sits in the hallway between their bedrooms. They're more like sisters than aunt and niece, or like mother and daughter, only Stella isn't the mom.

"Text me if you're going to be out super late," Stella says as Addie is leaving, because that seems like the thing to say.

"Okay."

"And...you know. Use protection."

Addie cringes. "Jesus Christ. Stop."

She hasn't been gone fifteen minutes when Elizabeth calls her and says, "If I bring chocolate cake, will you let me come over? You know, since we're friends now."

Stella knows she's teasing, and she grips the phone. "Addie isn't here."

"I know."

Stella looks around the house. It's not up to Elizabeth's standard of clean. It's not even up to Stella's standard of clean, and that is a low bar.

"You can't judge me. You can't judge the state of this house."

"I never would," Elizabeth says solemnly.

"Yeah. Whatever, then." Stella hangs up.

She's still in sweats and a T-shirt, so she changes into well-worn jeans that have a bit of stretch, and a different, cleaner T-shirt. Then she walks around and gathers up trash. Mail and food wrappers and used tissues and balled-up receipts. She lights a candle that Addie keeps on the coffee table, the one that smells like the beach.

She's standing in the kitchen, looking at the remaining mess, when Elizabeth knocks once and then lets herself in.

Friends, Stella reminds herself, trying not to get her hackles up at the familiarity.

Her mama used to have friends like this. Women would pop over with a pie, especially just after her daddy had gone off on another deployment. Stella looks Elizabeth up and down, looks at the pink box in her hands, then does what her mama used to do: takes the sweet gift and starts a pot of weak coffee.

Now that Elizabeth is here, Stella isn't sure what happens next. It's early for cake—Stella hasn't eaten dinner yet—but she cuts two big wedges and puts them on plates. Stella pours the coffee, and they sit at the kitchen table.

"How are the guys?" Stella asks, just to say something.

"Good," Elizabeth says. "I... We don't have to talk about work."

Stella nods and shovels cake into her mouth. Her face aches with the sweet taste, and it soothes her like a balm.

It's a relief not to talk about work. Even the thought of working at a job again makes Stella's anxiety spike. She doesn't know if she could bear talking about what she used to have.

"Addie says you're planning on painting," Elizabeth says, looking around.

Stella shrugs. "Someday."

Elizabeth drags her fork through a smear of icing on her plate. "Stella," she says, her usual cool, calm voice changing into something wobbly.

"What?"

"I need you to know something," Elizabeth says, "if we're going to be spending time with each other. It may change things, and you may decide that you don't want to see me again, and that's your choice, but it feels dishonest not to tell you." Elizabeth is looking down at her hands.

The bees begin to hum under Stella's skin, and she wonders if Elizabeth has bees too, if she's always had bees, and if this weird magnetic pull isn't so out of the blue and one-sided as it seems. Is Elizabeth feeling confused and frustrated and out of her depth too? If only Stella could name the feeling, label it, find the correct box, and shove it under her bed to deal with when grief isn't her constant companion. Something is preventing her from seeing clearly, from understanding herself. Or maybe she's just too… sad.

"Okay," Stella says.

"Stella"—Elizabeth enunciates each word deliberately—"I saw your husband die."

Stella feels strangely calm about this announcement. Disconnected, like she's watching herself. She reaches out to touch Elizabeth's arm and says, "That must have been so terrible for you."

Elizabeth looks up, surprised, her eyes wet.

"You didn't need to tell me," Stella assures her. Her voice sounds far away. "I'm not mad. I wouldn't have been mad even if I'd figured it out on my own."

Elizabeth nods, swallows hard. "Okay."

"If anything, I should be mad at—I don't know—myself? Him? The shooter?"

"God?" Elizabeth offers.

"Yeah," Stella says. "Fuck that guy."

Elizabeth barks out a surprised laugh, and Stella feels a prickle of satisfaction.

"It was awfully unfair what happened." Elizabeth dabs at her eyes with her napkin. "You and Chief Halligan had an enviable marriage."

Stella dabbles in revisionist history, but she can't pretend that her marriage was all sunshine and roses. "It wasn't," she admits. "It was a marriage. It was hard." She shakes her head. "I was a handful at the best of times."

Elizabeth reaches out and softly touches her hand. Stella jumps, knocks her fork from the plate to the table.

"How many people have you seen die?" Stella asks. For some reason, she has to know.

"Oh," Elizabeth says softly, "more than one."

"Elizabeth," Stella says after a stretch of silence.

"Hmm?"

"I'm not really…I don't know what to do," Stella says. "I'm not sure what comes next."

Elizabeth nods. "I know, honey."

After that, it's hard to stay mad at Elizabeth, so she stops. It's hard to hate her, so she doesn't. It's hard to begrudge her friendship with Addie, so she supports it instead.

"Have Elizabeth over, if you want," Stella says when Addie suggests a girls' night: watching movies, ordering in.

"Really?"

"Yeah," Stella says. "Why not?"

"Well," Addie hedges, "it's a Thursday. She might be busy."

"She might be," Stella agrees. "Doesn't hurt to ask."

"Okay." Addie pulls her phone from her back pocket to order. Stella wants a burrito; Addie wants ramen.

"Liz says she ate, but she'll come later, and we should start the movie without her." Addie hesitates, then says, "I think she's working on a rough case."

"They're all rough after you've been doing it awhile. Some police departments rotate detectives out of their homicide divisions before it wears them down."

"Do you think that's better?"

"No." Stella answers instantly, then explains. "It means no one specializes. It means rookies work every case. It's better for the cops, but not for the public."

"How do you pick between doing what's best for the public or for your employees?"

"You always choose the public," Stella says. "If you don't, it comes back to bite you."

"And what if the job makes you sick?" Addie fusses with a lit candle on the coffee table, turning it slightly so that the label is square with the edge of the table. The ceramic bottom, not quite smooth, scrapes against the wood.

"You leave," Stella says, "or they make you."

They eat their food and are forty-five minutes into a superhero movie that Stella doesn't even care if they finish. She can't follow the plot because she hasn't seen the four preceding movies that set up the flimsy premise of this one. Addie has tried to explain, but finally Stella waves her off, relieving her of the responsibility.

She goes to the kitchen to open a bottle of wine and drinks a glass alone at the table, looking at the open door of the dryer in the laundry room. They've been pulling underwear from it all week. Underwear is the easiest thing to put away. It can be carried in one armful and dumped into a drawer without folding it, and yet they haven't done it, neither one of them, and the other laundry is backing up. Now she goes over and pulls out the tangle of underwear and bras.

And that's when Elizabeth enters after a light courtesy knock. As she walks in, she glances at Addie watching TV, then turns to see Stella in the laundry room, her arms full of unmentionables.

Stella can't decide if she should be embarrassed or not. It's just one more thing.

"Hi." Elizabeth raises her eyebrows, but she doesn't comment.

Stella stuffs the clean laundry back into the dryer, shaking her head at her terrible sense of timing.

Elizabeth takes off her jacket and lays it across the back of an empty chair, dropping her purse next to it. She's wearing a camel-colored pencil skirt, a white striped blouse, and navy heels. She pushes her glasses up onto her head, tucking her curls off her face, and rubs the bridge of her nose, then settles onto the couch opposite from Addie and closes her eyes. When Stella comes out to greet her, Elizabeth looks up. "Can I have some wine?" she asks and closes her eyes again.

"Sure," Stella says. She fills a stemless wineglass halfway and sets it on the coffee table. Elizabeth snaps her eyes open when she hears the glass touch the wood.

Stella sits in an armchair across from the couch. "Are you hungry?" she asks.

"No," Elizabeth says. "Thank you." She takes a sip of the wine and then carefully toes off her high heels.

"We can watch something else." Addie stops the movie. "I don't think Stella was real invested in this one."

"I was not," Stella says. "Sorry."

"What do you want to watch?" Addie asks Elizabeth.

She shakes her head. "I don't care, sweetie."

Stella is feeling a little out of her depth but says, "I'm sick of TV. Let's connect your phone to the speaker and put on some music instead. Maybe we can play a game."

Addie and Elizabeth turn and look at her.

"Do you have games?" Elizabeth asks, sounding incredulous.

"There's a box of games in the garage, I think. Ron had a dominoes set that I kept. And some playing cards and poker chips. Stuff like that."

"I'll go look," Addie offers and goes out the front door to the detached garage.

"You okay?" Stella asks when she's closes the door.

"I'm just…" Elizabeth shakes her head. "There was this case a few months ago. The chief knew the guy and even thought he was probably guilty. The rest of us *knew* he was guilty, and he and I had words about it. Can't go easy on your buddies, Chief. That's not how justice works."

"Oh yeah. I've had that very same fight with a number of men in law enforcement," Stella says.

"Now this guy has lawyered up, and the chief keeps sticking his nose into the DA's office, and they're questioning me about whether *my* case is going to hold up because my sleazy boss is throwing his weight around. It makes me look bad, it makes my department look bad, and it makes the LAPD look like a disaster, which, frankly, it is."

"If the chief of police has a parade of sleazy friends that he has to continually cover up for, then, yeah, that can be exhausting," Stella says.

"And I wish you were still there because I know you would have run interference for us, and none of this would have happened."

Stella is surprised to learn that Elizabeth thought so highly of her. They bickered their way through most of their tenure together, and compliments were scarce. For the first time, Stella wonders if she was the cause of the tension between them, if Elizabeth had been trying and had grown tired of being rebuffed.

"If it was just the job, if it was just the murders and the families and the…the horror, you know, that would be one thing, but it's this shit that really wears you down." Elizabeth picks up her wineglass and drains it.

"You didn't have to come over. If you're tired, you can go and I'll make excuses."

Elizabeth looks up at her. "I'm glad to be here, Stella. It's a nice reprieve."

"Oh," she says. "Okay."

"I know you understand." Elizabeth settles her glasses back down over her eyes and tucks her hair behind her ears. "That's really nice, actually."

Addie comes in the front door and presents a black leather case. "Dominoes!" she announces. "Everything else in that box looked like it was for professional gambling."

"Dominoes it is," Elizabeth says.

Addie puts a bowl of pretzels onto the kitchen table and scrounges around for paper and pen to keep score. They have to look up the different games because everyone remembers different versions. They settle on Mexican Train, then they look for something to be their trains. Elizabeth goes to her purse to retrieve her wallet, a cream-colored Michael Kors number with a rose gold zipper, and digs out three pennies.

Stella snorts. "You don't have any quarters in there, Elizabeth? Sacagaweas? Gold doubloons?"

"I'll be expecting those back," she says, then winks at Addie as she returns the wallet to her purse.

Addie's music is not what Stella would have picked—she doesn't know any of the songs—but it melts gently into the background and fills up the little house, and it's all okay for a while. Cozy and warm. Addie wins at dominoes and that seems right too.

Stella is sitting on her bed in a T-shirt and underwear, wondering what to wear to therapy, thinking that maybe she'll just skip it, when she hears a familiar knock. Then she hears the door open.

"You guys should think about locking your door!" Elizabeth calls out.

"What are you doing here?" Stella yells back. "I'm not decent."

"I'm taking you to your appointment. I cleared it with Addie."

"Addie isn't my secretary. You can talk to me, you know." She looks around her room, but she still doesn't know what to wear.

"Would you have said yes?" Elizabeth asks.

Probably not. It was embarrassing enough the first time.

When Stella doesn't answer, Elizabeth comes down the hall and looks into the bedroom. "We're going to be late. Why aren't you dressed?"

"Come on in, I guess," Stella says sarcastically. "I don't know. Everything fits weird."

"Well, you eat like garbage," Elizabeth points out, "and you never leave this house."

"Wow. Thank you."

"It's not healthy is all I'm trying to say."

"Yeah, I got that."

Elizabeth sighs, leaves Stella's bedroom, comes back in a few moments with a pair of folded jeans. Addie's jeans—light wash, rips in the knees.

"I don't know—"

"Put them on. It's just an appointment. You don't have to impress anyone." Elizabeth tosses them onto the bed, crosses her arms, and waits, her pretty purse hanging on her arm and her hair clipped back.

"You look like an ad for Banana Republic."

"Thank you," Elizabeth says.

Stella shakes out the jeans and steps into them. They're tight, but they're supposed to be. She gets her toe caught in the rip in the knee and loses her balance briefly. She has barely slipped on her shoes and picked up her purse before Elizabeth hustles them out the door and into her car.

"Why are you doing this?" Stella asks when they're on the road.

"Because I want to. It doesn't impact my schedule much, and if a crime scene comes up, well, we can navigate that, but you know how I like to delegate." Elizabeth glances into her side mirror and changes lanes.

"That doesn't answer my question," Stella points out.

"I feel better doing it," Elizabeth says.

"Because you saw Ron die."

"Because I know it's difficult for you, and because we're friends, and yeah, because I feel a little responsible," Elizabeth admits.

"You aren't *responsible*. Jesus," Stella says. "Maybe *you* need therapy."

"I get therapy, Stella."

"What?"

"I have a stressful, dangerous job that is emotionally draining, three children carrying trauma from my alcoholic ex-husband, and I recently watched a colleague get murdered. I get regular therapy." She glances over. "Did you work prosecuting criminals for seven years and never go to therapy? Ever?"

It was much longer than seven years, but she lets it go and says, "I'm going now, aren't I?"

"I guess that's something."

Stella and Dr. Barrett talk through her homework, then she finds herself talking about Elizabeth again, about how she hated her and then tolerated her and then sort of needed her and has now found herself wanting her around.

"Friends," Dr. Barrett says, smiling "You're friends."

"Yeah, I guess." Stella wonders if this is what friendship feels like. Thoughts of Elizabeth swarm her all the time, and that can't be normal. "She brings me to these appointments because she feels bad that she saw my husband die and I didn't."

"Why would she have wanted you to see your own husband die?"

"Not that. She feels bad that she was on the inside," Stella says. "That's all. And I was outside."

"You'd been promoted," Dr. Barrett reasons. "You'd moved on to bigger things, which is completely normal. Is that the same as being on the outside?"

"You're either in the room and on the case or you aren't." Stella crosses her arms, digs her fingernails into her skin. "I'd left the room."

When Stella finishes the session, Elizabeth is sitting on the retaining wall again, waiting, this time holding Starbucks for them both. Stella's drink is a chocolatey thing topped with whipped cream and fudge drizzle. Barely coffee at all, really.

"Thank you," she says.

"You're welcome."

Elizabeth taps her plastic cup to Stella's, and they head back to the car.

CHAPTER 5

Addie couldn't get her full shift off for her birthday, so Stella takes her out for an early dinner, and Elizabeth and Josh meet them afterward for dessert. Addie announces her plans to spend a week in Nashville with her parents. They talk about Thom and Joyce coming out to Los Angeles instead, but Addie says, "Maybe it's not the right time for guests."

That stings a little, even though she was right to say it. Stella is getting better, but she's still deep in her grief. Time has passed, distancing her from Ron's death. She's in therapy, and she's even made a friend. Or remade one. Or made an acquaintance into something different.

Whatever the hell Elizabeth is.

But she still has bad days. Days where she can't get out of bed, where she loses time, where she can't even brush her teeth or her hair without crying. She certainly doesn't feel like she's back to normal.

It's good for Addie to go see her parents, and maybe it's good for Stella too, to have the house to herself again.

She drives Addie to the airport. Drops her off at the departure terminal with her rolling suitcase and her backpack. Promises to pick her up again.

"I'll text you," Addie says. "Call me if you need me."

"I'll be fine," Stella says again. "It's one week. Don't you worry about me."

When she gets home, the house seems quiet and empty and dark, even though it's only midmorning. She pulls her phone out of her purse to check what day it is. Thursday. Not that it matters. Her mama used to say, "Every day is Saturday when you're retired!"

Maybe she can get serious about her finances this week. Figure out how to bring some money in. Figure out who might be willing to take her on, even after all this. If there are any options left in this city for her.

But now she has a headache, so she puts off thinking about it for one more day and goes to bed.

The next day, Elizabeth calls. Stella is eating lunch in the backyard. Her therapist says she can't stay inside for the entire day anymore, so sometimes she sits out back so she can honestly say at her next appointment that, yes, she did leave the house.

"It's been one day," she says by way of greeting.

"Huh?"

"Addie's only been gone a day. You think I can't make it one day?"

"Listen, I don't have time for that," Elizabeth says. "Are you still trying to sell your car?"

"Oh." She's a tiny bit put out that Elizabeth isn't calling just to check up on her. "Yeah, I suppose I've got to."

"Which one—the SUV or the hybrid?"

"I don't know," she says, rubbing her temple. The sunshine she was enjoying suddenly feels too warm, and the turkey sandwich turns heavy in her stomach. She pushes her plate away. "I haven't decided."

"Well, how would you feel about selling one or the other to Detective Ramirez?" Elizabeth asks.

Marco Ramirez was Stella's favorite of Elizabeth's little band of detectives. He's quiet, often broody, but extremely observant and great at making mental deductions. He's also great on the stand. Most lawyers have a hell of a time trying to trip him up.

"Marco wants to buy my car?" Stella asks.

"He needs one, and I know you're selling one. I thought maybe I could broker a deal."

"Does he know what he wants?"

"I think he'd probably take either one, frankly, if it means a friendly face and not having to deal with a dealership or Craigslist," Elizabeth says. "How would you feel if I brought him by after work?"

"Today?"

"Yeah."

Stella hears voices in the background. Someone—it sounds like the gruff-voiced Esposito—says something to Elizabeth.

"Okay," Stella says. "Sure. I guess."

"Great. We'll see you then. Bye."

And Elizabeth hangs up. Stella pulls the phone away from her ear and looks at the screen just in time to see Elizabeth's name blink away.

She abandons her lunch things and walks around the side of the house and through the gate to the detached garage. A lot of her neighbors still have garage doors that need to be unlocked with a key and lifted, but Stella's has been updated. She keys in the code to open it.

The hybrid stays parked in the garage now, the SUV in the driveway. Addie parks on the street. They cleared out just enough space for it, but anytime they need something from the garage, they edge around the car. There's just enough room to open the driver's side door and slip in. It would probably be smarter to move the SUV to the street and back the hybrid out, but that seems like a lot of work, and it will be hours before Elizabeth gets there with Marco, so instead she turns on the dome light and looks around inside.

She removes the clip-on holder for her cell phone and picks at a corner of the DA parking permit decal until she can peel it away. The door has some candy wrappers stuffed in it, and she pockets those to dispose of later.

She can't give up the SUV, can't sell that last part of Ron just yet. Maybe the hybrid is more economical, but she doesn't feel as safe in it. If Marco wants a car, it will have to be this one.

She makes a mental note to tell Dr. Barrett at her next appointment that she made an actual decision. Maybe not the best one, but a firm one. Shouldn't that count for something?

Stella wakes up to see Elizabeth crouched next to her by the couch, her hand on Stella's shoulder. Her brow is furrowed in concern. Maybe it's because she woke Stella from a sound sleep, but she looks strange, otherworldly, with her intense green eyes and her perfect skin.

"You okay?" Elizabeth asks.

"Elizabeth?"

"Come on, sit up." Elizabeth presses the back of one hand briefly against Stella's forehead. Her car keys jingle in the other. "You're warm. Are you running a fever? I'll get you some water."

"I'm fine. I'm fine." Stella sits up, swings her feet to the floor, then realizes there's someone else in the living room. Marco is standing by the door, looking like he'd rather be anywhere else. "Shit. The car."

"Hello," he says. "Sorry to… Sorry."

"I lost track of time."

Elizabeth has moved to the kitchen, moving around the little house as if she's been here a hundred times before. She comes back with a glass of water and a bottle of Advil. "Why didn't you tell me you weren't feeling well?"

Stella ignores the question. But now she understands why Elizabeth looks different.

No glasses.

She takes a single pill from the bottle and sips some water, then wipes her hands on her sweatpants. Realizes she's still wearing what she slept in last night.

"I'm, uh, just gonna go change and then… Y'all have a seat." She scoots down the hall to her room.

She puts on clean underwear, a bra. A pair of purple leggings, a black T-shirt. She hasn't showered in two or three days, so she puts deodorant on under the shirt. Then she slips into the bathroom and looks at herself.

Her hair is a dry and frizzy mess, but that's a given. And she's a little flushed. It's hard to tell if she's feverish or if she feels bad because she always feels bad. She can't always parse what's emotional and what's physical.

She brushes her teeth, splashes water on her face, pulls back her dirty hair. She'll shower after they leave.

Elizabeth has made a pot of coffee, and she and Marco are sitting at the kitchen table with mugs in front of them.

"It's nice to see you, Marco," Stella says when she reemerges. "How are you doing?"

"I'm fine, ma'am."

"Oh, I'm just…Stella now." She makes an effort to smile.

"Are you hungry?" Elizabeth asks. "You want to order in? We could have something to eat and then do this car stuff."

Stella shakes her head. "Stop fussing."

"Okay," Elizabeth says.

"Marco, I don't know what Captain Murphy told you, but I don't think I can part with Ron's car yet, so—"

"Oh, that's okay," he says nervously. "I wouldn't…I don't…"

"You okay with a hybrid?"

"I'll take a look, yeah." He looks tired. His tie is a little crooked, and he has more than a day's growth on his face. Elizabeth seems stressed too. Stella wonders about their caseload.

Elizabeth reaches down into her purse and pulls out a folder. "I took the liberty of looking up Kelley Blue Book prices for both cars, Stella." She opens the folder, pulls out some pages, and slides a set to Stella and Marco each. "You'll see average estimates, some estimates with mileage variations, and I've jotted down what I think is a fair price if Marco pays you a cash lump sum versus monthly payments."

"If you're okay with payments," Marco says.

"Yeah, that's fine," she says. "Do you want to look at it? You may not even want it."

"Sure."

Elizabeth looks over at Marco and then lifts one shoulder.

"The keys are over here." All her keys are sitting on the counter in the kitchen. Addie's too. "I'll go move the SUV, and then we can pull the hybrid out of the garage, okay?"

"Here," Elizabeth says, reaching for the keys. "I'll do it."

Stella is perfectly capable of moving the cars, but it's so much easier to hand the task over to Elizabeth. They file out of the house, and she and Marco stand on the porch and watch Elizabeth back the SUV out of the driveway. Elizabeth's car is parked in front of the house behind Addie's, so she drives the SUV down to the end of the block and turns around to park across the street.

"Open the garage, Stella," she says when she gets back to the driveway.

"Right." Stella should take the keys and back it out herself, but Elizabeth marches into the garage before she can protest. The hybrid backs out noiselessly.

"It's gray," Marco says.

"Yeah."

"I just thought it'd be…something else." He looks at her and grins. "Pink or something."

Stella elbows him. "That's a bit much, even for me," she says.

Elizabeth gets out of the car, leaving the keys in the cup holder.

"Want to go for a drive?" Stella asks.

"How about I drive us all to dinner," he says. "I know a place that makes a good chimichanga."

"Yeah?" Stella says.

"You up for it, ma'am?" Marco says to Elizabeth. "Dinner out? On me?"

"Of course."

Stella goes inside to put on shoes. She pulls on a gray zip-up hoodie. There's no time for makeup, but who does she have to impress?

She rides in the back seat behind Elizabeth. Marco says he likes how quiet the ride is. There aren't many miles on the car because she hasn't had it that long and has spent most of the last year not driving it.

"How's your mom, Marco?" Stella asks.

Marco says nothing, and finally Elizabeth answers. "Marco lost his mother last month, Stella."

"Oh," she says. "I'm so sorry."

"Thank you," he replies softly.

It kills the conversation, but Elizabeth reaches behind her seat and pats Stella on the knee.

Marco buys the car. They agree on a year of payments, and he writes the first check before he leaves. She pries the key off her key ring and gives it to him.

Elizabeth slowly packs up her paperwork and slips the folder back into her purse but doesn't get up.

"You don't have to go," Stella says when she realizes maybe Elizabeth doesn't want to leave. "No sense in you going back to an empty house."

"You don't mind?"

"No," Stella says. "I just thought you were tired."

"I am tired." Elizabeth sinks back on the sofa. "But I can be tired here too."

"There's ice cream, I think." Stella opens the freezer. There's a package of chicken thighs that surely needs to be tossed and some empty ice trays. "Or not. Maybe I ate that."

"I'm stuffed from dinner anyway."

"Do you want to put on something more comfortable?" Stella offers.

Elizabeth looks down at her outfit—a sheath dress and coordinating blazer, black heels and nylons.

"We could watch something. Veg on the couch," Stella adds. "Light a candle, really go wild."

Elizabeth smiles, and something in Stella's chest swells.

"Sure," she says.

Now Stella must find something clean for Elizabeth to wear. She digs around in the dresser until she finds a set of pajamas that her mama sent for her birthday years ago. The top is a short-sleeved, button-down shirt, pink with a floral print, and the matching pants are soft. She doesn't wear them often because they seem too nice. But too nice is just right for Elizabeth.

She brings them out to Elizabeth, who is halfway through putting old dirty dishes from the sink into the dishwasher.

"Oh," Elizabeth says when she sees the pajamas. "How sweet."

"I need to shower. Are you okay with that?"

"Of course."

"I know you'll make yourself at home," Stella says. "I won't be long."

A shower feels right, even if it makes Elizabeth wait for her. She's grungy and greasy. Overripe.

She washes her hair first, shaves while the conditioner sets. She uses Addie's body wash that smells like apples instead of her usual plain white bar of soap. She feels like she needs to smell more than just clean to sit next to Elizabeth on the couch.

She turns off the water and drips in the shower for a few seconds, then pulls back the curtain and reaches for her towel. It smells a little musty, like it needs to be washed. She hears a soft murmur, like Elizabeth is talking on the phone. Stella dries off briskly, wraps herself in one towel, wraps her hair in another, then slips down the hall to her bedroom. She digs through the dresser and pulls out some clean shorts, blue with white polka dots, and a white tank top. She throws a chunky sweater on top and goes back to the bathroom to deal with her hair. She spends some time detangling her curls and puts some cream in to help control them as they dry.

Elizabeth is still on the phone when she comes out.

"Here she is." Elizabeth holds Stella's phone out to her. "It's Addie. I answered it."

Stella puts it to her ear. "Hi, sugar."

"Hi," Addie says. "Are you and Elizabeth having a girls' night?"

"Looks like," Stella says. "How are you? How's your daddy and mama?"

"Everything is fine here. It's nice to be home, and I also can't wait to leave."

Stella chuckles. "Yeah, that's kinda what it's going to be like from now on."

"Elizabeth said you sold the car?"

"The hybrid," Stella says.

"Well, that's great. The two of us don't need three cars."

"Do you think I should have sold the big one?"

"No, not if it's the one you like best."

"I didn't even know I liked it," Stella admits. "Ron never let me drive it." She almost never talks about Ron outside of therapy anymore, and saying his name feels weird.

Addie marches right past it. "We'll have more space in the garage," she says. "Maybe we can go through stuff in there when I come back."

"Sure, honey. Have fun, and don't worry about me, okay?"

"Okay," Addie says. "I love you."

"I love you too. It's late there. Get some sleep."

Stella joins Elizabeth on the couch. "So, what do you want to watch? We have Netflix, the Amazon one, and Hulu, I think. And cable."

"You want to watch *Bake-Off*? That's on Netflix."

"What's that?"

"Oh," Elizabeth says, "it's British people baking things in a tent in a field while being politely judged. It sounds boring, but there's something gentle about it." She takes the remote from Stella. "We'll start at the beginning."

"You know what Addie likes to watch?" Stella says. "People doing their makeup on YouTube."

"I guess that's popular. People can make money from it."

"It is weirdly captivating," Stella admits. "They're all basically commercials for expensive products, but I get it, I guess."

Stella has her doubts about watching people bake, but she's drawn in by the cinematography, the happy and bright music, the pastel tent full of nervous but kind bakers.

"Hey," Elizabeth says after a few minutes, "you want me to braid your hair?"

Stella turns to look at her, incredulous. "You want to *what*? Are we having a sleepover?"

"Wow. A simple no would have sufficed." Elizabeth turns back to the screen.

"I'm…I'm sorry. I didn't mean to be a bitch. I just don't see why you'd want to do that," Stella says.

Elizabeth smirks. "Ah. We never mean to be a bitch, do we?" She turns back to the TV. "It's fine. I just figured that you put your hair up into that ratty bun because you don't want to deal with it. A good braid could last you three days."

"Oh."

"Care to reconsider?" Elizabeth picks invisible lint off her borrowed pajamas. "We should do it before your hair dries."

"Fine." She should stick with no. Her and her ratty bun have been through a lot together. Plus, she's managed to suppress whatever it is that Elizabeth makes her feel, now that she comes around so often, but the thought of Elizabeth's fingers in her hair makes the bees hum.

A traitorous thought occurs. *Has Elizabeth ever slept with a woman?*

Likely not, but the urge to ask starts to gnaw at her, and now she has two things to push down hard on.

Anyway, she already knows the answer. Elizabeth was married to her ex-husband for a long time and casually dated Sam Warren after she divorced him. And it turns out that Elizabeth is Catholic, not the type of woman who sleeps with other women, even if she wants to.

She gets her hairbrush and two elastics from the basket on the back of the toilet, searching for two that match. She hands them to Elizabeth.

Elizabeth has pushed the coffee table away from the couch and placed a throw pillow between her feet for Stella to sit on. Elizabeth slips the purple elastics onto her wrist as Stella plops at her feet.

"Who knew you were a hairdresser?" Stella says, reaching for the remote to restart *Bake-Off.*

"My daughter is a ballerina," Elizabeth explains. "Braiding became part of my life very quickly."

Stella has never met Elizabeth's older children. In fact, she knows very little about her, despite how much time they spent together over the years. But Elizabeth seems to know everything about Stella.

As Elizabeth brushes her hair out, Stella keeps her eyes glued to the screen. It feels nice to have someone doting on her, extra nice that it's Elizabeth. She can smell Elizabeth's perfume—or maybe it's body wash.

"You need a haircut. Your ends are a disaster." Elizabeth sections off the hair.

"Oh, I'm sure," Stella says. "Curls hide all manner of sins, though."

"Until you get up close."

"The only one getting up close is you," Stella retorts, then feels herself coloring. Offhand comments are nothing when they stand alone, but enough of them create a breadcrumb trail that leads right to the truth.

Elizabeth sets half of Stella's hair over her shoulder and starts braiding the other side.

She can't remember the last time someone besides Addie touched her, and Elizabeth's fingers in her hair feel nice, but the yanking and pulling hurts a little too because she's braiding tightly. It's a good hurt, though. She slumps against one of Elizabeth's knees.

Elizabeth ties off the first braid. Shifts a little to get to the other side. Stella leans against her other knee in response.

On the screen, someone's bake goes wrong, and all the other contestants crowd around the doomed baker to help.

"Everyone on this show is so nice," Stella says. "I just want cake now."

"Yes, that is an unfortunate side effect of this show." Elizabeth drags her fingers along Stella's temple, gathering strands of hair that have already curled up wild. Stella leans into her touch, then realizing what she is doing, freezes.

"Did I hurt you?" Elizabeth stops moving her hands.

"Just a little snag," Stella mumbles by way of excuse.

"You don't have much gray. Which is impressive."

"It's just hard to see with all the blonde," Stella says.

Elizabeth sighs and then says, "I'm totally gray."

"Really?" Stella asks. She knew Elizabeth's auburn hair was a dye job, the color sometimes darker, sometimes lighter, but it's hard to imagine her totally gray, and she's surprised that Elizabeth admitted it. Her makeup and hair are always perfect, her clothes professional and flattering.

"I guess at some point I'll have to let it go. I mean, at what age do you start to look ridiculous and out of touch?"

"Your hair is beautiful. You don't seem out of touch."

"Well," Elizabeth says, "thank you."

Stella feels Elizabeth moving her fingers against her neck, adjusting the first braid, then braids, and ties off the other side.

"Turn around," Elizabeth says.

Stella looks away from the colorful confections on TV and turns around on her pillow to face Elizabeth. She's still tucked between her knees, but Elizabeth seems unconcerned. She surveys her work and then carefully pulls some hair free with the brush to form two small tendrils that frame Stella's face.

"Perfect," Elizabeth says. "Now, pin them up during the day to help keep the frizz away, but I'd sleep with them down. It'll be more comfortable."

"Yes, ma'am." Stella grins and then moves to turn back toward the TV.

"Stella, wait. Can I ask you something?"

"Sure." Stella's heart starts to hammer, anticipating the same question that's been clawing at Stella.

"Would it be all right if I stay the night?" Elizabeth face is unreadable, neutral.

"Stay?" Stella repeats, both confused and elated.

"The night. I could sleep on the couch. I just...don't feel like going home to that empty condo."

"Oh! Yeah, sure. Of course. You can sleep in Addie's bed or with... I mean, you don't have to sleep on the couch."

Elizabeth sighs, as if relieved at the answer after asking a difficult question. "Thank you."

"You're doing me a favor," Stella confesses. "I don't like waking up to an empty house."

Stella pushes herself off the floor, her knees cracking as they straighten. She tosses the pillow back onto the couch.

"Hot chocolate?" She needs something to ease the craving for sweets.

"Sure," Elizabeth says. "Want me to pause the show?"

"Nah, I can see it from the kitchen."

She pours milk into the pan and adds chocolate, stirring it slowly as it thickens, the way her mama used to. She pours the drink into mugs, then pauses with the dirty pot in front of the sink to look at her reflection in the warped cabinet glass. The French braids make her look more like Addie than herself. She reaches up and tugs on the end of one.

"You like them?" Elizabeth has twisted around on the couch to watch her.

Stella nods at her reflection. "I do."

CHAPTER 6

THEY FALL ASLEEP WATCHING *BAKE-OFF*. The show has stopped and Netflix is on a still screen, asking if anyone is still watching. Stella sits up and looks around. Her back is aching. The candle on the coffee table flickers, and there's at least a solid inch of liquid wax around it.

She turns to look at the clock in the kitchen and jumps when she sees Elizabeth curled up at the other end of the couch, then remembers that Elizabeth asked to stay the night.

Stella reaches up one hand to touch the end of her braid. Where are Elizabeth's glasses anyway? Stella hasn't seen them all night. Not even when she was moving the SUV or squinting at the menu at dinner with Marco.

Stella carries their empty mugs to the kitchen and sets them in the sink. The clock on the microwave says *1:36*.

She pokes her head into Addie's room, feeling along the wall until she finds the switch. The only light is a string of white lights that Addie tacked along the ceiling, but it's enough to see by.

The bed is rumpled, so she pulls back the comforter, hauls up the sheet, and straightens it out. The sheets aren't crisp and clean, but they're clean enough. There's some makeup on the floor by the mirror. Stella leans over to pick it up and drop it into the clear acrylic container that's also on the floor. Her back twinges again as she straightens, and she rubs at the sore muscle.

She goes to one of the cupboards in the hall where linens are stored. The cupboard closest to the bathroom has toiletries: cotton rounds and Q-Tips, boxes of tampons and pantyliners, hair products, curling irons, hair dryers, and straighteners. Tucked into the back is a pack of toothbrushes. She peels the plastic away from the cardboard and digs one out with a blue and white handle. She lays it on the edge of the sink.

She returns to the living room. Elizabeth is still asleep. Stella wills her to wake up by thinking hard at her, but it doesn't work. She turns off the TV and deliberately drops the remote down on the coffee table, but Elizabeth doesn't stir.

Stella reaches out and pats Elizabeth's hip.

Elizabeth blinks, pushes her hair out of her face, squints up at Stella. "What time is it?"

"After one," Stella says. "Time for bed."

Elizabeth sits up with a groan.

"Where are your glasses?"

"They broke. I'm waiting for a new pair."

"You can see without them? Well enough to get by?"

"Reading is a struggle. Driving at night isn't great."

Stella sits on the opposite arm of the couch, her stomach sinking. "That's why you wanted to stay the night."

Elizabeth sighs. "No, it's not."

"Then why?" Stella presses.

"I thought it might be nice, since we were both alone tonight." She cocks her head at Stella. "I can go if I misread the situation."

Stella backpedals. "Of course not. I'm just—"

"Suspicious of everything I do. I know." Elizabeth runs her hands through her hair.

There's no sense in arguing, since she's right, but it's annoying all the same. "I don't mean to be," is what Stella settles on. "I'm working on it."

"I know." Elizabeth says softly.

"I found you a toothbrush. You can use our makeup remover, if you want."

"Thank you."

"It's all in there. Go ahead." Stella waves her hand at the bathroom door. She's tired, ready to crawl into bed, but she wants to make sure Elizabeth is settled first. She blows out the candle, watches as the smoke swirls and dissipates, then locks all the doors, Elizabeth's earlier words echoing in her mind.

She turns off the lights in the living room, the kitchen, and the laundry room. Only the lights in Addie's room, the lamp on Stella's nightstand, and the line of light under the bathroom door remain.

She stands in the dim hallway, her back against the wall, and takes a deep breath, then another one. Feels a lump rise up in her throat, and her eyes fill with tears. They overtake her whenever she feels too much of anything. Fear, happiness, sadness, boredom, anticipation, hope, or anything else.

When Elizabeth comes out of the bathroom, her hair tied back, her face scrubbed clean, she finds Stella with her face in her hands.

"Come on," Elizabeth says softly. "Let's go to bed."

Stella allows herself to be led to her bedroom. Elizabeth pulls her covers back and eases her into the bed, then reaches out and turns off the lamp.

"I'm just down the hall if you need me." Elizabeth touches one of Stella's braids, giving it a soft tug, and leaves the door open behind her.

Stella keeps her eyes open until the light in Addie's room goes out.

Elizabeth has left by the time Stella wakes up late the next morning. The coffeepot is prepped and ready. All Stella has to do is push the button. There's a note on the back of a receipt.

Thanks for everything. Call me.
Liz

Stella isn't going to call her. Send her a text, *maybe*. And anyway, Elizabeth will come with her to her next therapy appointment, right?

She'll have to talk about Elizabeth spending the night, about crying in the hallway.

When she goes to the bathroom, the blue and white toothbrush is in the holder next to her pink and white one.

The day before Addie comes home, Elizabeth calls. "Can I go with you to pick her up?"

"You wanna go to the airport with me?" Stella holds the phone against her shoulder while she unpacks groceries.

"Yes," Elizabeth says. "I love picking people up from the airport. I love the idea of someone you love coming home."

Stella pops a grape into her mouth. "Whatever floats your boat."

"What time are you going to leave?"

"Her flight gets in at seven forty-five. That's not too late for you?" Stella asks.

"No."

"I'll need to leave around seven. You never know what traffic will be like."

"Okay. I'll head over right after work," Elizabeth says. "See you then."

Elizabeth offers to drive the SUV to pick up Addie. Her new glasses look a lot like her old ones, though the frames are a little thicker, a little darker. She looks even sharper, smarter than she did before.

They've barely left the house when Stella asks, "Are you dating anyone?"

Maybe it's Elizabeth's new glasses that have nudged her off her game. Maybe it's her perfume filling up the car. Maybe it's the fact that Elizabeth isn't wearing nylons with her gray skirt and Stella can see her bare leg. Or maybe it's that her hair is pinned up elaborately.

It's like Elizabeth put a lot of effort into looking pretty. But pretty people don't have to try to look pretty, so maybe Stella's projecting her own feelings.

"No," Elizabeth says. "Not at the moment. Why do you ask?"

"Just curious. Sorry. It's none of my business."

"It's fine." Elizabeth grips the steering wheel so tightly that Stella sees her knuckles turn white. "You know I was seeing Lieutenant Warren for a while."

"I'd heard that, yes."

"I realized that I had a type and…despite Sam's sobriety and best intentions, my bad taste in men was always going to work against me," she says. "I'm just not in the mood for men anymore."

"Men?"

"Precisely." She flips on the turn signal, cuts over a lane, and speeds up in time to hit the on-ramp to the freeway. She focuses on driving until they've merged. "Do you think about dating?"

"Oh..." Stella isn't sure if thinking about Elizabeth all the time counts as thinking about dating. "Sometimes," she lies.

"I think that's good."

"I agree, though. Men. Ugh."

She glances over to see Elizabeth smirking.

"I'm at a point in my life where I don't need a relationship to be happy," Elizabeth continues. "If someone comes along, fine, but if not, that's fine too." She waves her hand as if she really doesn't care, but it sounds more like she's trying to convince herself.

Stella looks down at her hands. Her rings glint in the evening light. "I don't know why I still wear these. I'm not married anymore."

"Grief is strange and won't be rushed. If you aren't ready to take them off, then you aren't ready."

"Sometimes I don't even miss him," Stella admits. "I'm mostly sad about the way it happened. Other times, I can't even remember why I'm sad. It's just my default."

She spins the rings on her finger and then pulls them off, twisting them at the knuckle. She holds them in her open hand. There's an indentation on her ring finger, and the skin is paler.

"How does that feel?" Elizabeth asks.

"Feels all right, I guess." And this time it's not a lie. "What do I do with them?"

"Put them in your jewelry box. Look at them if you want to, or never look at them again if you don't."

"Do you still have rings from your marriage?"

"I had a gold band that I sold with a bunch of other things after Paul gambled our rent money away. He promised to replace it but left before he did," Elizabeth says.

"You *do* have bad taste."

"Mm-hmm."

"The stone is nice," Stella says, looking again at the wedding set in her palm. "I could have it taken out and put in something else. Or I could give it to Addie when she gets married." Stella pulls her purse onto her lap and unzips the inside pocket, drops the rings in, and zips it closed. "Something to talk about with Dr. Barrett," she says with a nervous laugh.

"How's that going?"

"Okay." Talking about therapy is only slightly less uncomfortable than actually going. "I feel like we don't talk about anything, but then the hour is over and I'm exhausted."

"She must be good."

"I talk about you." Stella doesn't know why she says it. "I mean, I have."

"Me?"

"Just that we used to work together and weren't friends, but now maybe we are, and you and Addie… Well, you're at my house all the time." Stella shrugs. "She says we're friends."

"We are friends," Elizabeth confirms, then asks, "Do you want me to come over less?"

"No! At first, I did, but now…I like it." She looks out the window. There are more cars on the freeway now, and they've slowed down. "I'm not good at friends. I never have been."

"You're doing fine," Elizabeth says. "But you should be honest with me about coming over. About how you feel."

She opens her mouth to respond when a car cuts in front of them. Elizabeth slams on the brakes to avoid hitting it and leans on the horn.

"Asshole," she mutters.

So Stella doesn't say how she feels, and that's probably for the best. Maybe God sent that asshole in the BMW to save her from herself.

Addie is waiting outside the arrivals terminal when they pull up. Stella jumps out and hugs her.

"I'm sorry we're late. Traffic," she says.

"Of course," Addie says. "I haven't been waiting very long."

Elizabeth pops the hatch, and Addie hefts her suitcase in.

"You want to sit in the front?" Stella asks.

"No, no. The back is fine."

When everyone is settled in the car, Elizabeth turns and smiles at Addie. "Welcome home. How was the flight?"

"Long. Can someone please feed me real food?"

"That can be arranged," Elizabeth says and pulls away from the curb.

"How were Thom and Joyce?" Stella asks.

"Fine. They send their love."

"Did you see Uncle Brick?" Stella asks.

"Yeah, I saw pretty much everyone. We had a barbeque so people could come over. Everyone asked about you. I said you were doing fine."

"Nice of you to lie," Stella mutters.

Elizabeth glances at her.

"I don't know. It's just weird now that Grandma and Grandpa are gone. And their house isn't there."

"I know," Stella says. "It's weird for me too."

They sold the house after Stella's daddy died. No one could afford to keep it up, and neither of her brothers wanted to move into it, so it made more sense to let it go. Stella got a little money from the sale, but her daddy's health was so bad at the end that most of the money went to the nurse who came every day to the house, and by the time they paid all the bills and for the funeral, there wasn't a lot to split three ways.

Elizabeth suggests hamburgers. They go to Burger Lounge in Santa Monica and park in one of the nearby city-owned lots. There's a line to order, so Addie scouts out a booth by a family and snags it when they leave. She texts Stella her order.

Stella tries to pay, but Elizabeth says, "You paid for parking." Addie actually paid for parking with an app on her phone, but Stella has learned to choose her battles with Elizabeth.

Stella isn't a huge burger person, but Elizabeth and Addie seem to enjoy them. Addie looks exhausted, but she keeps up a running conversation about her time in Nashville while they eat. They're discussing whether to pick up something for dessert when Elizabeth's phone rings. Stella can see the screen from where she sits. It's Lieutenant Esposito.

"Oh," Elizabeth says, sounding a little sad.

"Go on. You know you have to answer it," Stella says.

She swipes to pick up the call. "Captain Murphy." She sticks a finger in her other ear and squints as if that will make her hear better. "Uh-huh. Okay," she says. "I have to take the Carters home, so I'll be there in about forty minutes."

Addie starts bussing the table. "Should we Lyft?" she whispers to Stella.

"The dead are already dead," Stella says. "They'll keep an extra twenty minutes."

Elizabeth hangs up. "Sorry."

"It's quite all right," Stella assures her.

"Lieutenant Esposito says hello to you both," Elizabeth adds.

As they walk back to the car, Addie says, "Thank you for dinner, Liz."

"Yes. Thank you," Stella says, then adds, "Sorry dessert is off the table."

"I don't need it anyway," Elizabeth says. "But I'm glad we got to spend some time together."

Addie loops her hand through Elizabeth's arm.

Stella trails behind them, jealous and nervous and afraid.

Stella sips at a lukewarm cup of coffee and does the daily crossword puzzle. It's not quite noon, and Addie has just gotten up. Stella let her sleep in. She has to work tonight and is probably still beat from a day of travel.

"Can I ask you something?" Addie says.

"Sure, darlin'."

"Did Elizabeth sleep in my bed?"

"Oh, shoot, I should have asked you, huh? Or changed your sheets. I'm sorry."

"No, it's fine. I'm surprised that she spent the night."

"It was no big deal. We both fell asleep on the couch watching Netflix. I told her she could stay." It's not exactly the truth, but Stella can't bring herself to tell Addie that it was Elizabeth who asked to stay, that Stella had been awake half the night, her temples throbbing from the tight braids and her mind racing, knowing that Elizabeth Murphy was one room away. "How did you know?" Stella asks.

"My pillow smelled like her," Addie says. "It was actually kind of comforting."

The buzzing under Stella's skin grows more insistent.

"Addie, listen. I'm sorry I was upset about Elizabeth at first. Because she's been really good for me, I think."

"I think so too," Addie says. "I still don't understand why you didn't like her."

"It's complicated."

Addie hovers like she's going to press the issue, but then she moves to the stove, frying bacon, making hash browns, and heating a saucepan of water to poach eggs. Breakfast for lunch.

Stella could not successfully poach an egg if her life depended on it, but Addie manages to poach two while paying attention to three other things. And then, when she plates it up, it looks so nice and it tastes *good.* Stella perforates the egg with the side of her fork and yolk rushes out and seeps into the bed of hash browns it sits on.

"My friend from the bar, Genevieve," Addie says, "works at the Wood Ranch in the Grove."

"What's that?"

"It's like a chain barbecue restaurant. She says they need more servers, and she could put in a good word for me."

"You want to quit the bar?" Stella asks.

"I'd quit for a better job."

Stella takes a bite of bacon. "Are you worried about money?"

"I think I could contribute more, especially with you not working."

"I'm gonna go back to work," Stella says, defensive.

"I know that. No one is rushing you," Addie says. "Anyway, I have to do something for a year until I can go back to school. I may as well save up, right?"

"If that's what you want to do, you should do it."

"What do you think you'll do when you're ready? Go back to the district attorney's office?"

"No. I don't know what, but not that."

"Maybe Elizabeth can help you." Addie sips her coffee.

"Elizabeth has done enough for me." Stella picks up her plate and moves to the sink. The more she lets Elizabeth into her life, the more she can't picture her life without Elizabeth, and that would put her into a potentially painful situation. "I can't ask her to take on my whole life as a pity project."

"She doesn't feel like that." Addie leans back in her chair.

"Yeah? How does she feel, then?"

"You should know exactly how she feels," Addie points out. "She works all the time, she doesn't have any friends, her kids have all moved out. She broke up with her boyfriend. Maybe she needs us as much as we need her."

"It is a lonely job," Stella concedes, and returns to the table. "And you can love your team, but it's difficult to be both their boss and their friend."

"You guys have so much in common. And if I take this job, I'll be around even less."

Stella pulls her half-empty mug of coffee toward her. "You think I don't notice that you cook for me when you have something to tell me?"

Addie grins. "I learned that from my mama."

"Your mama is wise," Stella says. "Okay, I'll give Elizabeth a call, initiate the next move in this game of friendship. Will that make you happy?"

"Yep," Addie says.

Maybe Stella gave in too easily, but Addie's happiness should win every time.

Stella waits until Tuesday when Elizabeth takes her to therapy.

"You want to go out and get a drink?" she asks without preamble.

Elizabeth glances at her. "Now? Honey, I have to go right back to work after this."

"No, not now," Stella says. "Clearly not now. I just mean sometime. Do something not in my house. Wear real clothes. Drink some wine or something."

"Oh. Yes, that would be nice. How about tomorrow? Unless we catch a new case."

"Okay. Good."

Halfway through her therapy session while talking about how much her parents liked Ron, Stella realizes that asking someone for drinks is like asking them on a date. She stops speaking midsentence.

"Stella? You okay?" Dr. Barrett asks.

"Yeah," she says, then adds, "I'm not sure."

Dr. Barrett frowns and scribbles something on her notepad.

CHAPTER 7

Stella finds another check from Marco in the mailbox. It's in an unstamped envelope with her name on it scrawled. He must have dropped it off in person.

Having extra money makes her feel a little frivolous, and she decides to buy a dress for her drinks with Elizabeth. Not to impress her—Elizabeth's seen her in dirty pajamas and ratty sweats for months now. But Stella doesn't have anything nice anymore. She got rid of the majority of her work clothes in the great purge: the dated blazers, the worn-out skirts, the scuffed-up shoes. She has some basic pieces—black and gray sheath dresses, a couple of suits that don't fit anymore, some patterned dresses—but nothing that feels right for late June. Anything with a lining will be too hot, but anything for warmer weather doesn't seem dressy enough.

She showers, taking time to shave her legs, under her arms, and even her bikini line, though it ruins the razor that wasn't very sharp to begin with. She slathers lotion all over her skin—legs and arms and shoulders and torso. She puts product in her hair and blow-dries it. Wraps sections around a barrel brush and then curls what she blew out straight. She used to fix her appearance all the time before going to work. How did she ever have the energy?

It's still early in the day—Elizabeth won't pick her up for hours. She suggested meeting at a restaurant, but when Stella confessed that she didn't know how to get there, Elizabeth said she'd come get her.

She goes to the Nordstrom Rack on South Figueroa. She'll find something nice there that won't break the bank. It's a little overwhelming, clothes shopping alone. Ron was good at picking out things for her, like vintage dresses that were modest enough for work but had personality.

She paws through the racks until something the color of merlot catches her eye. It's a velvet wrap dress with the front higher than the back. She rubs the soft material between her finger and thumb. It's a bit much for drinks with a friend, but it's beautiful. She pulls a size four off the rack.

She tries it on and is suddenly overwhelmed with having to buy it. She needs to get out of the busy, bright store as quickly as possible. She checks out and hurries back to her car.

She stops at CVS on her way home—she comes here less often now. She doesn't even recognize the man at the register. This time, she's not here for candy. She heads toward cosmetics. Her makeup was so old that Addie had to go through and throw away what was expired.

The multiple displays are daunting. She tries to think about the makeup videos she's watched with Addie. There was one blonde woman who used a lot of products from drugstores, so Stella scans the displays until she finds the foundation mentioned on her videos.

One decision made, she moves on and picks out a bronzer, new makeup brushes, and liquid eyeliner in a felt-tipped marker. She buys two mascaras because Addie threw out her old ones while pretending to barf.

She checks out to the tune of nearly seventy-five dollars. When she gets home, she puts foundation on her face, hides the dark circles under her eyes, smooths on eye shadow and blush, and applies lipstick. It feels good to put effort into herself again. She allowed herself to collapse into a comfort-only lifestyle, and when she admitted that to Dr. Barrett, the therapist reassured her it was okay, that sometimes self-soothing in the face of overwhelming grief is the only way forward.

But Stella has wallowed for nine solid months, and it feels like the things that brought her comfort then are starting to hold her back.

She puts on the wrap dress, looks in the mirror, and is surprised at the woman she sees.

Addie comes home to find the new Stella puttering around, passing the time until Elizabeth picks her up.

"Wow," she says. "Look at you!"

"Oh, it's nothing," Stella says, a faint smile belying her modesty.

Addie is still in her work clothes: black pants, white button-down shirt. Her tie hangs around her neck unknotted. She looks tired. She always seems exhausted, no matter when Stella sees her, but Addie is determined to work hard to save the money she needs.

"You look amazing," she says, pulling the tie from around her neck and whipping her shirt off. She throws it toward the washer; it lands on the floor just outside the laundry room.

"Elizabeth and I are supposed to…I don't know. Get a drink." It feels like she's describing a date, though it's not, and she's dressed up like it's a date, though it isn't. "I thought maybe I could try to match her level."

"I like it," Addie says as she walks past Stella to her bedroom. "You passed her right up." She comes back out in a black tank top and bare feet.

"I don't know what shoes to wear," Stella admits.

"Let's see what I have," Addie says. She disappears into her room and comes back with a pair of combat boots, but Stella protests. She's too old for that look.

Addie shows her a pair of gladiator sandals, but it's like the shoes and dress are fighting for dominance. Next, she brings out a pair of scuffed-up black platform pumps with a skinny heel. "I wore them to a bachelorette party," Addie says, rubbing at a mark with her finger. "It got a little rowdy. They'll clean up, though."

Stella tries one on. It's uncomfortable—it's been a while since she wore anything other than a kitten heel—but it looks the best with her dress. She points to the other pump. "Let me have it. I need to practice."

She's teetering around the house when her cell phone rings. It's Elizabeth. "Hello?" she answers breathlessly, wrenching off the shoes so her feet will stop screaming. The cool kitchen floor feels like heaven against her bare soles.

"Stella, hi," Elizabeth says. "Listen."

Stella knows what's coming next. They've caught a new case or some new development on an old one, and whatever plans Elizabeth and Stella made are now on hold.

Elizabeth promises to call her later and apologizes again before hanging up. And even though Stella knows the job, knows how these things go, she's disappointed.

All dressed up and nowhere to go.

It's her own fault for getting ready two hours early for something that was bound to fall apart. She looks down at her phone long after the call ends. She built herself up over nothing and wasted an entire afternoon.

Addie comes out of her room wearing a black sweater over her tank top, her purse on her shoulder. "I'm going to get drinks with—what's wrong?"

"Nothing," Stella lies. She can't bear to admit the canceled plans and her disappointment, can't endure any more sympathetic tuts in her direction. "Go have fun with your friends."

"Are you sure?"

Stella nods.

"Have fun with Liz," Addie says. "I won't be home until late."

Stella watches her go. She refuses to cry, swallowing the urge. It's not Elizabeth's fault. Stella knew better than to get her hopes up about anything. Life always finds a way to snatch happiness out from under her.

At eleven thirty, Elizabeth calls again. Stella, slumped into the couch still wearing her velvet dress, almost doesn't answer; it's late, and she could let Elizabeth think she's asleep. But she swipes over just before the call goes to voicemail.

"Hello?" She tries to sound stern.

"Can you come pick me up?" Elizabeth sounds bone-weary.

"Where are you?"

"Good Samaritan."

"Are you okay?" Stella barely listened to Elizabeth's excuse for canceling, never considered whether the new case might be dangerous. Instead, she wallowed in self-pity, mad at herself, mad at the universe for disappointing her.

"Sam got shot," Elizabeth says. "He's okay, but he's going to be here for a few days."

"Shit." Stella is off the couch and heading toward her bedroom. "I'm on my way."

She takes off her bad-luck dress, dropping it on the floor. Pulls on jeans and a tank top, throws on a cardigan, and grabs her purse.

She's halfway to the hospital when she realizes that the last time she was there was when Ron died. She shakes it off, puts it aside to think about another time. Compartmentalizing, Dr. Barrett would say. She says it like it isn't a great thing, but it seems like a good idea right now.

She drives into the nearby parking garage, going around and around with the little paper ticket between her teeth. The garage is packed, and when Stella finds a narrow spot, she carefully backs into it.

Her flip-flops echo loudly in the stairwell as she hurries down. Out in the open night air, the large hospital in front of her, she hesitates, not sure where to go, then heads to Emergency, wishing she could brandish a badge to muscle her way in to wherever Elizabeth is waiting. But she's always been very persuasive. Maybe she doesn't need the badge.

She waits in a line four people deep before she gets to the window. "I'm here to see a patient who was admitted tonight with a gunshot wound," she says. "Samuel Warren. He's an LAPD officer."

"Visiting hours are over." The woman behind glass doesn't look up.

"I understand that, but the officer who brought him in called me for a ride home. She's waiting to for test results before she leaves, and she's not going to leave until she's sure he's okay. Are you saying I can't offer them support?"

The woman looks up with a mixed expression: boredom and impatience. "Okay, ma'am. What was his name again?"

"Warren," Stella says. "Samuel."

The woman types, then stares at her computer monitor. Stella can feel the people behind her shifting restlessly.

Finally, the woman says, "We *are* still waiting on some test results." She types something else and then looks up. "I need a picture ID."

Lieutenant Warren has been transferred to a room. Stella hastily shoves her ID back into her wallet and enters the main hospital. It takes several minutes to find the elevator to the wing he's in.

The wide halls are lined with medical equipment. Stella winds her way through, careful not to bump anything, counting numbers until she finds the room. The door is open. The first bed is empty. The next bed has a curtain pulled closed around it. She steps in uneasily, not certain if she has the right room until she sees a pair of familiar black pumps under the curtain. She steps in quietly and stands under the wall-mounted TV.

Elizabeth is sitting in a chair by the bed, looking at her phone. Warren is asleep, his shoulder heavily bandaged.

"Hey," Stella says softly.

Elizabeth jumps, slamming a hand over her heart. "You scared me."

"Sorry. I was trying not to." Stella nods toward Warren. "How is he?"

"He's out." Elizabeth answers softly. "They repaired the damage. The bullet hit him in the shoulder, went right through."

"Did you get the guy, at least?" Stella drops her purse down to her elbow to relieve her shoulder.

Elizabeth hesitates, as if deciding how much she wants to share. "It was… He was a kid, actually. Thirteen, maybe fourteen. Circled back to the scene with his father's gun. I think he was trying to scare us. I could see his hands shaking. Castillo called for backup, which was—I don't know—maybe not the right call."

"They killed the kid," Stella confirms dully.

Elizabeth nods. "It was totally unnecessary."

Stella has never seen her look this tired. She still has on makeup, but the sheen is gone. Her clothes are rumpled, her hair flat.

"I can go get you food. I can pick up a change of clothes if you want to stay. I can take you home. Whatever you need."

"Home," Elizabeth says decisively. "He'll be out all night, and Esposito is coming first thing in the morning."

Elizabeth leans over Warren, whispers something to him. Then she kisses his forehead.

Stella has been fond of colleagues before, even felt protective of them, fighting for them when she had to, but she was never maternal, never warm. And she certainly didn't date them.

Stella follows Elizabeth through the hallway back to the elevator. She's quiet on the ride down. She doesn't relax until she gets into the SUV, then leans back against the headrest with her eyes closed.

"Are you okay?" Stella asks stupidly, but she can't think of what else to say.

"I thought this day was going to go differently." Elizabeth rolls her head to look over at Stella. "I was looking forward to drinks, actually."

"Me too." Stella says. "Sometimes I miss prosecuting homicide cases, but not the ones like this."

"Stella, do you think you could take me to your house?"

"Yeah," Stella says. "If that's what you want."

"I just...don't think I can face it tonight." Elizabeth doesn't say what "it" is. An empty condo, perhaps, or something else that haunts her.

"You don't have to," Stella assures her.

It's nearly one in the morning when they get to the house. Addie isn't home yet. Stella gives Elizabeth the same pajamas as before, and Elizabeth excuses herself to shower first. Her borrowed toothbrush is still in the holder.

Stella is carefully pouring fresh cocoa, using the wooden spoon to guide it into mugs, when she hears the bathroom door open. Moments later, Elizabeth is in her kitchen with wet hair, pajamas on, feet bare.

They take their mugs to the living room. Elizabeth falls asleep with her feet in Stella's lap before she finishes her cocoa.

Stella is still awake when Addie comes in. "I see the date went well."

"Not exactly," Stella says, the back of her neck going hot and tingly when Addie calls it a date. "A case went bad. Lieutenant Warren got shot in the shoulder."

"Oh, shit." Addie sets her purse down on the table by the door. "Is he okay?"

"He'll be fine," Stella says. "She wanted to come here."

"She can have my bed again," Addie offers. "I can sleep with you."

"I think we might just stay here." Stella puts her hand gently on Elizabeth's foot. It twitches at the contact, but Elizabeth sleeps on.

"Okay." Addie pats Stella's shoulder as she passes behind the couch.

Stella thinks about turning on the television for company or putting on some music, but instead, she sits in the candle-lit living room and lets Elizabeth sleep.

CHAPTER 8

After a shooting that affects an entire division, no one is expected to arrive bright and early the next morning, but Elizabeth shakes her awake around five.

"You fell asleep with your makeup on," she says.

Stella slept slumped down on the couch with her feet propped on the coffee table. Her left knee pops when she lowers her feet to the floor. She heads to the bathroom to wash her face, intent on driving Elizabeth home.

Elizabeth has changed back into her own clothes. The pajamas are folded neatly on top of the washer. There's dried blood on the hem of Elizabeth's sleeves.

"You should borrow something," she says. "You shouldn't have to wear that."

"It's fine. It's a short drive."

They're three-quarters of the way to her condo when Elizabeth says, "Wait. Let's think about this. My car is still at the office. We should've gone there first."

"I can take you home and then take you to work when you're ready."

"Are you sure?" Elizabeth asks wearily. "I've asked so much of you already."

"No, you haven't," Stella assures her. "I'm happy to do it."

She glances over and sees Elizabeth rubbing her forehead. A tension headache, no doubt. Maybe a holdover from last night. They did sleep awkwardly on the sofa, their necks at strange angles. Stella's too old for that, so Elizabeth, who's older, must be too.

Elizabeth's condo is dark and a little musty. She pauses in the front hallway to push a button on the thermostat and turn on the lights.

"I can make some coffee," Stella volunteers.

"That would be great," Elizabeth says. "I'm going to hop in the shower to rinse off. I won't be long."

"Take all the time you need." Stella has nowhere she needs to be.

Elizabeth's kitchen is organized and well-stocked. Stella finds mugs in the cupboard right above the coffee maker. At home, she would just dump the coffee into the filter and hope for the best, but now she counts the scoops of coffee beans as she drops them into the grinder and measures out the water for the coffee maker.

The grinder is quiet, efficient. Like Elizabeth.

While the coffee is brewing, Stella perches on one of the stools at the kitchen counter, looking out the window of Elizabeth's eleventh-floor condo. It's a little overcast, so there's not much of a view this early in the day, other than the swaying tops of palm trees and the buildings in the distance. When the coffee maker beeps, she picks out two matching mugs and fills them up. She finds almond milk in the fridge and a few packets of sugar in the cupboard. They've known each other for years, worked late nights and early mornings, but Stella was so concerned about keeping her distance that she doesn't know much about Elizabeth, not even how she takes her coffee, so she leaves it black.

She knocks lightly on Elizabeth's closed bedroom door, and when she hears no response, pushes it open slowly. She can hear the shower behind the closed bathroom door. She leaves the mug on the bureau because Elizabeth won't miss it there, then returns to the kitchen to wait.

When Elizabeth emerges dressed in a black pantsuit, her hair down around her shoulders, she's holding the mug Stella left her. She looks lovely, despite how tired she must be. "Sorry," she says again.

Stella shakes her head. "Don't be."

She drops Elizabeth off in front of the police administration building. "Call me if you need anything," Stella says, but they both know she won't.

The squad will be too busy finishing up the case to spend any time with Sam Warren, so Stella looks up the visiting hours on her phone, then showers, puts on clean clothes, fixes her hair, and puts on a little makeup.

Warren is out for tests when she arrives. He's wheeled back in about fifteen minutes later, looking groggy. His shoulder is still heavily bandaged, but he smiles when he sees her.

"Hiya, counselor."

"Just Stella now," she says. "How are you feeling?"

"Like someone took a shot at me."

Stella smiles at him. "Glad you came through it."

"Me too. Getting too old for this shit, though."

She laughs. "I hear you."

They make a little small talk until he starts to drift off. "You don't have to go, right?" he asks.

"I can sit awhile," Stella says. "Get some rest."

It's almost an hour before Detective Aaron Morris shows up. He's holding two cups of coffee. He looks exhausted and so much older than the brand-new detective with the boundless energy of a puppy that Stella remembers.

"Carter!" He looks surprised to see her. Of course, Elizabeth would never talk about Stella at work. For some reason, that makes Stella uneasy.

"I was just keeping Sam company."

"The captain is downstairs, parking."

Stella nods. "How's the case?"

He shrugs. "Sad, mostly."

Stella waits for Elizabeth to arrive because now it would be rude to leave, but she gives Aaron the chair. She tucks her phone in her pocket and shoulders her purse so that she looks like she's about to leave when Elizabeth finally arrives. Her hair is in a plastic clip behind her head, and her lipstick is wearing thin.

"Oh!" Elizabeth smiles fondly when she sees Stella. "What are you doing here?"

"Just keeping Warren company," Stella says. "But you're here now, and he's pretty drugged up, so I'm gonna skedaddle."

"Oh." Elizabeth sounds disappointed. "Sure."

Stella waves at Aaron. "Bye, Morris." She turns to Elizabeth. "I'll see you later?"

Elizabeth nods.

Stella is halfway down the hall when she hears Elizabeth hurrying after her. "What's the matter?" she turns and asks.

"Nothing. I just wanted to say thank you."

"For what?"

"For last night. For taking me to work and coming today."

"You're welcome."

"Can I…stop by after work?" Elizabeth asks.

"Of course, but you must be exhausted."

"Come to my place, then," Elizabeth says. "If you have time."

"All right," Stella agrees. "Text me when you're headed home."

Elizabeth flashes her a smile. "I'll see you later."

Stella walks back to her car, a little dazed. She's usually good at reading people, but she has always struggled to understand Elizabeth Murphy, and their friendship is not making that any easier.

Stella daydreams all afternoon about why Elizabeth wants to see her again this evening, enough so that she hustled down a hospital corridor after they'd already said goodbye. After they spent both the morning and previous evening together. And the day before that too.

Does that mean she wants Stella in the same way that Stella wants her? And what way is that, exactly? If Elizabeth confesses that she has feelings for Stella too, what happens next?

When Elizabeth finally texts, it's nearly seven. Addie is at work, and Stella has been drifting around the house, eating a handful of chocolate chips whenever she wanders into the kitchen. Stella offers to pick up something for dinner, and Elizabeth says no, they can cook. Says "we," as in Stella and Elizabeth together. Or preferably, Stella can sit on a kitchen stool and watch Elizabeth cook.

On her way out, she grabs a bottle of wine. Maybe they can have that drink after all.

Elizabeth smiles when she opens the door. She's wearing leggings and an oversized button-down. Soft music plays in the background, interrupted by a loud beep.

"That's the oven," Elizabeth says and turns around, leaving the door open.

"Hello to you too." Stella follows Elizabeth to the kitchen and sets the bottle of wine on the counter with a clunk.

Elizabeth turns at the sound. "Is that for me?"

"I mean, you can have some, I guess." Stella sits at the counter and sets her purse down on the stool next to her. "What's all this?" she asks, indicating the salad vegetables on the counter, a raw chicken on the cutting board, and a loaf of French bread on a baking sheet.

"Just throwing something together," Elizabeth says. "Nothing serious." Elizabeth resumes hacking into the chicken, cutting it into pieces. She then seasons it, covers it with foil, and shoves it into the oven. We're going to eat late. I'm sorry."

"I've been snacking all day. It's fine." She watches Elizabeth move easily around her kitchen. "You aren't too tired for all of this?"

"I drank so much coffee today that I feel kind of wired, actually."

"You'll crash," Stella warns. "Probably when you least expect it."

"I know." She tosses lettuce, chopped tomatoes, and sliced cucumbers into the salad bowl, then hesitates a moment before cutting up a pear into long, thin slices. "You're alone in your house all the time, and I'm alone in mine, so I figured..." She shrugs.

"I feel like I don't ever see Addie anymore," Stella says, changing the subject. "I'm a little worried about her."

"I think not being in school makes her feel anxious and bored. Working helps her fill the time while she waits."

"I know about being anxious and bored."

Elizabeth pushes the pear slices with the broad side of her knife into the salad bowl. "Have you thought about what you want to do next?"

Mostly Stella has been thinking about Elizabeth. She knows she needs to find a job, but she's managed to compartmentalize that particular worry away.

"Yes," Stella says. "Sort of. I don't know. I don't think anyone will want me now. Not like this."

"I disagree."

"As nice as that is to hear, I'm not sure your opinion matters all that much."

Elizabeth covers the salad with plastic wrap and shoves it in the fridge, then pulls a wine opener out of the drawer. She pulls Stella's bottle to her, uncorks it gracefully, and pours them each a glass. They let it breathe before taking their first sip. Then Elizabeth says, "Stella, I have an idea about what you could do next, but I don't want to overstep the boundaries of our friendship if you don't want me to get involved."

Stella's stomach flops over. Now she knows why Elizabeth invited her to dinner this evening. It's to gauge what she can do to help her pathetic friend get back into the workforce. Stella wants to say no, she doesn't need Elizabeth's help, much less her chicken dinner or her green salad with fruit.

Except that Stella does need help. Dr. Barrett has reminded her several times that asking for help isn't a bad thing and that receiving help doesn't make her weak. Behind that voice, she can hear Ron's, screaming that she's manipulative, that she only married him for the perks an LAPD deputy chief could offer a homicide ADA. That she's a selfish user who will never change.

"I guess it depends," Stella says.

Elizabeth tilts her head. "On me or the job?"

"On the job." Stella is suddenly hot, her palms sweaty.

"I have a friend," Elizabeth says, "an acquaintance, actually, who does consulting work. Her main client is the UC system. UCLA mostly, but she goes to other UC campuses on occasion."

"Consulting," Stella says uneasily.

"Guest lecturing, conferences, that sort of thing. Sometimes law firms will hire her to testify as an expert witness. She told me the other day that she's swamped all the time, and she's thinking about hiring someone to help her." Elizabeth studies Stella pointedly, her green eyes piercing through her glasses.

And her green eyes are all Stella can see. The rest of her is fading away, like part of a dream. She manages to choke out, "Uh-huh."

"Do you want me to give her your contact information?"

"Me?"

"Yes, you," Elizabeth says with a laugh. "You're the only person I know who could do this kind of work. You could start part-time to try it out, ease into it if it suits you. Addie said you don't want to go back to the DA's office and that you don't seem interested in a private practice."

Stella needs more information but nods at Elizabeth anyway. "Okay."

It must be the right answer because Elizabeth smiles and says, "Great. Good."

Stella excuses herself to use the restroom and locks the door behind her. She grips the edges of the counter with both hands and looks up at her reflection. It could be anyone looking back at her, except that the strange woman in the mirror blinks at the same time she does.

She feels herself sliding back down into despair. It always has one hand around her ankle, no matter how much better she thinks she's doing, how hard she tries. She can't get free. She's inherently unlovable. Elizabeth's friendship is based on pity, and Stella is using her, just like she's always used people. Ron was right all along. She comes out of the bathroom when Elizabeth knocks and asks through the closed door, "Are you okay?"

Stella opens it and forces a smile. "Sorry. Yes. I'm fine."

She doesn't know how long she was in there, can't explain where the time went, so she doesn't try.

At her next therapy session with Dr. Barrett, Stella asks, "What do panic attacks feel like?" She brings up the subject with some trepidation, not wanting to tip her hand or give too much away.

Dr. Barrett looks surprised at the question. "Do you feel like you're having panic attacks?" she asks.

"Well, I'm not sure," Stella says. "What do they feel like?"

"Different for different people," Dr. Barrett says. "Most people feel their heart race. They feel trapped or anxious. Light-headed. Sometimes they have trouble breathing."

Stella shakes her head. "I've had those before, but it's not what's happening now. I thought maybe… Could it be a different kind?"

"Why don't you tell me what you feel when you have an episode," Dr. Barrett suggests.

"I mean, it's not an *episode*," Stella says defensively. "I just feel extra, uh, extra nothing."

"Extra nothing," Dr. Barrett repeats.

"You ever look in the mirror and not recognize yourself? You know it's you, but if someone came up and said you were someone else, you'd think, yeah, that could be?"

"What you're describing sounds more like dissociation. You become detached. Things don't seem quite real. Maybe you lose time."

Stella nods. "That. That happens sometimes."

"Dissociation is a way your brain copes with too much of something. It's a way of protecting yourself from a stressful situation. Sometimes it happens to people who experience a trauma. It's a short-term survival mechanism."

"That makes sense," Stella says.

"It's not a good long-term solution, though. We can't just check out of a situation when it gets too difficult."

"Killjoy."

Dr. Barrett half smiles. "I'll print you out some literature on dissociative disorders and some therapeutic tips for when it happens. We can practice coping techniques." She sets her notebook aside and swivels her chair around to type something into her computer and then turns back to Stella. "What were you doing the last time it happened?"

They've been talking around Elizabeth for weeks now. Stella circles back to the friendship now and again, to the feelings she's been juggling for years. But she hasn't come out and told Dr. Barrett about her attraction to Elizabeth.

Anyway, that has nothing to do with her husband's death. What's the point of confessing her one-sided feelings?

"I was at dinner," Stella says. "I went to the restroom and looked at myself in the mirror. I didn't recognize myself."

"Were you with Addie?"

"No."

Dr. Barrett waits until Stella gives in, unable to bear the silence any longer.

"I was with Elizabeth," Stella says. "She wants me to—I mean, she *offered* to connect me with a job opportunity." She phrases it so Dr. Barrett will think the anxiety comes from reentering the workforce, though she doesn't think that was the cause of her bathroom spiral.

"You weren't expecting her to offer that?" Dr. Barrett says. "She brings you to your appointments. You're friends now. She's close to your niece. Why wouldn't she offer assistance in finding you work?"

"She would. Of course she would."

Dr. Barrett sets her pencil and notebook on the side table. "We have one more session scheduled on the LAPD's dime, Stella. I want to use that next session to talk about Elizabeth."

Stella hears the blood rushing in her ears.

"I know that makes you uncomfortable," Dr. Barrett says, "but I think it's an important piece of your recovery. I'm telling you now so you can prepare."

"I haven't been lying to you," Stella says quickly.

"I don't think you have," Dr. Barrett reassures her. "And you don't have to talk about anything that makes you feel unsafe. But I have some questions for you about Elizabeth, and I hope you will continue to be honest with me."

Stella nods, her face hot and her chest tight. She fumbles for the strap of her shoulder bag.

"Stop and see Kathy on your way out. She'll give you those printouts we discussed."

Her blood boiling, Stella stomps out to the receptionist's window. Kathy is over by the printer. "Hang on a minute," she says.

Stella looks out to the waiting room, where Elizabeth is flipping through a magazine.

"Here you go, hon." Kathy is holding out a short stack of paper. Stella takes the pages and shoves them noisily into her bag with a mumbled, "Thanks."

Elizabeth looks up, drops the magazine onto the end table, and stands. "Ready?" she asks.

"Why did you wait inside?" Stella demands.

Elizabeth stares at her a moment and then says slowly, "It's a hundred degrees out there."

Stella is dressed in denim shorts and one of Addie's T-shirts. Pictured on the front is a skateboarding skeleton. Elizabeth is wearing a sheath dress, and her hair is in a French twist in deference to a late June heat wave that has settled upon Los Angeles.

"How was your session?" Elizabeth asks.

Stella shrugs, her bag pulling on her shoulder. "I don't know if I like Dr. Barrett anymore. I might skip the last session."

Elizabeth presses her lips together.

"One more isn't gonna make much of a difference," she continues.

"So you think you'll stop therapy altogether once your LAPD sessions run out?" Elizabeth asks.

"Yes."

"Because I could talk to—"

"Stop helping me! You don't have to save me every time I fuck up!" Stella blurts out, then immediately regrets her outburst.

Elizabeth falls silent. She pulls the key fob from her handbag and unlocks the car.

They drive in silence for a while. Stella can hardly wait to be home in her bed, the whirring fan providing white noise while she naps.

Elizabeth's stony silence should make Stella feel even worse, but her feelings are maxed out. Finally, Elizabeth says, "You know, I screw up sometimes too."

Stella snorts.

"I was under the impression that these sessions were helping you. I didn't mean to make you feel like you had to go. I didn't mean to crowd you."

Stella nods, unable to apologize, unable to admit that she's crowding herself. Instead, she sulks, punishing Elizabeth with silence for the rest of the drive home.

Stella wakes up to Addie sitting on the edge of her bed the next morning. "What happened yesterday?"

"Huh?" Stella asks groggily. She's still so tired, tired to the bone, even though she went to bed at ten and it's nearly twelve hours later.

"What happened with Elizabeth?"

"What? Nothing. She took me to therapy."

“And then you were mean? Because you’re always mean after therapy?” Addie asks.

“I wasn’t mean,” she says, rubbing her eyes.

“Elizabeth called me and said I could come over to her place whenever I wanted, but that she probably won’t be coming here anymore. So you must have done *something*.”

“Okay. Yes, I’m a fuckup. Are you happy? I fucked up,” Stella snaps. “I drove her away.”

“Stella!” Addie says with a sigh. It’s unusual for Addie not to call her Aunt Stella, so Stella knows she’s in for it now. “I’m sure we can—”

“Listen, you date her if you want to. I don’t care. I don’t need a friend right now.” Stella rolls over to face the wall. If Addie will leave her alone, she can go back to sleep.

“Date her?” Addie says. “Why would I—oh.”

Stella tenses, unsure what Addie has figured out. She tries to do some damage control.

“Friendships don’t always work,” she says. “We gave it a shot. Go see her if you want. No hard feelings.”

“All right. We’ll talk about this when you’re feeling better.”

Stella feels the weight of the bed shift as Addie stands up, hears her footsteps as she walks away.

They’ll never talk about this. Because Stella knows, after nine therapy appointments, that she is officially beyond help.

CHAPTER 9

Stella skips her last therapy appointment. Her phone rings five minutes after she's supposed to be there, and she watches the number go to voicemail. She taps the delete button, but still hears the beginning of the message.

"Hi, Stella. This is Kathy from Dr. Barrett's office—"

Elizabeth didn't show up to take her to the appointment anyhow. They haven't spoken since the last one two weeks ago. Stella knew Elizabeth wouldn't come, but a small part of her hoped she'd pull up outside of the little house anyway, knock on the door and say, "You ready?"

When Addie gets home from her lunch shift, she sits down at the kitchen table where Stella is nursing a cup of coffee. The skin under her eyes is dark.

"Are you okay?" Stella asks.

"Wood Ranch offered me more hours." She drums the top of the table with her fingers. "I could have an extra day off, but it would mean working another double. We could spend more time together, though."

Stella looks at Addie, her chin resting on her hand. "Is that what you want?"

"I think we could both use it."

"I think so too," Stella agrees. "We need a spa day."

"I've been thinking about a different haircut," Addie says. "Some sort of change."

Stella chuckles. "I used to change my hair after someone broke up with me. Like that was gonna fix my broken heart."

Addie's face crumples, and she starts to cry.

It takes a half gallon of ice cream and a bottle of wine before Addie starts feeling better, but as the evening progresses, Stella feels worse and worse. She's been self-absorbed and blind. Addie lives an entire life outside of this bungalow, and Stella doesn't know a thing about it because she can't look past the tip of her own nose.

And what stings worse is, Elizabeth probably *does* know all about Addie's love life.

Stella finally learns a little about Addie's heartbreak—a boy she works with seemed great and then abruptly stopped being great. A boy who was charming but drank too much. Who drove drunk and nearly got Addie killed on the 405. Who was great at apologies but couldn't follow through on anything he promised.

Stella tells Addie she wished she would talk to her more, trust her with her secrets, but Addie says she didn't want to be a burden while Stella was going through a difficult time.

"It's not like my husband died. I just picked a loser," she says.

Stella's glad Addie will be able to spend more time with her, but she still goes to bed feeling like gum on the bottom of someone's shoe. Around three a.m., after hours of tossing and turning, she gets up and drags her comforter off the bed and onto the couch.

She turns on the television to Addie's YouTube account. The first video is some beautiful girl putting on makeup, someone who probably doesn't live far from where Stella is now. Stella lets the girl's confidence and beauty soothe her until, eyes half closed, she floats into another morning.

Addie makes appointments at a salon for their first spa day, the first day they spend together in a long time. Stella's hair is as long as it's ever been since she was a little girl with two braids down her back. But the ends are in bad shape—she can break them off easily—and her roots are a mixture of dirty blonde and gray. Now that she has an appointment, she can see how awful it looks.

They have a nice but subdued time together. Stella gets some subtle highlights to help mask her gray, has three inches of hair cut off, and gets a blowout. Addie is going all blonde, and her hair takes longer to lighten, so Stella goes to a nearby Starbucks for coffee while she finishes up.

Two uniformed officers are sitting near the door, but she doesn't notice them at first. She waits in line, orders the coffee, and is lingering at the pickup bar when she finally sees them. They're looking right at her, a man and a woman, staring her down.

Maybe it's her pretty hair, styled to its absolute best. She tucks a piece behind her ear and pretends she doesn't see them. The man gets up and approaches her.

"Mrs. Halligan?" he says.

And boy, is *that* jarring. Stella never took Ron's last name because it required too much paperwork, too many appointments, too much time, and it hadn't been that important to her. And now she's his widow, both married and not. The purgatory of marriage.

"Oh," she says at last. "Not... Yes, I suppose I am."

"My name is Officer Damaris Lopez," he says. "I worked with the late Chief Halligan."

She forces a smile. Shakes his big, warm hand.

"I just wanted to say how sorry we all are for your loss."

"Why, thank you, Officer Lopez. Thank you so much."

"If you ever need anything," he says, reaching into his pocket and pulling out his wallet, "please don't hesitate to call." He hands her a business card.

Now the woman officer approaches.

She's about Stella's height and half her age. "There are a lot of LAPD officers that were unhappy with how things were handled. That man should never have been let into the building. He should have never gotten close to Chief Halligan."

"Stella!" the barista calls out.

"I can't comment on that, but thank you. That's...that's my coffee," Stella says.

"Nice to see you, ma'am," Officer Lopez says, and they leave.

Stella carries the coffee back to the salon in a daze. Her first instinct is to call Elizabeth to discuss the bizarre encounter, but of course she can't do that. Addie says she needs to apologize, but she's not ready yet.

Addie is getting a blowout when Stella comes back. Her new hair color is light with artfully done highlights that stand out dramatically against her tan. Stella sits in the empty chair next to her to wait.

Stella wants to tell Addie about the experience at Starbucks, but she can't. It's too strange, would take too much explanation. She wouldn't know where to start. Anyway, it would just trigger another lecture about Elizabeth. And she can't tell Dr. Barrett either, since she quit therapy.

She'll just have to carry being called Mrs. Halligan around with her for a while. Roll the name around inside and see if it cuts her up or comes out a pearl.

Stella's phone rings on Monday morning just after nine. She doesn't recognize the number, so she sends the call to voicemail. She lingers in bed, dozing between bouts of scrolling on her phone. In her waking moments, she thinks about getting up.

She's staring at the sink of dirty dishes when she remembers to check her voicemail.

"*Hi, Stella. My name is Mallory Anderson, and I'm calling because Elizabeth Murphy suggested you as a potential consultant for my business. I'm looking for someone to help with my caseload, and I think your experience would be perfect. I'd love to talk to you about it if you're interested. Please give me a call back at this number, or you can text, if that's easier, and we can set up an appointment. Thanks. Bye.*"

Stella is surprised to get the call—after her outburst, she thought Elizabeth would have changed her mind about helping. But while Elizabeth is many things, she's not petty.

Stella decides to text the woman later.

She takes her coffee out to the backyard. When she gets out there, she sees that Addie's window is open.

If only they could talk through the screen, whisper secrets like confession. It might be easier to share if they weren't face-to-face. But of course, Addie is still asleep. Stella drinks her coffee, then goes back inside the house.

She decides to text Mallory Anderson before she loses her nerve. The woman must be quite a bit younger than Stella because it would never occur to her to text even if a cell phone was her only means of communication. She and Ron had a landline, but when she moved, she didn't bother to install another one.

Hi Mallory, this is Stella. I'd love to meet with you. Just let me know when & where.

Mallory responds over an hour later, and Addie's awake by then. She looks tired and wrung out but beautiful as only a woman in her twenties can—youth's dewiness overriding whatever stress she's going through. The blonde hair suits her. She's very much a California girl now.

"You still like it here, Addie?" Stella asks.

"Huh?" One hand holds a mug of coffee while the other holds her phone.

Stella is cooking a pot of oatmeal on the stove. It's something she can put a lot of sugar into while pretending it's a healthy breakfast. "California," she prompts.

Addie thinks for a moment. "Yeah. Parts of it."

"You ever think about going home?"

Addie shrugs. "No. It would feel like going backward. There's not a lot for me there anymore. And the waiting around while I decide whether to go back to school is kind of boring. Besides, I like living with you, and I don't mind the restaurant. And the weather is awesome."

Stella agrees. She peers out the kitchen window and blinks at the sunshine. It's hot this late in June, especially at this time of the morning.

"What do you want to do for the holiday? You got plans?"

Addie squirms, and Stella senses her guilt. But she can wait that out easily. She's got years of watching interrogations under her belt.

"Josh invited me to watch fireworks with him," Addie finally says.

Stella's phone chimes with a text notification.

"Josh and Elizabeth."

"Yes," Addie admits. "And you are one hundred percent invited."

Stella snorts.

"You *are*. Liz said so specifically."

"She doesn't want to see me, and that's fine. But you should go."

"This is all so stupid," Addie says helplessly.

Stella retrieves her phone and opens the text.

Nice to hear from you! How about 6/30 at the Starbucks on Westwood near UCLA. Let me know if 1:00 pm works.

She responds immediately.

Great. See you there.

"Listen," Addie says when Stella puts down her phone. "This was always going to be a hard year. For you, for me, for Elizabeth. But having a spat doesn't mean giving up on the relationship."

"We barely made it to be friends."

"That's not true. Come on, Aunt Stella. Come with me. You can see the Hollywood Bowl fireworks from Elizabeth's condo. We don't have to stay long."

"I dunno. Maybe." Stella knows she's being stubborn but can't seem to find her way out of it. And *maybe* means no, of course. She'll figure out a way to weasel out of it when the mounting pressure forces her to be creative. But a big part of her wants to see Elizabeth and misses what they had going. She misses Elizabeth's soft voice, her easy, calm manner. But she does not miss feeling like a burden Elizabeth needs to bear.

And that's what keeps Stella from reaching out or apologizing—that feeling of being pitiable and pathetic. And if she leaves the house, she runs the risk of people calling her Mrs. Halligan again.

"Who was texting you?" Addie asks. She's salvaged Stella's oatmeal from the stove and is pouring it into bowls.

"Some lady who maybe needs help with her consulting business," Stella says.

"Wait, like a job?"

"Maybe."

"Consulting for what?"

Stella reaches for the sugar dish and puts a liberal spoonful on top, then reaches for the brown sugar. "Law enforcement stuff. Expert witness work. Maybe teach some classes at a local university. I'm not sure exactly."

"That sounds awesome," Addie says. "Perfect for you."

"It'd be nice to do something part-time for a while until I figure out… you know, my life." She opens the refrigerator, pulls out a mostly empty bottle of maple syrup, and squeezes it into her oatmeal.

Addie looks pointedly at Stella's bowl. "At some point the oatmeal becomes a pretense."

"Oh, hush." Stella stirs the concoction and takes a bite. It's so sweet, her teeth buzz.

"Where'd you find this lady?" Addie asks. She puts a handful of dried cranberries into her oatmeal.

"Oh, you know. The internet," Stella lies.

There was a time when Stella wouldn't have gone on a job interview in anything other than a blue or black suit, maybe a gray one, but it's too hot for a full suit and her options are limited. She settles on a pink and black patterned cap sleeve wrap dress that will keep her cool in the heat. And it still fits, despite her middle age spread—which is what she's calling her terrible eating habits now.

She showers and washes her hair, puts on makeup, and gets dressed. She programs the address of the Starbucks into the GPS. She leaves early, afraid to be late. She texts Mallory that she's there, buys herself a venti mocha with extra whipped cream, and sits at a small table near the window. Fifteen minutes later, someone approaches.

"Stella?"

Mallory smiles warmly. She's probably in her early forties. She's more attractive than beautiful, and tall and broad-shouldered. She looks androgynous in her charcoal-colored suit. She wears her dark hair in a bob, and her blue eyes are easily her most striking feature.

"That's me," Stella says, standing to shake her hand.

"It's over a hundred out there." Mallory sets her purse down on the empty chair and sheds her suit jacket, exposing her bare arms. "I'm going to go order something, if you don't mind."

"Of course. Go right ahead."

While Mallory is at the counter, Stella realizes that she hasn't prepared at all. She didn't update her résumé—hasn't even looked at it since taking the job with the DA's office. She has no references. And she has no idea what kind of questions Mallory will ask, no way to know if her answers will be satisfactory.

By the time Mallory comes back with an iced drink in her hand, Stella has started to panic.

"First of all," Mallory begins, "thank you so much for meeting me today."

"I-I'm not sure what you're expecting, exactly," Stella confesses.

"I have been a one-woman operation for going on six years now," Mallory explains. "I like making my own schedule. I like deciding how much I'm going to work."

"Who wouldn't like that?"

"Lately, though, I'm getting so much work that I can't keep up. I have regular clients I don't want to turn away, and potential new clients that I'm interested in working with. Frankly, I need another set of hands on deck. Elizabeth Murphy couldn't recommend you highly enough, and she's a hard nut to crack, so here we are."

"Here we are," Stella repeats, forcing a smile. She flushes with guilt for not being the person Elizabeth expects her to be.

"So let me tell you about how I'd like to move forward." Mallory sips her drink and then leans in. "I have a number of regular appointments that can be farmed out. Professors at UCLA, USC, and Loyola Marymount, for instance, who want an expert to speak to their students on a semi-regular basis. Then there are expert witness jobs—and from what Elizabeth told me, you're probably more qualified for that than I am anyway. Providing expert testimony for court cases, as you know, can be difficult to schedule, so having you available for those lets me keep a more predictable calendar."

It occurs to Stella that this is not a job interview, that Elizabeth's word is enough for Mallory Anderson to hire Stella sight unseen.

“That all sounds fine. I’ve been on a sabbatical of sorts for the last nine months, which isn’t really that long, but I feel like I’m out of the loop.”

“I heard about what happened to your late husband”—Mallory looks at her with a familiar expression of sympathy mixed with relief that it wasn’t her loved one—“and I’d like to offer my condolences.”

“Thank you. I do feel ready to start doing something again.”

“Let’s try it, then. Fall semester starts in August. Criminology classes always want forensic law experts to come chat with their students. When those jobs start coming in, I’ll divert them to you.”

Stella nods.

“I’ve drawn up some numbers here.” Mallory pulls a folder out of her bag and slides a piece of paper toward Stella. “The figures show the average going rate for the profession, then here’s the adjustment for my fee.”

Three hundred dollars an hour for classroom visits, four hundred and fifty for expert witness cases at trial, four hundred if the lawyers just want to consult.

“This seems reasonable,” Stella says.

“I’m happy to start you slow, let you… Well, if we go on for a while and you decide you want more work, you can let me know.” Mallory cocks her head. “Do you want time to think about it?”

Stella sits up straighter. “No. No, I’m in.”

Mallory grins. “Great! When the requests start coming in for classroom visits, I’ll let you know. Now I have to run to another appointment. It was so nice meeting you.” And she hurries out, leaving Stella alone in the coffee shop.

When Stella was first getting started in her career, finding a job was extremely competitive, with tons of hoops to jump through. Even when she was recruited for a job, there were background checks and psychiatric evaluations. This is the first time that someone has simply handed her work with no strings attached.

Still a little stunned at the turn of events, Stella picks up her coffee and goes home.

Addie keeps pestering her to come watch the fireworks at Elizabeth's, but Stella feels like she needs to clear the air first. And that means she needs to *apologize*—the thing she hates most in the world.

This fight with Elizabeth is stupid. It's not even a fight, really. It's Stella being hard to like, as usual. Elizabeth didn't do anything wrong besides being so pretty that it made Stella jumpy.

The Fourth of July holiday falls on a Tuesday. The Sunday before, Stella wakes up determined. Addie is asleep and will be for hours. She puts on black yoga pants, her purple sweater that is starting to fray at the edge of the sleeves, and a pair of flip-flops. She drives over to Elizabeth's, marches up to the building, and jams her finger on the buzzer before she loses her nerve. Except that in the four seconds before the open line rings, she almost bolts back to her car.

Then she hears Elizabeth's voice. "Hello?"

"It's Stella," she says, more timidly than she intended.

"Oh," Elizabeth says. She unlocks the security door. Stella pulls it open, then rides the elevator up eleven floors. She turns the wrong way when she gets out and backtracks. She knocks on Elizabeth's door. It's too late to run now.

When Elizabeth opens the door wearing a dress, jewelry, and makeup, Stella is struck again by how beautiful she is.

"Hi," Elizabeth says neutrally. "What are you doing here?"

"I just came to say that, you know, that, uh"—she clears her throat—"I'm sorry for being so awful to you. You didn't deserve that."

"You're sorry?"

"I am."

"Thank you. I accept your apology."

"You do?"

"Yes. Do you want to come in?" Elizabeth stands aside and opens the door wider.

This is further than Stella thought she would get, but she steps in. "Are you going somewhere?"

"Yes, but I have a few minutes," Elizabeth says. "Would you like some coffee? I still have some in the carafe."

"Where are you going on a Sunday?"

"Mass."

Elizabeth brings her coffee fixed just as Stella likes it.

"Are you planning on coming for fireworks? I made sure Addie knew you were invited."

"Oh, I dunno," Stella says, though now she wants to come. "I don't want to be any trouble."

Elizabeth arches one eyebrow. "You wouldn't be."

Stella sips her coffee. She wants to tell Elizabeth about Mallory, about the job she has now. Wants to apologize for the past and thank her for the future, but she has lost her words.

"Do you want to come with me?"

"Huh?"

"To church," Elizabeth clarifies. "Would you like to come along?"

Stella hasn't set foot in a church since she was in high school. She grew up experiencing different Protestant religions: Baptist, Lutheran, Methodist, Presbyterian. Her father being in the army, they had moved around a lot, and her mother chose churches based on which one had the most beautiful building.

Strange that they had never landed in a Catholic church, but some lines just weren't crossed, and the Catholic-Protestant divide was one of them.

Stella still has no real interest in going to church, but sitting next to Elizabeth for an hour is a different story.

"Yes," she says, surprising herself. "That sounds nice."

CHAPTER 10

She finds herself standing in Elizabeth's bedroom while Elizabeth looks for something to go with her sandals, as she politely calls them. At least they're black flip-flops, which means they'll go fine with the cotton-poly forest green A-line dress that Elizabeth brings out of her closet. The color is much more suited to Elizabeth, but the fabric and shape will work for Stella's body type without too much of a struggle.

"You sure?" Stella asks, taking the dress.

Elizabeth points her to the bathroom.

Her bathroom is, surprisingly, a tiny bit messy. A coil of dark hair in the sink, a tube of lipstick on the counter, the towels wrinkled and damp. Stella is reassured to know that Elizabeth is just as human as everyone else.

Stella emerges looking like a woman in a borrowed dress. Wrong shoes, unkempt hair, no makeup except for concealer under her eyes to hide the bags.

"That looks nice," Elizabeth says. "Come on. We've got to go."

They take the SUV—Stella can't leave it parked in the guest spot forever—but Elizabeth will drive. And with Elizabeth behind the wheel, Stella feels pressure to fill up the conversational space, but her mind is blank. Elizabeth, meanwhile, hums along to the radio while she drives. Thankfully, the church is close.

As Elizabeth parks, she asks, "Have you ever been to a Catholic mass before?"

"Only to serve a legal motion," Stella says.

Elizabeth laughs. "Well, try to avoid that today, hmm? And don't feel pressured to participate in anything you don't want to. It's fine to just sit."

Stella bravely follows her in. Elizabeth greets a few people and introduces Stella as her friend. She immediately regrets coming. She could be home right now, lying in bed or eating crackers or sitting in the backyard or anything other than smiling wanly at strangers.

They make their way to a pew close to the front and slide in. Elizabeth leans over and tells her that this is the church she raised her kids in. She stopped going for a while but found her way back a couple of years ago. She doesn't attend consistently, and when she does, she sometimes has to leave in the middle of mass, but people know she's a homicide officer and don't ask questions.

When mass begins, the congregation stands and sits and occasionally kneels as a body. They sing a few hymns, but the singing is nothing like in the churches Stella went to growing up.

When Elizabeth gets up for communion, Stella stays behind, not knowing what's expected. After the pew clears out, Stella sees that she is not the only one not taking communion. An old woman sits at the opposite end of the pew. A walker rests in the aisle next to her.

The woman gives her a big smile. Stella hesitates, then smiles back. The woman motions for Stella to sit beside her. Her fingers are gnarled, the knuckles large with arthritis. Stella scoots across the empty space.

"I've known Elizabeth Murphy since she was married," the woman says.

"Oh?" Stella says politely.

"She's never brought a *friend* before." The woman winks.

"Oh!" Stella says. "That's…so nice to hear. Thank you so much." She starts to scoot back to her place, but the woman continues.

"In my day, you had to hide it, you know. It could ruin your life. I'm so glad I've lived long enough to see that…things are better. Not perfect, but better. It doesn't have to be a secret anymore." She raises her fist as high as her shoulder and shakes it feebly.

"I'm happy too, ma'am," Stella says, but she feels ashamed and alone. She still carries the secret. Even Elizabeth doesn't know about it, though she can barely hide her desire. It may be a different time, and maybe they're too old for it to ruin their lives, but it could still change things significantly.

She watches Elizabeth make her way back to the pew, her heart in her throat, and she's terrified the woman is going to say something to Elizabeth and reveal what Stella has kept hidden. But Elizabeth smiles warmly at the old woman, then takes her seat next to Stella. "That color suits you, by the way," Elizabeth whispers. "It looks nice."

"It's yours. You should like it," Stella manages to say.

"Still." Either Elizabeth doesn't hear the snip in her remark or chooses to ignore it. She brushes her hair back from her shoulders and bows her head. And for just a moment, Stella considers sending up a prayer of her own.

Addie drives them to Elizabeth's condo on the Fourth of July. It's never been Stella's favorite holiday, but now that things are a little bit better between her and Elizabeth, thanks to Stella's pathetic apology and Elizabeth's forgiving nature, she's happy to be included in the celebration.

When they arrive with a fruit salad—their contribution to the meal—Josh opens the door for them. Marco is watching the Dodgers game, beer in hand. He looks up and smiles when he sees Stella.

Elizabeth takes the fruit salad from Stella. "Maria and her husband are supposed to stop by," she says. "I think they had another barbecue to go to first."

Addie and Josh are friends by now, and Marco is glued to the television, so Stella follows Elizabeth to the kitchen. There's not much to be done—all the snacks are out—but Elizabeth keeps picking things up and setting them back down and wiping already clean counters.

"You need a drink," Elizabeth says, nodding at Stella's empty hands. "I have beer, soda, white wine…or I could make you something else." She opens a cupboard next to the refrigerator. "I have vodka, rum…"

"Surprise me," Stella says. "Not white wine."

"I could drink a cocktail," Elizabeth says, pulling out a bottle of vodka and a metal shaker from a cabinet. She fills it with ice, measures out the vodka, and slices a lime. She opens the refrigerator and pulls out a bottle of cranberry juice. The result is a pink concoction in a thin-stemmed glass garnished with a lime wedge. They clink their glasses together.

"I met with Mallory Anderson," Stella says after tasting her drink.

Elizabeth raises her eyebrows, though she can hardly be surprised. "Did you? How did that go?"

Stella doesn't buy it, but answers anyway. "Fine. We're gonna try some things out starting next month."

"I'm so glad that worked out for you."

"Maybe. We'll see." Stella drinks her cocktail and feels it burn down her throat as she swallows. Whoever taught Elizabeth to make a cocktail—either her Irish Catholic parents or her alcoholic ex-husband—wasn't screwing around.

They take their drinks back out to the living room. Stella follows Elizabeth's gaze to the window. The sun is sinking into the horizon. "Do you want to go up to the roof to watch the sunset?" Elizabeth asks. "That's where the best views of the fireworks will be anyway."

"What about Maria and her husband?" Stella asks.

"We'll wait down here," Addie says. "Right, Josh?" She elbows him.

"Yeah. No problem," Josh says.

"We'll save you seats," Elizabeth promises. She hands Stella her drink. "You hold this, I'll grab a blanket in case it gets chilly." Elizabeth gets a blanket out of the closet, and they take the elevator to the roof.

They walk out into a little vestibule that's shielded from the elements. Elizabeth unlocks a glass door that opens up to a wooden deck with a patch of grass that turns out to be AstroTurf. There are a few picnic tables, some lounge chairs, and planter boxes.

"This is nice," Stella says.

They sit down side by side at a picnic table and look out at the sky. The setting sun is still bright enough that Stella wishes she had brought sunglasses or a hat, but she settles on shielding her eyes with her hand.

"Thanks for coming," Elizabeth says.

"I'm glad to be invited."

"I was starting to worry that I'd…I'd ruined things." Elizabeth sips her drink.

"I'm always worried that I ruin things." Stella means the comment to be glib, but it's the truth. "You didn't do anything wrong. I'm the mess."

"You aren't a mess—"

"Okay. Hard to like, then," Stella says. "Ungrateful."

"Self-pitying?" Elizabeth observes.

Stella raises her glass. "That too."

"Bullheaded? Blind? Completely insufferable?"

"Yeah, okay. I get it," Stella mutters.

"I think so many people have told you that you're hard to like that you not only believe it, but you work hard to make it true."

"Dr. Barrett assured me our sessions were confidential," Stella complains.

"Addie says you quit therapy."

"That sky is real pretty."

Elizabeth ignores the diversion. "It seems to me that therapy was helping you."

"I don't know if it was or wasn't." Stella studies her nearly empty glass. "That's the honest truth."

Elizabeth backs off. Swallows the last of her drink and places the empty glass on the table. She looks out at the sky.

"Do you want to go to mass with me again next Sunday?"

"Oh," Stella says, surprised. "Do you want me to?"

"It's nice to have someone to go with," Elizabeth says. "But of course, if I catch a case…"

"Yeah. I remember." She looks out at the sky again, now more orange and purple as the sun sinks lower. "Sure. I'll go."

Their time alone ends when Addie and Josh emerge onto the roof. They're followed by Maria, her husband, their lanky teenage son, and Marco carrying an armload of beers.

"America! Woo-hoo!" Josh says, taking a bottle from Marco and raising it in salute.

Elizabeth rolls her eyes and reaches under the table to squeeze Stella's knee lightly, then gets up to greet her guests.

When they get home, Addie goes right to bed, but Stella stays up. She turns on her laptop and brings up a Wikipedia article on the Catholic Church, thinking she'll read it for a bit of background, but after thirty minutes of wading through all the history, she gives up.

She certainly wouldn't choose to be Catholic, but then again, if all her religious choices were spread out in front of her buffet style, she wouldn't choose anything. For Elizabeth, though, being Catholic is as much part her background as being a Californian, a mother, a redhead. Some things can't be undone.

TV Land is playing old episodes of *Cagney & Lacey*. She saw every episode when the show originally ran, so she keeps the volume low, letting it keep her quiet company. She watches several episodes, but the show is more stereotyped than she remembers, and it's making Stella's skin crawl. When she finally turns it off and glances at the clock, it's nearly four a.m.—she's becoming nocturnal.

She can hear Dr. Barrett's voice in her head. *Give it a name, Stella.*

Okay. Her depression is making her nocturnal.

She could go to bed and wait for sleep. Maybe she'd drift in and out a little, but after watching the fireworks, she probably wouldn't sleep. They were too loud, too bright, and reminded her more of gunshots than freedom. Each staccato burst made her flinch. She refused a second drink, which was just as well because she had to drive a tipsy Addie home.

As they were leaving after the fireworks, Elizabeth hugged Addie, sweeping back her blonde hair and kissing her forehead. Stella watched, burning brightly with jealousy, but no one seemed to notice, least of all Addie. She chatted loudly all the way home and then collapsed into bed with her clothes and makeup on.

Briefly Stella wishes she lived someplace where she could sit on a front porch. California has a lot to offer, but outdoor space isn't one of them. Not in the city, anyway.

She pulls on her shoes. The closest CVS doesn't open until seven, but there's one two miles away that's open twenty-four hours. She goes to the bathroom to look in the mirror. Tells her reflection to shove it and grabs her purse. It's not the first time she'll shuffle through a CVS in flip-flops and pajamas, and it's not going to be the last.

The parking lot is mostly empty when she arrives. She squints against the fluorescent lights as she tosses chocolate into her basket. She pauses in the card aisle. Ron's birthday is coming up. He was born on the twenty-first of July, on the cusp of Cancer and Leo. She never believed much about astrology, but she had a roommate in college who studied it, and Stella managed to pick up enough to know that Ron's sweet side was Cancer, his temper was Leo.

"So stupid," she mutters, glancing at the birthday cards. She barely managed to buy a card for him when he was alive, and she rarely took the time and effort to buy him a gift. Anyway, he had everything he wanted. He mostly wanted to go places for special occasions, but she was always working.

She leaves the cards behind. She's been explicitly trying not thinking about what Dr. Barrett calls the year of firsts. The first birthday without him. The anniversary of his death. "They'll sneak up on you," she warned. "The first time you go someplace you went to together. The first day you make it through without crying. The first time you have sex again."

It's been weeks since her last appointment, and now here she is at five in the morning in a CVS thinking over Dr. Barrett's words.

The anniversary of his murder is only two months away.

In the makeup aisle, Stella puts a few things into her basket, then goes to the candy aisle before checking out.

"Would you like to buy a bag for ten cents?" the clerk asks.

"Sure," Stella says. She can never remember to bring in her own bags from the car, and even then, Ron used to hate to buy bags so he would wait while she trudged out to the trunk to see what she could scrounge up. He'd carry it all in his arms before he'd consent to purchasing a bag.

"Have a good night," the clerk says and then glances out the glass door. "Day."

"You too," Stella says, and shuffles out.

Sitting in the car, the bag next to her on the seat, her eyes start to burn like she's going to cry. She swallows the lump in her throat, and after a few minutes, nothing happens, so she goes home.

Elizabeth picks her up Sunday morning. Stella is wearing a dress, has made up her face, done her hair. She's wearing real shoes. She's ready to make a better impression on the Catholics of Los Angeles.

"Can we sit by that old lady again?" Stella is ready to face her fear, to be seen and known and understood. "The woman who sat in our pew last week. I don't know her name, but she had a walker and she's known you since you were married."

"That's Dot Northcott," Elizabeth says. "Her attendance has been sporadic. She's not very well."

"Oh." That information takes some of the wind out of her sails. She was determined to be brave, and now only God will see her for what she really is.

"Can I talk to you about a theoretical case?" Elizabeth says about five minutes into the drive.

Stella is well aware that it's a case Elizabeth is working on. "If you can't talk to me, then who?" Stella asks.

Elizabeth generally describes the murder, the suspects, the steps that have been taken. "If this were your case, what would you have done?"

"The same," Stella says, but Elizabeth looks over like she knows Stella is not telling the full truth. "Maybe I would have gone after the boss a little harder, but you followed the money. You got the facts you needed to get."

"I didn't get a confession."

"Most people don't confess," Stella reminds her. "Statistically speaking."

"And if I had you to put them on the stand?" Elizabeth asks.

"Everyone has different gifts, Elizabeth. You can envy the gifts someone else has, but you do so with the understanding that they're envious of your gifts. I may be good at finding the truth and sniffing out lies, but I'm not good at much else. And my gift is as much of a curse as it is a blessing." Stella has always been defensive about her professional life. There were always people, mostly men, who were jealous of her abilities and tried to sabotage her.

"All right, you don't have to get worked up." She glances over and smiles. "Your accent gets thicker when you're passionate about something."

"Anyway, I never could do paperwork like you," Stella says, falling back on humor to defuse the situation.

"Oh, wonderful. Bureaucracy is my gift."

"And you have great hair."

Elizabeth rolls her eyes. "Thanks."

When they arrive at the church, Stella scans the church for the old woman, but she isn't there. They sit in the same pew as the previous week. Stella feels less self-conscious this time. She still doesn't really know what's happening, and the priest says a few things in the sermon that she doesn't agree with, but the ritual is nice, and she likes having something to do. And she likes doing something with Elizabeth.

Afterward, Elizabeth says, "Do you want to get some lunch?"

"We could go to where Addie works," Stella suggests, though it means going all the way to the Grove, paying for parking, battling weekend shoppers. As soon as the words are out of her mouth, she wants to stuff them back in and go home.

"That's a great idea!"

Elizabeth and Addie still see each other when Stella's not around. They simply like each other, no strings. Elizabeth is a competent maternal figure for Addie, and Addie substitutes for Elizabeth's missing daughter, the one who lives across the country and rarely calls.

It would be easier for Stella if she could accept her friendship with Elizabeth at face value and not long for something she doesn't understand herself. Anyway, if Elizabeth came to her and said, "I find you attractive. Let's do something about it," Stella would probably freak out and run away.

She looks across the car and studies Elizabeth's beautiful face, her hands, her hair, her lap.

Elizabeth must feel like she's being watched. "What?" she asks.

In a perfect world, Stella would tell her the truth, tell her that she makes her blood buzz and her skin hum, and only Elizabeth's hands on her will calm her.

Instead, she says, "Nothing."

The restaurant is busy, and they wait to get into Addie's section. Stella explains that she's Addie's aunt and that they're not stalking her.

"Well," the hostess says, "you do look like her."

When they finally get a booth, Addie comes up and, without looking up, says, "Welcome to Wood Ranch Grill. My name is Addison. Can I get you started with something to drink?" She's digging in her apron for her pad of paper and a pen.

"Two shots of tequila, please," Stella says.

Addie's head snaps up. "Oh, my God! Hi!" she says. "You guys came for lunch at my restaurant! And right here in my section."

"We did," Elizabeth says.

“We were free,” Stella says. “It was Elizabeth’s idea.”

“No, it wa—”

Stella cuts off Elizabeth with a hard look.

“Well.” Addie puts a hand on her hip. “Isn’t this so nice? What can I get you? You were kidding about the shots, right?”

Stella shrugs. She’d drink one.

“Water, please,” Elizabeth says.

“Yeah, water is fine,” Stella says. “No, wait. A Coke.”

“Coming right up.”

Elizabeth opens her menu and holds it away from her face. Then she pushes her glasses to the top of her head and pulls the menu in closer.

“You need bifocals.”

“I have bifocals,” Elizabeth mutters.

“Then you need a new prescription.” Stella digs in her purse for her own glasses, which are swimming around at the bottom of her big bag. She could use a new pair too. “We could split something.”

“I was thinking a salad.”

“Ugh. Never mind.”

“We can split a sandwich. I can get a side salad,” Elizabeth says.

“You should get what you want.”

“I want to share with you. Whatever you want.”

“Why are you being so nice?”

Elizabeth sets her mouth in a thin, hard line. “Because I like you, even though you’re testing my patience right now.”

Stella looks back down at her menu. “Fair enough.”

“Have you gone back to Dr. Barrett yet?” Elizabeth says from behind her menu.

“Since we talked about it three days ago? No.”

“Hmm,” Elizabeth says. “It seems like you still have plenty to talk about with her.”

Stella slaps her menu down. “What’s that supposed to mean?”

“It means you still don’t trust me! I’m over here acting perfectly normal, and you think I have some underhanded reason for being nice.”

“I talked about plenty of other stuff,” Stella says. “I didn’t need to talk about you in therapy.”

“Maybe you do.”

"If you must know, talking about you is exactly why I left! Why on earth is everyone so obsessed with me talking about you?" Heat crawls up the back of her neck and into her cheeks.

Addie arrives with two waters and Stella's soft drink. She unloads them from her tray and then tucks the tray under her arm. "Y'all ready to order?"

"Not yet," Elizabeth says. "Can we have five more minutes?"

"Of course," Addie says. "Do you want some recommendations? The burgers are good, the pasta is crap, the sandwiches are okay if you don't get them with brown mustard—"

"Thank you, sweetie, for the drinks," Elizabeth says. "We just need a few more minutes."

"Okay," Addie says and goes to take an order from another table.

Stella picks up her menu and opens it to cover her face.

"Stella."

She pretends to be focused on studying the sandwiches. Turkey avocado with provolone and a basil aioli sounds good.

"Stella Anne Carter," Elizabeth says, "why on earth would you quit therapy over talking about me?"

Stella lowers the menu. "Do you talk about me at therapy?"

"Yes."

"Oh," Stella says with genuine surprise. "What do you say?"

"Well, none of your business, *really*, but I talked about you when you left for your promotion, and I talked about you extensively after…after your husband passed. And now I talk about how I can get you to trust me again."

"I see." Stella turns her attention back to her menu. "Turkey avocado. Would you eat that?"

Elizabeth glares at her. She takes her glasses off her head and tosses them onto the table. Even in the dim light of the dark paneled restaurant, her jade green eyes are striking.

"Listen," Stella says. "I do trust you. I do. I'm brimming over with trust. Can we please not talk about Dr. Barrett anymore?"

"Do you want me to go with you? Because I will."

"I can drive myself now, if I want to."

"I mean, do you want me to do a session with you? Would that help?"

"Jesus Christ, I do not want that."

Elizabeth sits back. "I see."

"Look," Stella says. "You're a normal lady living a normal life. I, on the other hand, have done a lot of irregular things and am currently living an unnormal life. Some things are better kept with the lid on, okay? Okay. Good talk." She waves at Addie. "Yoo-hoo! We're ready."

Addie comes over, pad and pen in hand. "Yes. What can I get you, Aunt Stella?"

"Turkey avocado and a side salad. We're gonna split it." She looks at Elizabeth for confirmation, but Stella, who's an expert at reading people, can't read Elizabeth's face at all. "Right?"

"Yes," Elizabeth says. "We're going to split it."

"Okay," Addie says, and jots down the order, then scoots away, appearing not to notice Stella's red cheeks and Elizabeth's stony face.

CHAPTER 11

"So…lunch, huh?" Addie says when she comes in later that night after working a double.

Stella is sitting on the sofa, looking at her phone. A candle burns on the coffee table. The television is off because she turned it off when she saw Addie's headlights. She doesn't want Addie to think she's been watching television for the last eight hours, even though she has. She managed to unload the dishwasher and wash her bedding and the mattress cover, but only because she spilled coffee in bed this morning.

"You guys seemed to be having a pretty intense discussion." Addie flops down next to her on the sofa. "Everything okay?"

Stella puts her phone down. "We went to church, we had lunch, she dropped me off at home. Nothing exciting."

"Uh-huh. Uh-huh," Addie says. "That's so interesting. Super interesting, actually."

"Why?"

"Because I talked to Elizabeth during my break, and she says you had another fight about therapy."

"Damn it, Addie, I wish you two wouldn't pair up against me."

"Hey, I'm Switzerland," Addie says, putting her hands in the air. "I can't help it if I'm stuck in the middle."

"You can tell Elizabeth I'm not going back to see Dr. Barrett."

Addie kicks her shoes off, leans back on the sofa, and sticks her feet on the coffee table. "Can we talk about Elizabeth?"

"Nope."

"Aunt Stella, I know you like her," Addie says.

Stella feels her face get hot.

"It's okay. You don't have to freak out."

"I'm not freaking out." The words sound like they come from someone else, squeaky and strange.

"It's fine to have feelings for her, even if you've never felt anything like it before," Addie says gently.

Stella stands up. "I'm not doing this."

Addie sits up, gently grabbing her arm to keep her from leaving. "You either do it with me or your therapist," she says, "because it's starting to ruin your life."

"My life is..." She wants to say *fine*—she can feel the word in her mouth—but her life isn't fine, and it sounds delusional to say it is. So she says instead, "It's too late to change things now."

"It's *not* too late."

Stella shakes her head. "I don't want to talk about it."

"Is it Dr. Barrett? Because we can find you a different therapist."

It is and it isn't. Their conversations circled around Elizabeth nearly every session, getting closer and closer, but every time they got too close to the truth, Stella shut down. Dr. Barrett wasn't a bad therapist or an unlikable woman. Stella just didn't want to talk about Elizabeth. She wants to wake up one day with her feelings about Elizabeth gone. By magic or lobotomy.

"Dr. Barrett was fine," Stella says. "I just ran out of things to talk about."

"What's it like," Addie asks, "being so absolutely full of shit?"

"Not as uncomfortable as you'd think," Stella answers. The dryer buzzes loudly. "I have to make my bed."

"Okay." Addie releases Stella from her grip. "We can do this another time."

"Or not!" Stella calls over her shoulder.

Mallory emails her with three jobs in August. One at UCLA, one at UC–Irvine, and one special consulting job for the LA County District Attorney's office.

I know it's not exactly what we discussed, and you may not want to return there, but I think you'd have good insight for the DA.

Stella writes back, says she'll take the jobs, even the one for the DA. She's in no position to be choosy. She writes down the dates and times, the names of the people she's meeting, and prints out campus maps, putting stars next to the buildings where she'll be teaching.

She spends the two weeks before her first assignment preparing as much as possible, as if the last twenty years of law experience don't qualify her for the work ahead. Like that former life belongs to someone else. Like she dreamt all the days of getting up early, making a pot of coffee, rushing around to find her shoes and bag and sweater while Ron reminded her for the hundredth time that if she would only set up the coffee to brew the night before or lay out her clothes and pack up her purse the night before...

Stella never convinced him that she just wasn't a night-before kind of person.

She hopes she remembers enough about that life that, whatever questions she gets asked, the answers come to her. Hopes she's not the fraud she's starting to believe she is.

Stella's home alone in the late afternoon when the doorbell rings, and there's Elizabeth on the porch.

"Hi." Stella is surprised to see her.

They're in a better place than they were when they weren't talking, but their fight at the restaurant set them back a spell. Elizabeth hasn't shown up unannounced in a while, and she's no longer comfortable walking in with a knock. And she hasn't spent the night in ages.

"Sam came back today," Elizabeth says without preamble.

"Yeah?" Stella asks. "How's his shoulder?"

"Good. Healed." Elizabeth drops her purse by the door exactly as Addie does. "He told me he still loves me and wants to get back together."

Stella steps aside. "Why don't you come in?" She wishes Addie was home; she's much better at navigating these sorts of things. Emotions. Elizabeth.

"I'm sorry to drop in on you unannounced." Elizabeth sheds her jacket and chucks it over the back of the couch. "Do you have wine?"

"Of course I have wine."

There's a half empty bottle of red from the night before on the counter. She pries the cork out, pours a generous amount into two wineglasses, and carries them to the living room.

Elizabeth accepts the glass, but then just holds it in her lap. Stella sits on the other end of the couch with one foot tucked up under her so she can face Elizabeth. "So, uh, do you want to get back together with Sam?"

Elizabeth looks at her in horror. "No!"

Stella's internal bees start to hum, and she exhales the breath she didn't know she was holding. "So then what's the problem, exactly?" She sets her wineglass down. Her hand is shaking, but Elizabeth doesn't seem to notice.

"I told him no thank you. But it's going to…"

"Oh," Stella says. "It's going to fuck up your division."

Elizabeth nods. "I really like this job, for the most part, and I don't want things to change."

Stella shrugs. "I do not, historically, embrace change all that well—"

Elizabeth snorts, but Stella ignores her.

"But sometimes things change because they need to change. Because it's time."

Elizabeth narrows her eyes. "Who are you?"

Stella leans in and whispers, "I'm the clone."

Elizabeth reaches out and takes Stella's wrist in her hand. Her fingers are cold.

"Hey," Stella says. "It's gonna be fine. Do you want to spend the night?"

Elizabeth nods. Her eyes fill with tears and her face crumples.

Stella takes the wineglass out of Elizabeth's other hand and sets it down next to hers. Then she cautiously scoots closer to Elizabeth and opens her arms.

Elizabeth flings herself into her arms and buries her face into her neck.

"Oh, hon. It's gonna be okay." She holds Elizabeth, patting her back as she weeps. Stella wonders who had last held Elizabeth in their arms. Her children live far away, and she isn't dating anyone. Stella has Addie for the occasional hug. Maybe Elizabeth gets hugs from Addie too, but Addie is young, and Elizabeth is more of a maternal figure for her, so she wouldn't go crying on Addie's shoulder.

Elizabeth mumbles something into Stella's neck.

"Hmm?"

"I'm sorry," she says.

"None of that." Stella lifts her hand and strokes Elizabeth's head.

Addie comes in soon after and finds them still embracing, Stella with her fingers in Elizabeth's hair. She lowers the bottle of champagne she's holding aloft and stops.

"Aunt Stella, what did you do?"

The bottle of champagne was intended to celebrate Addie's promotion to team lead. Elizabeth has stopped crying but won't stop apologizing. Addie decides to run a bath for her, telling her she looks exhausted and declaring that she'll stay the night.

While Elizabeth is in the tub, Addie puts together a dinner and Stella puts out a clean pair of teal cotton shorts and a black tank top. The tank top is one of Addie's workout shirts that says *I won't quit but I will cuss the entire time* in huge gold letters. Stella hopes it will make Elizabeth smile. She leaves the clothes folded on the edge of Addie's bed.

She comes up behind Addie, who is stirring a pot of boiling noodles at the stove, and rests her chin on her shoulder. "She showed up and just started crying." It's close enough to the truth. Addie doesn't need to know Elizabeth's workplace politics or love life.

"Her job is stressful," Addie says. "And I think she's lonely all the time."

"She's lived in Los Angeles her whole life. How is it we're the only friends she has?"

"Maybe we're just the only people she likes right now."

Stella steps back, peers into the pot of noodles. "What are you making?"

"Just some pasta. I think there's a jar of white sauce in the pantry."

Addie is good at making something out of nothing, and by the time Elizabeth emerges from Addie's room, she has set out pasta in a creamy pesto sauce, a salad, and garlic toast made from half a loaf of sourdough.

Elizabeth is wearing the clothes Stella found for her and one of Addie's hoodies. Her long legs are set off by the shorts. Her wet hair is brushed back, and her makeup has been washed off. Her eyes are not quite as big behind her glasses without mascara. "This looks so good," she says. "Thank you."

They sit down, fill their plates, and begin eating.

Stella breaks the silence. "Addie got made team lead at the restaurant."

"Oh, honey," Elizabeth says. "That's great. Congratulations."

"It's, like…not a big deal. More responsibility, not much more money."

"It means they like you," Stella says.

"It means I'm not a moron," Addie counters.

"Have you been looking at schools?" Elizabeth asks and takes another bite.

"I've looked at some websites. I can't even apply for another six months." Addie says and pushes some noodles around her plate. "Aunt Stella starts working again next week."

Elizabeth looks at Stella with surprise. "You do?"

"Just a panel thing at UCLA," Stella says. "A couple of other assignments. I'm starting off easy."

"What kind of panel?"

"It'll be me and a few law enforcement experts," Stella says. "We'll go through some cases with the class at the beginning of the semester and then review them at the end. Look at how their perspectives changed. I think. I'm not real sure yet."

"This is going to be a great fit for you." Elizabeth smiles, her eyes crinkling up at the corners.

"You could do it too, you know. You could retire and do consulting as easy as anything."

"I suppose," Elizabeth says. "I'm not sure I'm ready for that yet, though."

"You have options, is all I'm saying."

"Why would you leave the LAPD? You love it," Addie says.

"I wouldn't," Elizabeth answers. "Not yet."

Stella changes the subject. Talking about working makes her feel anxious. She asks Addie, "Tell me about your worst customer today." That always gets her talking because people are generally terrible, and they're especially terrible in Los Angeles. Addie's clientele is a mix of tourists and wealthy shoppers with a dash of employees from other stores.

"Oh my *God*, there was this DUDE." And she's off. She even gets a laugh or two out of Elizabeth, especially when she goes into the part where she has to explain to an adult man that blue cheese dressing isn't just crumbles of blue cheese inside of ranch dressing. That it is its own dressing, and that the man didn't believe her. Then she had to make what he thought was correct just to satisfy him.

"A grown-ass man!" Addie says at the end of the story. "And he had a wedding ring on! Someone *married* him."

Elizabeth chuckles. "Men are so stupid."

"They really are," Stella agrees. "Even the good ones."

"What good ones?" Addie asks. "Name one good man."

"You're too young to be this bitter," Elizabeth says, putting her hand against her chest dramatically.

"I'm advanced for my age." Addie stands and starts to clear the table.

Stella waves her off. "I got this. You cooked."

"I'll go change my sheets," Addie tells Elizabeth.

"Oh no," Elizabeth protests. "I have to get up so, so early. I can sleep on the couch."

"No!" Stella says. "That couch is terrible."

"Addie works so hard. She needs her sleep," Elizabeth says.

"It's fine—"

"Anyway, I should go home." Elizabeth pushes back from the table.

"NO!" Addie insists. "You need to stay here, hang out with us."

"That's sweet, but—" Elizabeth stands but hesitates, like she needs a little more convincing.

"You can sleep with me," Stella blurts out.

Addie stares at Stella in disbelief.

"Oh, I couldn't—"

Addie cuts her off. "That's a great idea. Aunt Stella doesn't need to be up at any particular time."

"What about your new job?"

"It doesn't start until next week," Stella reminds her.

"Besides, your bed is bigger," Addie says, barely containing her excitement. "And then you two can bond."

Elizabeth raises her eyebrows, then says, "I know you don't—that is, if it makes you uncomfortable—"

"It was my idea. You're my friend."

"Yes," Elizabeth says, "I am," though she sounds a little uncertain.

Stella cleans up the kitchen while Addie and Elizabeth talk in the living room. They keep their heads close together.

Stella stays focused on her task to distract herself as much as to give them some time together. She fills the dishwasher, starts it up. She empties the dish rack, then washes the pots and pans.

She's elbow-deep in soapy water when she feels Addie's hand on her shoulder.

"Elizabeth is brushing her teeth. I'm going to bed. I'm tired."

"Okay, sweetie." Stella wipes her forehead with her arm.

"You okay?"

"Yes, of course," Stella lies.

"Don't be weird. Let her do the talking."

"I'm not gonna be weird!" Stella hisses, though the second part is solid advice. She'll just lie in the dark and listen until Elizabeth drifts off. It shouldn't take long. All that crying would exhaust anyone.

By the time she makes her way to her room, Elizabeth is perched on the side of Stella's bed, waiting. Stella is suddenly aware of how awful her bedroom looks. The bed is nothing but a box spring and mattress. No frame. It's pushed up against the wall, like a child's bed. Her clothes are scattered on the floor. Her makeup is everywhere, even though she hardly ever wears it—unless she's trying to impress Elizabeth.

"I can still leave," Elizabeth offers.

"Why would you leave?"

"I'm too old to be crashing at friends' houses."

"Says who?" Stella counters and sits next to her on the edge of the bed. "Maybe people wouldn't feel so alone all the time if they had more sleepovers." Stella is trying to convince them both, but it's really not a bad idea.

Elizabeth tilts her head and smiles. "As long as you don't think I'm being pathetic."

"No more than me," Stella promises. "Aren't you exhausted?"

"Anxious, mostly. I think part of the problem is I haven't been sleeping well, and now I have to worry about whether my division will survive."

"You oversee a high-profile division with a solid case-win ratio. It's a feather in the chief of police's otherwise very bald cap. The cast of characters might change, but the division isn't going anywhere."

"I often ask myself, 'What would Stella do?' But the answer is that you would never have dated someone you work with in the first place."

"Elizabeth, I dated a string of losers, had a rushed divorce, and then married a cop, knowing exactly how dangerous the job is. Not exactly smart."

"That's not the same thing. I knew better—or should have."

"We all know better in retrospect," Stella says. "Come on. Lie down."

She pulls the covers back and waits while Elizabeth slides in close to the wall. Her dark hair stands out against the light fabric of Stella's bed linens. Elizabeth pulls off her glasses and hands them to Stella, who sets them on the nightstand.

"I have to brush my teeth." Stella turns off the lamp, and the room fades into soft darkness with only the light from the hall spilling across the floor.

The light in the bathroom is unkind at night. Maybe it's the bulbs bouncing their cold, energy-efficient light off the harsh white walls. She could get warmer lights, but they're expensive and quick to burn out. Or she could paint the walls blue or another dark color, something absorbent.

Or she could stand here as always, inspecting her skin in the mirror, her stomach pressed into the sink. It's not the wrinkles that bother her, exactly; it's the tiny lines. The pre-wrinkles. The skin that hasn't quite gone yet but is *going*. The skin in the process of decay.

She squirts toothpaste onto her brush and jams it into her mouth. Half the time, she doesn't even bother to brush her teeth before bed. It feels like this whole exercise is a performance for Elizabeth; in fact, maybe her entire life is about trying to impress Elizabeth, the one person she looks forward to seeing as much as she dreads it.

Back in the bedroom, she finds Elizabeth curled onto her side, facing the door, still awake. Stella admires the picture for a moment and then reaches across the wall, feeling for the switch that will turn off the hall light.

It's been a long time since she's had someone besides her niece in her bed. She and Ron slept apart as much as they slept together toward the end. She didn't like his snoring; he didn't like how she brought work to bed.

Elizabeth smells clean and delicate. Stella crawls into bed and lies on her back, staring up at the dark ceiling.

"I can hear you thinking," Elizabeth says sleepily.

"Oh yeah? What do you hear?"

"Who is this squatter in my bed?" Elizabeth says.

"Actually, I was thinking that it's nice to have someone in bed with me again." Stella rolls to face Elizabeth. "And something tells me you don't snore like a lumberjack."

"And if I do?" Elizabeth asks.

"I can live with that," Stella promises. "Or I might smother you in the night with my pillow."

"Quite the spectrum," Elizabeth says and yawns. "Life or death."

Stella looks at Elizabeth. Her dark hair falls across her face like a shadow. Stella reaches out and tucks it behind her ear. Elizabeth nuzzles her face into Stella's hand.

"I'm so glad I found you again," Elizabeth says. "I missed you after you left our division. I was so upset that you'd left."

"Sh-h-h." She holds her hand against Elizabeth's cheek. "I'm not going anywhere."

Stella starts to pull her hand away, but Elizabeth catches it, holding it as she falls asleep.

CHAPTER 12

Stella wakes up to light shining in through the window and the sound of Elizabeth whimpering. After several long moments of disorientation, she remembers that she's in her own bed, in her own room, in her own house. And Elizabeth spent the night.

The motion sensing light on the back porch—no doubt activated by a cat or a possum—illuminates Elizabeth. She is curled into a tight ball. She whimpers again softly, then makes another noise, more distressed this time, then mumbles, then says quite clearly, "No!"

Stella reaches out and puts her hand on Elizabeth's bare shoulder. Presses gently and then slides her hand down her arm. She repeats the motion twice before Elizabeth settles down. A minute later, the porch light shuts off and the room is dark again.

It feels like something Stella was not meant to see, and she realizes that Elizabeth's strength might be something of an act for Stella's benefit. She knows all too well the horrors Elizabeth faces in her work every day. She knows that Elizabeth's ex-husband abandoned his family. And she also knows that, not too long ago, Elizabeth witnessed her friend and colleague gunned down in cold blood.

She wraps her fingers loosely around Elizabeth's wrist. She imagines pulling Elizabeth toward her until her whole body is pressed against Stella's. That's as far as she will allow her libido to take her, despite the bees humming under her skin. Anything more seems impossible.

Elizabeth is quiet now, though still breathing heavily. Her fingers twitch, and Stella wraps her hand over Elizabeth's and holds it.

Stella feels like a teenager, excited to hold hands for the first time. Her heart beats like she ran around the block a few times. She's sweaty and hot, the bees swarming inside. Elizabeth seems to settle down, but now Stella can't breathe. The hand holding Elizabeth's is clammy, and her head is swimming. She pulls her hand away and scrambles out of bed. She stumbles into the nightstand, rattling everything on it. She can't seem to find the doorway.

"It's okay. It's all right. Take a deep breath. Sit down." Elizabeth speaks calmly and guides Stella to the edge of the mattress.

Stella sits down and leans forward, pressing her face between her knees. She used to be solid as a rock, unshakable. A man once tried to kill her, and she simply brushed herself off and went back to work. Now she's always on the edge, the edge of crying, of panic, of never leaving her house again. Even holding hands with Elizabeth sent her spiraling; the thought of Elizabeth's body against her own is overwhelming.

It all funnels back to pain again, like water circling a drain. Grief, anger, pleasure, all of it ends up in the same, rotten place.

Elizabeth is stroking her back, scratching at the base of her neck. Stella tries to breathe.

"I was having a bad dream too." Elizabeth's voice is thick with sleep.

Stella doesn't tell her that she was barely sleeping at all. "My marriage wasn't very good." The confession tumbles out of her mouth. "We weren't happy. I don't understand why it hurts so bad."

Elizabeth pauses stroking for a moment and then resumes. "It was a shock. We had such a shock, you and I."

Stella sits up slowly until she is sitting upright. She clutches her hands in her lap. Elizabeth sits up next to her. Their hips are pressed together.

"Tonight was supposed to be about you crying." Stella sniffles.

Elizabeth shakes her head. "Am I making it worse for you?"

"No."

"I should go home."

"No." Stella says it emphatically. "Please stay. I'll sleep on the couch."

"No, I will."

"Elizabeth, it's my house!"

"Okay but...did I do something wrong?"

"No. No, it's me. I'm wrong. I'm supposed to be helping you through this thing with Sam, and I'm just making it worse."

"I don't care about Sam," Elizabeth says. "I care about—I mean, Sam isn't who I love. And I came over to see you." She wraps her hands around Stella's.

"You're shaking," Stella whispers.

Elizabeth nods and, leaning in slowly, presses her forehead against Stella's shoulder. "I'm just so tired. Please stay with me."

"I will." There's no way she can ignore the pleading in Elizabeth's voice. "Absolutely I will. Maybe you should call in for a few hours."

Elizabeth nods, yawns. "Okay."

They lie down again, but this time Elizabeth curls up into her, keeps her face tucked, an arm draped over Stella's hip. Stella can feel Elizabeth breathing.

Stella only dozes. Wakes up every hour, watches the light change through the window, keeps watch over Elizabeth, who sleeps peacefully the rest of the night. That's something, at least.

Stella hears Addie humming in the shower. The pipes squeak when the water turns off.

Elizabeth is still curled up against her. Stella extracts herself, careful not to wake her up. She probably doesn't sleep in very often.

She shuts the bedroom door softly behind her, then heads for the kitchen and starts a pot of coffee. Addie appears a few minutes later in her summer robe, a towel wrapped around her hair.

"Good morning," she says. "You look…tired."

"Couldn't sleep."

"Too much sex?" Addie asks.

Stella freezes.

"Too soon for that joke. My bad." Addie pulls the towel off her head and starts drying the ends of her hair. "So what happened?"

Stella reaches into a cupboard, pulls down three of the biggest mugs. "Nothing," she says. "Nothing happened. Well, Elizabeth had a nightmare."

"Again?" Addie asks.

"Does she have them a lot?"

Addie shrugs. "Enough to mention it. It's been a weird time for her at work."

"She doesn't talk to me like she talks to you," Stella mutters.

"Have you tried?"

Stella doesn't answer. Instead of being there for Elizabeth, she wallowed in her own misery.

"She's still sleeping," Stella says. "I think we ought to let her."

"Aunt Stella, I think you need to loosen up a little around Elizabeth."

"I'm plenty loose."

"Whenever we talk about her, your shoulders go up to your ears. You both want the same things. You want to be friends. You want to be close."

The coffee maker beeps. Stella pulls the carafe out quickly, and several drops hit the burner with a hiss. She pours a cup for herself and Addie, then shoves the carafe back in. There's still plenty for Elizabeth.

Stella stirs cream and honey into her coffee. She wonders what Elizabeth will do when she wakes up, if she'll hang around all day. Elizabeth seemed desperate to have Stella with her in the night, but she'll surely wake up feeling foolish and want to leave in a hurry.

"Are you working today?" Stella asks Addie, knowing she is.

"Yes, and I need to get going." She picks up her mug. "Come sit with me while I do my makeup."

Stella follows Addie to her room, sets her mug down on the nightstand, and crawls into her bed. Addie settles in front of the mirror on the floor. Addie's bed smells like her perfume, and soon Stella drifts off to the soft music playing on Addie's phone and the clink of her cosmetics in the plastic bin.

And at some point, voices seep into her consciousness. She cracks an eye. Addie and Elizabeth are standing in the doorway, Elizabeth in her borrowed pajamas, her auburn hair disheveled from sleeping. Stella closes her eyes and listens.

"I don't know if I can do it anymore," Elizabeth says.

"You can. You have to," Addie tells her.

"It's too much."

"Trust me. She's coming around."

"I'm such a—"

"No, you aren't."

"I have to go home and get ready for work. Let her sleep," Elizabeth says. "Her insomnia is terrible."

Stella doesn't want Elizabeth to go. She wants her to stay, even if all they do is sit on the sofa or drive around doing mundane errands. But she's obviously distressed over something, something that Addie knows but not Stella, and she has no idea how to make her feel better. So Stella feigns sleep. Elizabeth leaves, and then Addie leaves; only then does Stella get up to face the day.

Alone, completely alone.

Stella drives to Elizabeth's to join her for mass on Sunday. She still finds the service boring, but there's comfort in the ritual of it all. She looks for Dot Northcott, the old woman she met on her first visit, every time she goes to mass. She saw her on the other side of the sanctuary last week in a wheelchair with a rolling oxygen tank on the back. Today Stella looks all around but doesn't see her anywhere.

And now, the service behind them, she's in Elizabeth's bedroom, watching Elizabeth flick through her closet for something suitable for Stella to wear on her first day of work.

"It's an evening college class. You don't have to be overly dressy," Elizabeth says. "What about that little dress with ties on the side? The one with coral roses."

"I don't want to wear that. Maybe I could buy something."

"No, I'm sure I have something appropriately *law enforcement* for you," Elizabeth says drily. She scrapes metal hangers over the wooden rod, then pulls out a dress. "Here it is."

It's a maroon A-line, fully lined, with a slight flare at the skirt, which suits Stella just fine. Her days of pencil skirts and tailored sheaths are on hold until she gets through the depression that seems to ease only when she's eating. The dress is a size four. She was a size two most of her adult life, with a metabolism so fast, she hardly ever felt full. Now she's not sure a size four will fit.

"Go try it on," Elizabeth orders.

"Now?"

"Yes, now. I'll step out."

The dress fits, though she doesn't bother to try to pull the zipper all the way up.

Elizabeth is waiting for her in the kitchen. "Looks good," she says.

"I've never seen you wear this," Stella comments.

"It's a little too… I mean, I like it, but I never know what to wear with it. A blazer doesn't go because of the way the skirt flares."

"A sweater would work."

"Except I rarely wear sweaters at work," Elizabeth points out.

"Okay. Well, I'll borrow it, if you don't mind"—Stella smooths her hands down the front—"even though now I feel weird about it."

"If I looked like you, I could wear anything, Stella. It's not the dress. It's me."

Stella thinks of the exchange as she gets ready for her first day of work. Elizabeth pretends she doesn't see the weight Stella has put on, how her sadness has dulled everything from her personality to her appearance to her intelligence.

She blows out her hair and curls it with a curling iron. She applies makeup, drawing a pretty decent cat-eye flick, thanks to hours of watching women on YouTube do their makeup and some practice of her own. She slips on a sensible low-heel shoe, and she's ready to go. She's so worried about being late that she arrives way too early, but after she finds parking that doesn't require a campus pass, she treks to the building, using a map on her phone, reading and rereading Mallory's email to make sure she has the right building, the right room, and the name of the professor. By the time she finds the building, she has only ten minutes to spare. Her palms are sweating, and she thinks about the talks she had with Dr. Barrett about dissociating. She knows it's not a good idea, but it sure seems like one right now.

Just outside the entrance to the building, her phone buzzes with a text from Elizabeth.

Good luck this evening! You're the most knowledgeable law enforcement lawyer I know. No one is a better expert than you.

She smiles at the screen. Another text comes through while she's looking at it.

Well, besides me.

"Brat," Stella mutters, her lips curling in a small smile. She tosses the phone back into her bag.

She walks down a long hall and opens the door into a large classroom with tiered seating. At the front of the room, next to a whiteboard and screen, is a table with four chairs set up behind it. Next to the table, two men are talking. They turn to look at her. "Am I in the right place?" she asks.

"You must be Stella Carter," one of the men says. "I'm Professor Paul Arenella."

She walks in and shakes his hand. "Thanks for having me."

"Thank you! We don't often get a special assistant from the district attorney's office."

"Former special assistant," she reminds him.

"That either." He gestures to the other man. "This is Max Clauser, our faculty director, and we're waiting on Assistant Sheriff Olmstead and someone from Social Services."

Stella finds her place at the table—the four seats have name cards—and sets her things down.

She watches the students as they file in and find places to sit. She was expecting a class of undergrads, but UCLA's criminology department is part of the law school, and most of them are adults who seem to have come straight from their full-time jobs. The social worker arrives last, five minutes late, and he looks more exhausted than anyone else.

Professor Arenella introduces everyone with a brief bio. Stella, at the end of the table, is last.

"Stella Carter has consulted for the federal intelligence community, including the CIA, served as a prosecutor for the state of Tennessee, and spent five years working with the LAPD's homicide division. Most recently, she worked as a special assistant for the LA district attorney's office. We are *extremely* lucky to have someone of her caliber here this evening. Let's have a round of applause for our panelists."

Stella smiles and tries to feel like she belongs. She doesn't feel worthy of the description, but she knows her résumé impresses people.

The class lasts two and a half hours. The students read through a variety of cases, and the panel answers questions. It's a good class. Each panel member has a different background. Cops look at things differently than lawyers, social workers differently than cops.

The cases seem straightforward, but each one contains a single tricky element that triggered some obscure law or that happened in an unincorporated part of the county or something else. At the end of the semester, Stella and the other panel members will return to review the same cases and compare the real results to what the students concluded.

Max Clauser has been talking for ten minutes about the legalities of one of the cases. He seems to like to hear himself speak.

"Wouldn't you agree?" he asks when he finishes, addressing the rest of the panel.

"Oh, I think when it comes to solving a case and catching a serial killer, it works better to ask forgiveness than to get permission," Stella says.

Clauser raises his eyebrows. A few of the students titter.

"I know I'm talking to a room full of future lawyers, most of whom will go on to work for private firms, but when it comes to public safety, law enforcement's highest priority must be stopping a serial rapist or murderer from causing any more harm. As a prosecutor, I watched cops do their damnedest to follow procedure. But sometimes they have to make a quick decision, do what they think is right to protect the public, and let the lawyers hash it out later on." She scans the faces of the audience. "That's you all."

The class breaks into laughter.

When the class is over, Arenalla thanks her again. "I'm so glad Mallory brought you on board. That was fabulous."

"Pleasure's all mine," she says, slipping on her sweater and picking up her bag.

Sheriff Olmstead intercepts her before she walks out the door. "I heard you were out of the game." His uniform accentuates his broad shoulders, and his badge catches the light. "Retired."

"Not exactly," Stella says. "Just taking a break."

He probably knows exactly what happened to Ron. It hit the public news cycle, so there's no way anyone in LA law enforcement wouldn't know.

"Well," he says, "welcome back."

She calls Elizabeth on the drive home, buzzing with excitement, talking quickly. She's talking through her hands-free Bluetooth connection. Elizabeth keeps asking her to repeat herself.

Finally, she says, "Just come over. Can you come over?"

"Okay." Stella gives in easily. "On my way."

It's late, nearly ten. Elizabeth will have to work in the morning. Stella hasn't seen her since Sunday, since the borrowed dress, and they've only texted a few times. They haven't talked about Elizabeth's nightmare or Stella's panic attack—much less spending the night in the same bed. Maybe it's best if they don't.

Stella parks on the street, a block away from Elizabeth's building, and she's suddenly tired. The adrenaline of the evening is wearing off, and she wonders if she should have gone home instead, but she perks up when she sees a smiling Elizabeth waiting in the lobby.

"I figured I'd ride up with you." She's wearing black leggings, a long, mossy green sweater, and slippers. Her at-home clothes. There's nobody else in the lobby, in the elevator, or in the long hallway of the eleventh floor.

Stella tells her everything. How the panel was mostly men, how she was the most qualified person there, how the borrowed dress seemed right after all, how good it felt to be doing something again. Not just making money, but actually contributing.

Elizabeth takes Stella's coat, sits her down at the table, then slides a piece of warm apple pie à la mode in front of her.

"For me?"

"Mm-hmm," Elizabeth says.

Stella quickly devours the pie and ice cream. And then Elizabeth says breezily, "Why don't you just stay? I'll text Addie."

Stella slips out of the borrowed dress and into the pajamas Elizabeth lays out. It's late, but she's tired and happy for the first time in a long time. She leans into the feeling.

Though Elizabeth has spent the night at Stella's a number of times already and even has her own toothbrush, it feels weird from this side.

Stella's house is simple and uncomplicated. Elizabeth's condo feels very grown-up and proper. Clean. Decorated purposefully. Stella feels mildly out of place, but Elizabeth is a good hostess. She finds a toothbrush, turns down the bed, shows Stella which side she'll be occupying.

Stella knows there's another bedroom here, Josh's bedroom, and he's away at school, but there's no talk of her staying there.

She brushes her teeth and washes her face, then ties up her hair. She dabs a bit of Elizabeth's expensive-looking body lotion on her face.

Elizabeth's bedroom has soft carpet and low lighting. The lights of the city can be seen in the distance out of her window. She's reading in bed, glasses on her nose. Stella feels a pang deep in her chest, so much so that she has to rest her hand over her ribs.

Elizabeth sets her book onto the nightstand. "When's your next thing for Mallory?"

Her question makes it easy to climb into the bed next to her and rest her head on the pillow. She brings up Mallory's email on her phone and discusses the next date.

"Trials are the real moneymakers," Elizabeth says. "When people start to realize that you're available as an expert, you're going to get very busy."

"I did expert testimony for the DA's office occasionally," Stella points out.

"They had to merit you as a special assistant. When they realize that they can essentially buy you, you'll have more work than you know what to do with."

Stella was a government employee for a large chunk of her career, and it didn't take her long to figure out it wasn't the perfect fit. She worked long hours serving the public for not much compensation. But she stayed for the steady paycheck and job security, leaving glamour behind.

The idea of working fewer hours for more money is…tempting.

"Is it selling out to do that?" Stella asks, worrying the edge of the sheet.

"I don't think so. Do you think so?"

Stella shakes her head. "I've spent my whole life worrying about money so…it'd be nice to make some. If this works out."

Elizabeth smiles. "And why wouldn't it?"

Stella is wrapped up in the warm light, the soft bed, the intimate bubble. She yawns.

"Are you ready to turn the light out?" Elizabeth asks.

"If you are."

Elizabeth reaches up to turn off the lamp, then rolls onto her side and exhales. "I haven't been sleeping well at all," she admits.

"Nightmares?"

"And insomnia. It's a little better when I spend the night at your house. Sometimes."

"Come over anytime," Stella says.

"Maybe we should buy a big house and move in together."

"Maybe," Stella says. "Can we get a dog?"

"A little one," Elizabeth agrees. "One that won't dig up my garden."

"A big bathtub?"

"Sure. How about a built-in wine rack?"

Stella smiles. "Now you're talking."

And they fall asleep imagining their dream house. Stella sleeps the whole night through.

She wakes up to sun streaming into the room. Elizabeth is already gone. She wanders into the kitchen. A pot of coffee is waiting on the burner. On the counter is a key with a note.

Lock up when you leave.
E.

CHAPTER 13

Summer rolls right into September. It doesn't feel much different because the heat doesn't break and Addie isn't in school. She works a grueling, never-ending eight shifts over six days. Stella has a little routine of her own, though.

Addie works late on Friday nights, so Elizabeth comes over after work. Sometimes she brings dinner or Stella orders in. On Sundays after church, Stella stays over at Elizabeth's condo for the rest of the day. She stays the night, waking up after Elizabeth leaves for work on Monday, then wanders home.

On Thursday, Addie's day off, Stella prepares her invoice for Mallory. Addie helped her design a simple one, based on a template she found online.

After the bookkeeping, they go out for brunch. The crowd is more elite and less crowded than on the weekend. Addie recognizes an actor. Stella has no idea who they are or what they acted in. She was never much aware of pop culture, but she feels even more out of the bubble now.

Addie orders an espresso drink, a glass of orange juice, avocado toast, and granola with yogurt. She's always been slender, but she's even more thin now. Her wrists are knobby, her collarbones stick out, and her face is drawn.

"What about waffles? French toast?" Stella suggests. "If your mother saw you, she'd cuss me out for not feeding you."

"Speaking of, they want to come out to see me. And you. Us."

"Thom and Joyce wanna come here?" Her brother has mentioned it now and again, but she's surprised he's actually going to follow through. "When?"

"In two weeks."

"Two weeks?"

"Yes," Addie says patiently.

"Thom and Joyce are coming here in two weeks?"

"How do I reboot you?" Addie snaps her fingers in the air. "Is it okay? Yes or no."

"You don't need my permission, Addie. It's your house too," she says.

"Right. I wish they'd given me more notice—" She stops abruptly when the server brings their drinks.

Stella pours creamer and adds sugar to her coffee before picking up the conversation again. "Two weeks is fine. That's enough time to clean, anyway. Where are we gonna put them?"

"I was thinking about that." Addie watches Stella stir her coffee. "Maybe Elizabeth would put you up while they're here."

"How long are they coming for?"

"A week."

"I don't know, honey. That's a long time to ask of Elizabeth," Stella says.

"She won't mind. You're over there all the time anyway," Addie says, downing half of her orange juice. "Mama and Daddy can sleep in my bed; I'll sleep in yours."

"I'm not there all the time," Stella protests. She feels the back of her neck flush. She and Addie haven't talked about the sleepovers at all. "Once a week maybe."

Addie shrugs.

"What are you gonna do with them for a whole week?"

"Touristy stuff, I guess," Addie says. "The beach. Maybe the Guggenheim or the Huntington."

Stella's brother Thom is a mechanic, and his wife works as a receptionist in a medical office. Good work, good people, salt of the earth and so on, but Stella can't picture Thom anywhere near art. Her brother Brick, certainly. He was always interested in art and literature. But Thom's needs are simple. All he ever wanted was to get married, have kids, and watch football on Sundays. He didn't know what to do with a smart kid like Addie, who, as she got older, acted out against the boring routine.

"Disneyland might be more your father's speed."

"Please don't make me go to Disneyland alone with my parents. Jesus. I would not survive that."

Stella tries to think if either of her brothers came out for Ron's funeral. Brick did, she thinks, but she really can't remember.

That Friday, Addie takes the night off.

"You're here!" Elizabeth says when she arrives. "What a treat!"

"I switched shifts," Addie explains. "I needed a Friday night off. Like a normal person."

Addie cooks steaks, red potatoes, and asparagus, moving comfortably around the kitchen. Elizabeth quarters the potatoes and then stands guard over them as they boil.

Stella spends so much time with Elizabeth that she forgot how comfortable Addie is with her. She treats Elizabeth like she's her real aunt and Stella is her unhinged landlord. She watches them chitchat and giggle and bump hips, trying not to feel sorry for herself, trying to enjoy the fact that her two favorite people love each other.

"Did you tell Addie about our dream house?" Elizabeth asks when the potatoes are boiled and drained. Addie adds cream and butter and salt.

Stella has not told Addie about their dream house because she's a little bit embarrassed about it. It's different when they're talking together at night, when it's cozy and so, so intimate that it makes her ache. It's even become something of an inside joke between them because if they're out shopping or at home watching TV and see something beautiful, one of them will say, "Put it in the dream house," like either of them could afford to drop four thousand dollars on a West Elm sectional sofa.

They both know it's a joke. Elizabeth won't sell her condo, and Stella can't afford nice things. Besides, combining resources isn't something friends their age really do. It seems juvenile and silly.

So Stella just says, "Nope."

"We decided that in a perfect world, we'd sell this house and the condo and buy a big sprawling mansion. You could live there, and Josh, and we could just, you know…" Too late, Elizabeth seems to realize that talking about the dream house doesn't translate well outside of the bedroom.

"If money were no object," Stella says.

And that isn't quite right either because that's not how it started. It started with the dream of selling their homes to buy a bigger place. But the real fantasy, the one that lives underneath, like the bees that hum inside her skin, is living together.

Elizabeth picks up the other thread gratefully. "You know, Travertine tile floors, every bedroom with its own bathroom, a swimming pool that someone else maintains."

"His and hers closets," Addie says. "Or hers and hers, I guess."

Stella glares at her.

Addie mouths *What?* behind Elizabeth's back and then turns on the hand mixer to blend the potatoes.

They take dinner to the backyard because it's a nice night, warm but not miserably hot. As the sun sets, the sky turns orange and red and then purple.

"Mama and Daddy are coming out soon," Addie says after they've eaten their fill.

"Are they?" Elizabeth asks. "That will be nice for you. Have they seen the house?"

Addie shakes her head.

"They asked to come out several months ago, but the house wasn't really ready for visitors," Stella says delicately.

"At least they won't have to pay for a hotel." Addie rests her chin on her hand, her face illuminated by the citronella candle on the table. "That means they can stay for a whole week and not just a couple of days."

"A whole week with my brother. Yay." Stella's only sort of joking. Maybe she and Thom struggle to connect because they are only eighteen months apart. Or maybe it wouldn't matter which brother came. Family visits have never been one of Stella's strengths.

"Well, you can always come stay with me if you need the space here," Elizabeth tells Stella. "You know, if you start to feel overwhelmed."

"Thank you. That's so kind," Stella says, ignoring the triumphant look on Addie's face. She ought to decline the offer, but she can't bring herself to do so. She's happiest when she wakes up in Elizabeth's bed, and she won't deprive herself of that feeling. "Maybe for a couple of nights, anyway."

Elizabeth's phone rings, and she pulls it from the pocket of her cardigan. "Oh no. It's Detective Morris."

Stella pushes herself away from the table and starts to gather dishes. Someone in Los Angeles is dead, and Elizabeth is about to be pulled away. She'll go to work until dawn, come home only to shower and change. No church this weekend. No sleepovers. Sunday will bleed into Monday.

"Don't worry about it," Stella says after Elizabeth hangs up and apologizes.

Elizabeth kisses Addie's forehead and reaches out to squeeze Stella's fingers.

"See you later, Carters." She closes the sliding door behind her.

The flight comes in at four o'clock on a Friday, the peak of rush hour. Commuter traffic is heavy from both directions. Addie drives the SUV, avoiding the freeway altogether. Stella can tell she's nervous.

"You remind me of me," Stella says. "I used to full-on panic any time my mama and daddy came for a visit."

"What did you have to be nervous about? You had your life together."

"That's a matter of opinion." Stella chuckles. "Daddy sure didn't think so."

"Grandpa loved you. He used to brag about you all the time."

"Grandpa used to send me letters expressing his disappointment," Stella counters. "Apparently, failing to meet your parents' impossibly high standards is a Carter family trait."

"They want me to move back home," Addie says.

"Sugar, you do what you want. You're a grown woman. There's nothing they can do about that."

Thom and Joyce have already picked up their bags by the time Stella and Addie arrive. Thom rides in front with Addie. Joyce sits in the back with Stella, her purse on her lap. "My word!" she says as she stares out the window.

"You ever been out here before?" Stella asks.

"I went to San Francisco once in the eighties," Joyce says as she rummages in her purse for hand sanitizer.

"Oh, so practically a native."

Joyce looks at Stella, confused.

"Never mind," Stella mutters to herself.

They're almost home when Stella's phone rings.

"That's Elizabeth's ringtone." Addie catches her eye in the rearview mirror. "Invite her to dinner."

"Honey, she's been working that big case... Shit, where is it?" She finally pulls the phone out of her purse. "Hello?"

"Are they here?"

"Oh hi!" Stella says airily. "Mm-hmm. Yes, ma'am!"

"How's our Addie holding up?"

"I'm not sure at the moment, but I can get back to you."

"We wrapped up the case, so if you need me to—"

"Tonight? Of course! Come to the house! Yes. Yes, that would be fine," Stella says. "See you then."

Elizabeth chuckles. "That bad? Okay, see you later."

Stella hangs up, drops her phone back into her purse.

"Who was that?" Joyce asks.

"Our friend Elizabeth. You'll like her, Mama. She's serious."

"Ah." Joyce tucks in her elbows and slants her knees away from Stella as if to protect herself. As if a decade in California might have turned Stella feral.

Thom says, "Over four dollars a gallon for gas is a crime."

"We almost hit five," Addie says.

"Now I understand the fascination with hybrid cars out here." Thom shakes his head. "How much does it cost to fill this thing?"

"Fifty dollars, if I'm lucky." Stella still doesn't drive much. Maybe a bit more now that she's taking on assignments for Mallory.

"Why on earth would you buy such a big car?" Thom asks.

"I didn't. This was Ron's car."

No one says anything for the rest of the drive.

Addie made up her room for her parents. Stella would have been happy to give hers up, but Addie felt they'd be more comfortable in her room. They spent two solid days deep cleaning. They washed every towel, every set of sheets, every bit of laundry. They vacuumed and swept and mopped all the floors. They picked up and put away almost every bit of junk scattered around. Everything else, they shoved in a drawer. Addie strung lights around the patio and bought cushions for the outside chairs. They even shopped. Stella's refrigerator has never been so full.

"And you own it?" Thom asks. They're standing in the backyard after putting their suitcases away and walking around the small house that suddenly feels cramped with two bedrooms, one bath, and no formal dining room. They'll have to cram five people around the kitchen table or eat in the backyard.

"Yeah," Stella says. "I lived in this neighborhood when I first moved to LA, but it was too far from Ron's office, so we moved somewhere more central. I moved back when I got the chance."

"How much did you pay?"

"Thomas Carter!"

"I'm just curious!" he says.

"I paid six thirty," she says. "Well, six twenty-nine, nine."

"For two bedrooms and one bath?" He takes off his baseball cap to scratch his head and puts it back on again. "Do you know how much house you could get for that much money in Hendersonville?"

"I don't want to live in Hendersonville."

"A mansion, Stella Anne."

"I don't need a mansion." She rubs her temple. "I'd just have to clean it and maintain it."

Thom stuffs his hands in his pockets. "Addison seems fine."

"I think she's doing well," Stella agrees. "She's a great kid."

"Joyce thinks she's too skinny," Thom says. Stella thinks Addie is just working too hard and skipping meals. But she does eat. Stella was skinny most of her life, and it's finally catching up with her. "And blonde."

"Watch it."

He gives her a lopsided smile. "How you doin' anyway? We never hear from you."

It would be easy to lie, but for once, she doesn't see the point. "It's been a hard year, Thom."

"Should we have come out sooner?" he asks with the same expression of sympathy and secret relief that Stella has been met with for the past year. The one that says, *Thank God that isn't me.*

"No, it isn't that. It felt like we just lost Mama, and then we lost Daddy. I wasn't prepared to lose Ron too." She never talks about Ron anymore, especially now that she's not going to therapy. She taps at her face with the back of her hand to catch the moisture.

"How could you be?"

"I think maybe I'm through the worst of it. I've been working a little, so that's good."

"That's great!" he says. "Doin' what?"

"Consulting. Which means I show up somewhere and talk about how I used to be a lawyer." She rolls her eyes and he smiles.

They turn when the door opens behind them. "There you two are!" Joyce says.

"Here we are, baby," Thom says. "What's on deck?"

Elizabeth lets herself in just as Addie is carrying the food out the back slider. Joyce seems surprised that she just walks in the door, but Elizabeth's warmth is disarming. "You must be Addison's mother!" She smiles broadly, takes Joyce's hand in both of hers. "I'm so happy to meet you!"

Stella introduces her to Thom, who remembers her from Ron's service. Stella will never admit that she doesn't remember him being there. Elizabeth compliments Addie until Addie begs her to stop. By then, Thom and Joyce like Elizabeth better than anyone else in the room. That's Elizabeth's gift. She can warm you right up or cool you right down. Stella has seen both sides.

The string lights that Addie hung come to life halfway through the meal and add to the ambiance. Stella sits next to Elizabeth. Their chairs are so close that their armrests are touching, and they spend the whole meal bumping elbows.

When Stella finishes eating, she excuses herself, thinking to start on the dishes, maybe find a little alone time to counterbalance a suddenly overwhelming number of people in her house. But the sink is piled high, there's still food in the pots and pans, and it's too much. Instead, she slips into her bedroom.

Stella can hear the conversation clearly through the open window. She stands along the wall, pressing against it. Addie is talking about work. Joyce is asking about the people she works with, the food she serves. Her questions come in rapid-fire bursts of three. Finally, after the third round, Thom says, "Jojo." Softly but with warning.

No one in Stella's family likes California. They don't understand why she took a job out here in the first place, why she stayed after that job ended, why she's still here when there's no husband to tie her down. And now she's lured their beloved Addison out here. Addie, the brightest star this family has seen since—well, since Stella herself.

When Stella was around Addie's age, she graduated from a prestigious law school and won an internship with a top law firm. Meanwhile, Addie is waiting tables and not going to school. And somehow, it's Stella's fault.

"Doesn't it matter that I'm a good waitress?" Addie sounds exasperated, her voice pitched high. "I understand that you don't like what I'm doing, but doesn't it matter at least that I do it well?"

This is the moment that Elizabeth walks into Stella's bedroom, looks around, and realizes that Stella is standing by the window in the almost darkness. Stella raises a finger to her lips, then reaches out to Elizabeth and pulls her in close, intending to pull her next to her against the wall. But instead, she pulls Elizabeth against her. Suddenly they're close enough to wrap their arms around each other.

For a few seconds, neither one moves. Then Elizabeth tightens her hold and tucks herself deeper into Stella's arms. Stella turns her head a little, breathes in the scent of Elizabeth's hair. Elizabeth exhales onto the back of Stella's neck.

"Of course it matters that you do well." Joyce's words are supportive, but she sounds irritated.

"But it doesn't matter if I'm happy," Addie concludes.

Elizabeth is moving her hand up and down Stella's back now, then she slips it under the hem of her loose T-shirt, stroking her skin. Stella catches her breath at the unexpected contact in a mix of panic and euphoria. Her hands are shaking, but she couldn't move even if she wanted to. Nothing could make her let go of Elizabeth in this moment, not an earthquake, a fire, or a herd of stampeding rhinoceroses.

"I know you want to take care of your Aunt Stella, but she ain't your responsibility, darlin'," Thom says.

Elizabeth nuzzles her nose behind Stella's ear, and Stella reaches up and grabs a handful of her hair, her nails grazing Elizabeth's scalp. She makes a sound in response, almost like a whimper.

"You don't think I wanted to get out of Tennessee before Uncle Ron died?" Addie asks.

Elizabeth strokes Stella's back, shifts her weight enough to gently press a thigh between Stella's. Now Elizabeth can brace her foot against the wall. Stella relaxes while Elizabeth presses against her, holding her in place. The room is tilting slightly.

"Baby—"

"You don't know anything about my life out here. And anyway, I'd rather be a waitress here than anything at all back home." Addie's voice breaks. "I was so bored and lonely, and y'all didn't even notice!"

Elizabeth shifts her weight again, pulls her hands free, and slides them into Stella's hair. And Stella knows that Elizabeth is finally going to kiss her. Elizabeth licks her lips. Stella's heart is racing, but she's not scared. She wants Elizabeth to kiss her slow and deep while her family argues on the other side of the wall. She's ready, ready to find out if the real thing is what she's imagined, or if they should part ways before they get in any deeper.

But instead of kissing her, Elizabeth just stares at her with a look of longing on her face. They're both breathing unevenly, trying not to make a noise. Then Elizabeth closes her eyes, her head falls forward and rests against Stella's shoulder. Stella holds it there, cradles it with both hands.

When Elizabeth doesn't move, Stella decides to break the spell. Surely, she only imagined the longing on Elizabeth's face. "We should go save her," she whispers.

Elizabeth nods against her and then, after a moment, steps away. Stella ushers her back into the hall.

Elizabeth stays for a slice of cake and then makes her excuses. As she leaves, she says to Stella, "See you later?"

Stella nods, though she's unsure. She's convinced herself that it was only a hug, that she's blown it out of proportion, that once again she's being needy and ridiculous. But the idea of spending the night in Elizabeth's bed is agonizing. Maybe she'll sleep with Addie tonight instead.

Thom and Joyce go to bed at nine, exhausted from the time change and the day's travel. Stella and Addie clean the kitchen. Stella washes pots and pans while Addie packs up the leftovers, puts things away. They start the dishwasher.

"Aren't you going to Elizabeth's?" Addie hops up on the counter and looks at Stella expectantly.

"I don't know. I don't want to crowd her."

Addie rolls her eyes. "Where did you two go after dinner?"

"Oh, I just needed a minute to myself," Stella says. "She found me and gave me a hug. That's all."

"Did that calm you down?" Addie asks, one side of her mouth curling up knowingly.

Quite the opposite. Stella's heart hammered for some time afterward. Like she'd been electrocuted. Like she'd sprinted around the block, leaving the back of her neck hot, her hands shaky.

"Addison," Stella says with some exasperation.

"Uh-oh."

"Elizabeth is lovely, but she's straight, and while I admit to you and to you *alone* that maybe I am going through something right now in that department, it's not fair to Elizabeth to force her into a role she's not willing to play!"

"Did she tell you she was straight?" Addie asks innocently.

"What?"

"Have you had that conversation?"

"No, but—"

"Then you don't know."

"She's only ever dated men!"

"*You've* only ever dated men!" Addie points at her. "So how can you be sure?"

Stella stares at her. "What has she told you?"

"Oh no." Addie crosses her arms. "I don't divulge your confidences, so I'm certainly not going to divulge hers."

Stella pulls out a chair and sits facing Addie. "You're kind of stuck in the middle of this, aren't you, sugar?" Stella says. "I'm sorry."

"Don't be sorry. Just don't give up."

And as if on cue, her phone beeps with a text from Elizabeth.

See you soon?

"Oh, my God. Just go already." Addie hops down from the counter and pulls a Diet Coke out of the refrigerator. "But you'd better come back for breakfast."

"I will. I promise."

Elizabeth greets Stella in her pajamas and robe. Her face is clean and shiny, her hair clipped back.

Stella carries in a little canvas bag with something to sleep in, yoga pants and a T-shirt to wear home in the morning. She has a toothbrush here already.

She changes into pajamas right away because Elizabeth seems ready to crawl into bed. Stella likes Elizabeth's bed. She feels like she's staying in a nice hotel when she sleeps over.

"Stella," Elizabeth says after she turns out the light.

"Hmm?"

"I'm sorry about earlier."

"What? Coming over? They loved you."

"No, I mean in your bedroom." Elizabeth's voice cracks a little.

"It was just hugging. We both needed a hug. That's all." She lets Elizabeth off the same hook she let herself off of earlier.

"I can't remember the last time anyone hugged me, touched me at all, even, and I feel like I maybe went overboard. I didn't mean to make you feel uncomfortable."

"I didn't."

Elizabeth sighs in relief. "You aren't upset?"

"No." It's a little deflating to hear that Elizabeth hugged her due to touch starvation rather than an overwhelming desire to put her hands on

Stella, but maybe that's for the best. She can love Elizabeth in one way while Elizabeth loves her in another.

"Come over here." Stella turns over and scoots to the middle of the bed, slides one arm under her pillow, and spoons into Elizabeth. Elizabeth wraps an arm around Stella and soon falls asleep.

Eventually Stella drifts off too, surrounded by the smell of her bedsheets, the scent of her hair. She's playing a dangerous game with herself, but it's worth it tonight. Elizabeth pressing against her eases the buzzing inside her down to a pleasant hum.

CHAPTER 14

Stella wakes up the next morning still in Elizabeth's arms and realizes it's the anniversary of her husband's death. What had Dr. Barrett said? That it wasn't always the big anniversaries that hurt but the small firsts. A whole year has passed, but in this moment, she's warm and comfortable with Elizabeth sleeping against her.

Stella turns to face Elizabeth, taking care not to extract herself from her arms. She's never been much of a cuddler—men run hot, and she hates to wake up sweaty—but she doesn't mind this. Elizabeth's limbs are light and delicate, her embrace gentle.

What would Ron think of how her life looks now? She spent the past year pushing Ron out of her thoughts. Maybe now it's time to give him a little headspace. Ron could be understanding when he wanted to be. It might make sense to him now why everything was always such a struggle between them. Why they always pushed back on each another. Why they were never quite happy. Ron always seemed happier than she was, but he couldn't have been happy with the half of her who filled her life with work so she didn't have to face the emptiness of her life with him.

She thinks back through her romantic history: all the boys she kissed in high school, the college boyfriends, her husbands. Everyone she's ever been in love with fell in love with her first. They wooed her, wore her down. And she'd gone along with it because that's what women did. Elizabeth's the only person she's ever fallen in love with on her own.

She can't lie to herself any longer. She's in love with Elizabeth. And there's no way Elizabeth feels the same.

She reaches out to brush hair out of Elizabeth's face. Studies the lines at the corners of her eyes, her button nose, the shape of her mouth. She looks at Elizabeth for a long time, looks at her like she's starving and hasn't eaten in days. And then she carefully slips out of her arms and out of bed.

Stella can tell that Addie knows what day it is, but she's smart enough not to bring it up, and Stella doesn't say anything either. They take Thom and Joyce around to see the sights, starting with Venice Beach. Even though Nashville isn't that far from the coast—no more than a day's drive—the Pacific Ocean is totally different from the Atlantic. They cram into Addie's car because it's smaller, thinking that would help with parking, but the beach is crowded and there are no spaces. They had planned to eat lunch in West Hollywood, but after Joyce declares that Venice Beach is too liberal, they decide instead to drive up the Pacific Coast Highway toward Malibu. They find a restaurant on the beach with tables on the patio facing the water. The only other diners are a family on the other side and an older couple, both reading the newspaper.

Halfway through the meal, Addie's phone buzzes. "It's Josh." She swipes to answer the call. "Hello?"

Joyce clears her throat in disapproval.

"So you're in town?" Addie asks.

The voice on the other end is loud enough to be heard but not clear enough to know what he's saying.

"The rumors are true. They're here." Addie covers the mouthpiece. "He wants to meet you guys."

"Who does?" Joyce asks.

"Josh is Elizabeth's youngest son," Stella explains.

"We're in Malibu. I'll text you when we get home." Addie sets her phone on the table and looks apologetically at her mother. "He suggested dinner later."

"He seems nice." Thom wiggles his eyebrows.

"Oh, I am fully not his type," Addie says. "Besides, he lives far away."

"Santa Cruz," Stella confirms. "It's a good six-hour drive."

On the drive home, Stella frets. If Josh is staying at the condo, it would be strange for Stella to stay there too. When she spends the night, everyone except Addie might assume she stays in Josh's room. And she likes waking up with Elizabeth. Sitting in their pajamas, hair still messy, drinking coffee in her kitchen. She likes pretending she has that life.

"You okay?"

Stella looks up to see Addie looking at her in the rearview mirror. "Yeah, sugar. Just fine."

"Because I know what today is."

"We don't have to talk about it," Stella says, but it's too late.

"Talk about what?" Thom asks.

"Ron died a year ago today," Stella says.

"Oh, honey." Joyce says sympathetically. "Why didn't you say somethin'?"

"So we can all be sad? I'd rather be doing something with you than moping at home."

"That's why Josh came home, I bet," Addie says. "So Elizabeth doesn't have to be alone."

"What does Elizabeth have to do with your husband?" Thom asks, his forehead scrunched up like he's trying to solve a puzzle with no clues.

"She was there when it happened. She saw him die, Thom."

"Jesus Christ," Thom says. "No wonder you two are thick as thieves."

"Well, I've known Elizabeth for years, but it put our friendship onto a new trajectory."

"I can't imagine." Joyce turns to look at Stella. "I just can't."

"I hope you never have to," Stella says. "I don't recommend losing your husband or watching someone die."

"Stella," Addie says.

Stella notes Addie's tone. It's a plea for her to stop. "Anyway, we don't have to see Elizabeth again. I see her all the time."

"If it would help you two to be together on a day like this," Thom says, "I'd love to meet her boy."

Stella should be closer to Thom, should put more effort into their relationship. He's really not a bad brother. She touches his arm. "Thank you."

They agree to meet Elizabeth and Josh at their favorite Mexican restaurant for dinner. They're already seated at a large round table when the Carters noisily arrive. Addie and her mother are bickering, and

Thom, who's a little toasted after drinking beer all day, speaks louder than necessary.

Stella feels bad for Addie. She's even-keeled, good-natured, and unflappable, and it's hard to see her on edge around her parents.

Thom married Joyce right out of high school when they were both barely eighteen, so Stella has known her for most of her life, but they've never really clicked. They were too different. Stella had big plans for herself after graduation, and Joyce just wanted to marry her high school boyfriend and have a van full of babies.

But they only managed to have Addie, and that took years of doctor appointments and thousands of dollars of fertility treatments. Why they talk down to her about her life choices and then act surprised when she doesn't want to move back home is a mystery Stella can't solve.

Elizabeth waves them over. She stands up to greet them and introduces Josh. Then Elizabeth says, "Come sit by me, Stella. You can squeeze in."

She looks beautiful, even in the restaurant's dim lighting. Under the table, they fumble for one another's hands and squeeze briefly before letting go. It must have been a hard day for Elizabeth too.

Josh cheerfully offers food suggestions, explaining what's good and what to pass on. Joyce and Stella exchange a look when Thom orders a margarita, but then Addie and Elizabeth order margaritas too. Joyce and Stella order soft drinks.

Josh gushes about his studies in journalism. Joyce, who worked on the high school newspaper, listens with genuine interest.

"Addie has a degree," Thom says. "Not that she's usin' it."

"Thomas," Joyce warns.

"Thank you, Dad," Addie says. "How unkind of you to say that."

"I ain't bein' unkind, doll. I'm just statin' facts!"

The waiter brings their drinks. Joyce takes Thom's margarita and moves her Diet Coke in front of him.

"Baby..."

"Stop embarrassin' yourself," Joyce says softly.

An uncomfortable silence settles around them. Josh stares down at the table. Elizabeth gazes off into the distance. Addie looks mortified.

"Addie," Stella says finally, breaking the silence, "I left my phone in the car, and I don't remember where we parked. Will you come with me?"

"Sure," Addie says.

"Order me something, if the server comes. I don't care what," she says to Elizabeth. "Excuse us."

She hurries out of the restaurant, Addie right behind her. When they're out the door, Stella turns to look at Addie. Tears have cut a path down her cheeks.

"Jesus, what the fuck was that?" Stella asks. "Oh, honey."

"He's just a dick when he drinks. Like all dads."

That's a comment they'll have to unpack later. She wraps Addie in her arms. "You're not wasting your life. You're doing amazingly well. It's hard to move away as far away as you did. But you have a good job, and you've been promoted! You help me with expenses, and you give me a reason to get up in the morning. I love you so much, sugar. I really do."

"Thank you," Addie says, pulling back. "I didn't even want them to visit. They're never happy with me."

"They're morons, and you're wonderful," Stella says. "I'm as proud of you as if you were my own daughter."

Addie nods, wipes her face with the sleeve of her hoodie.

"You okay? You could spend the night with Elizabeth and Josh," Stella offers. "I'll take care of Thom."

"It's fine," Addie says. "I have to work tomorrow, so you'll have plenty of time to eviscerate him then."

Stella chuckles, which brings a smile to Addie's face.

"Did you really forget your phone?"

"Nah, it's in my purse."

They return to the restaurant. Josh and Elizabeth have gone to the restroom. Thom looks sheepish, like his wife has already made the first deep cut.

"All right, phone acquired," Stella says, sitting down. "How about we don't drag the Carter name through the mud anymore in front of our friends, hmm?" She tries to keep the tone light, but the intent is clear.

"You sounded just like your mama then, Stella Anne." Joyce gives her a tight smile.

When Elizabeth and Josh return, everyone is on their best behavior, and they make small talk as they eat. Stella likes what Elizabeth had ordered for her, and when Stella steals a sip of her margarita, Elizabeth doesn't say a word.

They say goodbye in the parking lot. Elizabeth hugs Stella and whispers, "See you later?"

"I'm not sure," Stella says. "Maybe."

Elizabeth nods dejectedly. Stella thinks about her expression the whole ride home.

Stella sleeps with Addie that night instead of at the condo because it seems like the thing to do. Addie needs the support, and Stella is happy to oblige. Addie gets up and leaves for work a whole hour early just to get out of the house, leaving Stella to babysit her brother and sister-in-law for the day.

"Well," she says as they're sitting around drinking coffee, "y'all want to go to mass?"

"You go to a Catholic church?" Thom asks, surprised.

"Elizabeth goes," Stella says, "so I go along."

"Really?" Thom glances at Joyce.

"My therapist suggested I find a routine," Stella says. "Going with her to mass once a week is my routine, and now I'm kind of used to it."

"But a Catholic church?" Joyce asks.

"Not my first choice," Stella says, "but if you're raised Catholic, you're Catholic for life."

"You go," Joyce says. "We'll entertain ourselves here."

"How about if I leave you the SUV? Elizabeth usually picks me up anyway. Y'all must have some touristy thing you want to do. Addie won't be home until late afternoon."

Thom nods. "That'd be fine."

"Okay," Stella says. "Y'all mind if I shower first?"

Stella takes her phone into the bathroom and turns on the shower, then calls Elizabeth.

"Are you going to church today?"

"Are you calling me from the shower?"

"No. Kind of. I'm near it," Stella admits.

"So you're hiding in the bathroom?"

"Please save me from my family. Addie is at work, and if I leave them the car they can go somewhere on their own."

"We weren't planning on it, but I'll send Josh to get you, and we can decide what to do today."

"Thank you so much. Give me half an hour to get ready."

She takes a quick shower. It's still warm enough for a summer dress and a pair of flats. She applies a little makeup. Some foundation, powder, and blush. Mascara and lip gloss. Enough to add a little color and to feel alive.

Josh texts her when he arrives. After making sure that Thom and Joyce have everything they need, she hurries out.

"Oh, Lord, you are a sight for sore eyes," she tells Josh. "Thank you for the rescue."

"No problem," he says, pulling away from the curb.

"It was so nice of you to come up this weekend. You're good to take care of your mama."

"I'm sure I don't have to tell you she was in quite a state after the accident." Josh glances at her, but his words don't sting like they might once have. She can mostly talk about Ron without tears.

"I understand. It's hard to watch someone die." It's hard enough to watch a murderer die, but a colleague or someone you've known a long time is never easy. Ron was Elizabeth's boss, and they had a friendly working relationship that didn't include Stella. "She seems okay to you, though, right? I mean overall?"

"Yeah," Josh says. "She seems—dare I say it—happy."

"Was she not happy before? I mean before we lost Ron."

"I thought she was. At least sometimes," Josh says. "Her job is hard, of course. But that whole dating thing with Sam was, like, weird. Half the time they were dating, she didn't seem to know it, and once she figured it out, she pulled back."

Could it be that Elizabeth is more like her than Stella realized? Did she date men her whole life simply because they asked her? Or was she projecting? Still, it's reassuring to hear that Elizabeth isn't pining for Lieutenant Warren.

"It's not a good idea to date someone you work with anyway."

"But where else is she supposed to meet people?" he asks. "I keep trying to set her up with a dating app, but she won't even try."

"Maybe she thinks she's too old for that."

"At least she has you now. When I left for college, she had no one: no husband, no friends, she wasn't close to anyone at work, and my brother and sister never called. She talks about you all the time. She's really happy you're friends."

"Me too."

Stella smells bacon the moment they walk in. Elizabeth is in her black yoga pants and a button-down pale blue shirt with the sleeves rolled up to her elbows. Her hair is piled up and clipped away from her face. She's rolling out dough for biscuits. She grins when she sees them.

"Thank you for saving me," Stella says.

"Our pleasure," Elizabeth replies. "Make yourself at home. You know the drill."

Stella helps herself to coffee. Josh announces he's going back to bed until the food is ready.

"You can cut the biscuits while I make the gravy. Here." Elizabeth hands her a round biscuit cutter.

"I suppose I can't screw that up."

Stella washes her hands and then stands next to Elizabeth for her tutorial. "The dough is all rolled out. You should get about eight or nine biscuits out of this. That's plenty. It's not—" She stops short when Stella accidentally bumps hips with her, then clears her throat and continues. "It's, uh, not as good if you have to reroll the dough."

"Okay," Stella says, and nudges Elizabeth again, this time on purpose. Elizabeth pushes back, and then they're pressed up against each another.

Stella reaches for the cutter and holds it above the dough, positioning it as close to the edge as she can. "Here?"

"Right there."

She pushes the cutter down into the dough and pulls it back out. The dough sticks to the cutter, and Stella has to poke it out with her finger. "It's sticky."

"Mm," Elizabeth agrees. "Next time flour the cutter." She opens the canister of flour. Stella dips the cutter and coats the blade. The next biscuit comes out easier.

"You're so smart."

Elizabeth makes a pleased noise in her throat and turns to start the gravy, making a roux from the bacon grease. It needs to be stirred constantly while it thickens up, and she hands Stella a slotted spoon.

Now the biscuits are in the oven, the bacon is keeping warm under foil, and Elizabeth is cutting up a honeydew into perfect slices.

The rhythmic cycle of the spoon as she stirs lulls Stella's mind to wander. She imagines spinning around and pressing Elizabeth into the corner where the countertops meet. She imagines their bodies pressed together, her mouth slanting across Elizabeth's, Elizabeth kissing her back, then hopping up onto the counter and wrapping her legs around Stella's hips. Stella pulling the clip out of her hair and watching it tumble down onto her shoulders. Elizabeth's hands reaching out, pulling up the fabric of Stella's dress until it's bunched around her hips.

"Stella?"

"Huh? What?" Stella's face is hot. She can blame her pink cheeks on the heat from the burner.

"I said, how does it feel?"

"How does what feel?" Stella asks.

"The gravy," Elizabeth says. "Is it thickening up?"

"Oh. Uh, yeah, I think so."

"You zoned out for a minute there."

"I was just thinking about breakfast. Sorry. It's been a weird week."

"Your family seems nice."

"Do they?" Stella asks. "They were not at their best last night."

"I know Addie is struggling through this visit, but you were very diplomatic," Elizabeth says.

"I just don't know how I'm gonna do four more days of this. I have no earthly idea what to do with visitors."

"What did you do with your parents when they used to visit?"

"Worked," Stella says. "Sometimes they came to the courthouse."

"You never took off time for them?"

"I *tried*, but then people would commit crimes! Anyway, they got used to it, got to know my team. Ron took them sightseeing, but after several years, there wasn't much more to see." Stella sighs. "I was a bad daughter then, and I'm a bad sister now."

"No, you're not."

"Bad daughter, bad sister, bad wife. Was I even a good prosecutor? Who knows?" She bangs the spoon against the side of the pan.

Elizabeth wipes her hands on a kitchen towel and switches the burner off, then turns to face Stella. "You're not bad. No one is a perfect daughter or sister or wife. We just do what we can in any given situation."

"I know."

"And you were a very, very good attorney. That's why I requested you for my division in the first place," Elizabeth says.

Stella presses her lips together in an effort not to smile. "But Captain Murphy, *I* requested Homicide."

"Huh," Elizabeth says. "Guess it was meant to be." She's still holding Stella's arm, so she steps in and slides her hand around her waist, drawing her into a sideways hug. Stella squeezes her back. Then they move to a full body hug.

"Things get better and then worse and then better and worse again," Stella says softly, her chin hanging over Elizabeth's shoulder.

Elizabeth makes a sympathetic noise, holds her tighter.

They sway a little, hanging onto each other, until the timer on the oven beeps and they pull apart once more.

CHAPTER 15

ADDIE CALLS STELLA DURING HER lunch break.

"How's it going?"

"Oh, lovely. I went to Elizabeth's for breakfast, and I'm still here," Stella says. She's reclined on Elizabeth's couch after a slow, easy meal. They cleaned up the kitchen together. Now Josh is working on his laptop at the dining room table, Elizabeth is in the bedroom, and Stella is watching the television with no sound. She only turned on the TV because it felt weird to just sit.

"What about Mama and Daddy?" Addie asks.

"I left them the SUV and told them to use it if they wanted to do something touristy. I told them I was going to church, but then we didn't go."

"You just left them alone there?"

"Yeah. Why not?"

"Because they'll snoop! Oh, my God, Stella!"

Stella sits up, alarmed. "Well, what the hell do you have in there? You know I don't care about a little pot, but if you have hard drugs in the house, that's not okay."

"You don't understand," Addie says. "I need you to make sure they're not actually home. Please!"

"Okay, honey, but it would help if I knew what we were dealing with here." Stella has never heard her sound quite this panicked before.

"I'll tell you everything later. I promise."

"All right, sugar. I'll text you when I get there." She hangs up and pushes herself off the couch. "Christ almighty!"

Josh looks up from his computer. "What's the matter with her?"

"I have no earthly idea, other than she doesn't want her parents alone in our house."

Stella looks around for her shoes. They're not under the coffee table, not under the dining room table, not in the kitchen. She finally finds them by the front door with everyone else's. Elizabeth must have collected them and added them to the row.

She looks through her purse for her keys, then remembers that she didn't drive herself.

Stella goes to Elizabeth's closed bedroom door and knocks lightly. When Elizabeth doesn't respond, she turns the knob. She can hear the shower running in the bathroom.

"Shit," she says, returning to the living area. "You think your mama will mind if I take her car?"

Josh considers. "No. We can always come get it, I guess."

"If they're not home, I'll come right back," she says, then mutters, "I don't know what the hell I'm supposed to be looking for." She finds Elizabeth's purse by the door and digs out her keys. "Can you explain to her what's going on?"

"Yeah, yeah. Girl emergency. Got it." His attention is already back on the computer.

Stella takes the elevator to the parking garage and heads for Elizabeth's car, which Josh had picked her up in this morning. The LAPD car that Elizabeth uses for work is right next to it. Which Stella shouldn't drive. Officially. Except that the keys she took from Elizabeth's purse are for the LAPD car.

"Fuck it," she says, and hops in the silver motor pool sedan. She's at her house within fifteen minutes. She spends most of the drive hoping that Thom and Joyce went somewhere. Because if they are home and she finds them doing nothing suspicious, she's going to have to explain why she showed up only to turn around and leave again. And if they are doing something weird, she's going to have to deal with that too.

What could Addie have in that house that she's so desperate not to be found? Stella would know if she's hiding a drug habit. She's a little old to be freaking out about her parents discovering a vibrator, and she's old enough to drink without hiding it.

What's unsettling is that whatever she's hiding from her parents, she's been hiding it from Stella too.

The SUV is gone, and she promises God, or whoever is listening, that she'll stop sitting through church thinking about how boring and lame Catholicism is. For at least five services, anyway. Definitely three.

She almost flips a U-turn and heads back to Elizabeth's condo, but she can at least change her clothes while she's here. No sense in wearing a dress just to sit on Elizabeth's sofa. Sweatpants and a T-shirt will do fine for that.

Just to be sure, she calls out, "Thom? Joyce? Yoo-hoo!" as she pushes the door open. When no one answers, she goes to her bedroom, pulls her dress off, and puts on a clean pair of sweats, a black tank top, and her favorite sweater. She's just about to head out the door when something makes her look down the hall toward Addie's room.

Stella looks inside. Other than a large suitcase at the foot of the bed, everything seems normal. She walks in and pulls open the drawer of the nightstand. There's nothing in there but a package of hair ties, a bottle of Advil, some receipts, four different tubes of lip balm, and a damaged phone charger.

No vibrator, then. And even if she did keep one there, she would probably have hidden it during her parents' visit. Stella isn't sure she even has one because the walls of the house are so thin, they have no secrets.

She looks around the room, trying to think. Stella has pawed through her dresser plenty of times, looking for clean clothes to borrow. The closet is half open, revealing a pile of shoes and Addie's dresses and jackets. Like Stella's, her closet has two doors that slide over each other on a track with a plywood wall between the two sides.

One closet door is open; the other one is closed. A couple of boxes are stacked in front of the closed door. How is it she's never noticed these before? She lifts the flap of the top one. It's filled with old textbooks, and that's strange because she thought Addie had fully unpacked within her first month of living here.

She pushes the boxes out of the way and slides the other closet door open.

The inside has been rigged for high-quality artificial lighting, with a large white square to provide soft light and a ring light on a tall stand. Many rolls of different colored fabrics are propped up in the back corner.

Several boxes crowd the remaining space. One box says Maybelline. The box under that one shows the Wet n Wild logo. A third box was shipped from NYX Professional Makeup to Addie at a PO box. An expensive-looking camera with an expensive-looking lens sits on top of the stacked boxes.

Stella texts Thom and Joyce. It turns out they drove all the way to Anaheim for a baseball game that didn't start until one o'clock, so they'll be gone for several more hours. Stella and Elizabeth are ten videos deep into Addie's YouTube channel when they hear Addie come in the front door. She's home from work early. Stella pauses the TV.

Addie walks into the living room, her purse still on her shoulder and her eyes wide. "I can explain."

"I'm not sure what's to explain." Stella tosses the remote onto the coffee table. Addie's image on the screen is frozen, one eyelid covered in a shimmery gold shadow.

"Aunt Stella."

"You have over three hundred thousand subscribers. From what Josh says, that's downright respectable," Elizabeth says.

"He also said that with that many subscribers, there's no way you still have to wait tables," Stella adds. "Is that true?"

Addie sets her purse down. She's on the edge of tears. "Did you tell Daddy?"

"No, Addison, I did not," Stella says. "And I won't because it's your business to tell. But what I can't bring myself to understand is why you felt you couldn't tell me."

"Or me!" Elizabeth says.

"Well, uh—where are Mama and Daddy?"

"They went to an Angels game," Stella says.

Tears begin to fall from Addie's eyes.

"Honey," Stella says.

"I'm just gonna..." Addie turns and walks down the hall to her room. The door closes with a soft click.

"I'm so confused." Stella picks up the remote again and turns the television off. "Why should she be embarrassed?"

"I don't know. Josh says that the young women who make these beauty videos make a lot of money, and they can make even more just by mentioning certain products."

"We watch those videos all the time," Stella says. "Together! She had a hundred chances to tell me about it."

"I don't know," Elizabeth says again.

"Should I go in there?"

"Let's give her five minutes." Elizabeth puts her hand on Stella's knee. "You're doing fine."

"I feel like I did something wrong. Like if I had done better, she would've told me."

"Maybe she just wasn't sure it was going to work out."

Stella rubs her temples. She's starting to get a headache. "Maybe I was so caught up in my own problems that she felt she couldn't talk to me."

"Perhaps in the beginning. But she didn't tell me either."

Stella has long suspected that Addie confides more in Elizabeth—or did when she first moved out to California. At first it rankled, but now she's glad for it, glad that she had Elizabeth to lean on when Stella was so unreliable, so stricken with grief.

She has just opened a bottle of wine and filled three glasses when Addie comes out. She's changed her clothes, and her eyes are red and puffy. She holds a wadded-up tissue in her hand. She sits in the nearby armchair.

"I'm not mad at you, Addie. You're not in trouble," Stella says. "We're just confused, sugar."

"I know." Addie sniffles. "How many videos did you watch?"

"A few," Stella says. "The smokey eye one, the cut crease."

"What's in my bag, morning routine," Elizabeth adds. "Not that far back."

Addie heaves a big sigh. "I started the channel my senior year of high school. God, this is so embarrassing."

"Why?" Elizabeth says. "Josh says a lot of people make videos these days."

"I don't know. I started out doing song covers with my guitar and with my friends. Just for fun. And then sometimes I would do my makeup. And then it became more makeup than singing. But it was hard to keep up when I was in college, so I didn't make that many. And it's hard to grow your channel when you don't upload regularly." She sips her wine. "But then I started getting more serious. I made a schedule and even got on a few PR lists."

"What are PR lists?" Stella asks.

"Companies send her makeup for free," Elizabeth explains.

"And then more people started subscribing. Like, I made a of couple videos that got a lot of views, and then the channel just… I don't know, it just started to grow. When I hit a hundred thousand subscribers, I stopped thinking about going back to school. I wanted to move to LA. I knew you and Uncle Ron were out here, but I also knew I was never going to convince Mama and Daddy to let me. But when Ron died…" She starts to cry again.

"When Ron died, you had a good excuse to come out here." Stella finishes her thought.

"I didn't tell you because I didn't want you to think I used you. I know it seems like that, but you really did need someone, and I needed to leave Tennessee. It was just timing."

Now Addie is crying hard enough that she can't speak. She hides her face in her hands.

Stella looks at Elizabeth, unsure of what to do. But Elizabeth is no help. Her eyes are tearing up as well.

"Even if you had come out just for your career, I wouldn't have loved you any less or been any less happy to have you," Stella says. "Do I wish you had been honest from the start? Sure. But it isn't like I've always been honest."

"Amen," Elizabeth mutters.

Stella shoots her a look, then continues. "But now I'm worried because you've been carrying around this big secret and working yourself to the bone!"

"Do you—I don't mean to make things worse, but do you actually work at the restaurant?" Elizabeth asks.

"You ate at my table!" Addie says.

"I mean still."

"Yes! I mean, I left early today. I told them I was sick. But yes, I still work at the restaurant. I work four days a week, not six, though," she admits.

She dabs at her eyes with her wet tissue. Stella's about to get up to find a tissue box, but Elizabeth beats her to it, grabbing one from the kitchen counter. She takes one for herself, then holds the box out to Addie. Stella is still dry-eyed. Ordinarily, before her husband up and died, she was never one for crying unless it was to get her own way.

"What do you do on the other days?" Stella asks.

"I usually film at a studio downtown," Addie pulls the sleeves of her hoodie over her hands. "It's like a shared space. It's hard to film here."

"Because I'm always home," Stella says.

"Yeah. Sometimes I can in the middle of the night, but they don't come out that good," Addie says.

Stella steers the conversation back to the original issue. "Why don't you want to tell your parents?"

"They don't get it!" Addie says passionately. "They knew my friends and I used to do song cover videos, and they hated it. Said it was a waste of time, and maybe it was, but so what? They made me go to college, but nothing interested me, and I feel like I barely made it through. And then everyone said that my degree wasn't enough and that I had to go to graduate school, and I just can't make myself do it!"

"Sweetie, no one can make you get another degree. You're a grown woman." Elizabeth says, sounding very reasonable. "Especially your parents, who live on the other side of the country and wouldn't be paying for it."

"Really?" Addie sounds surprised, maybe because no one has ever said as much to her. She's so smart and so responsible and so good-natured that Stella forgets she's only twenty-four.

"Yes!" Elizabeth says. "Tell your parents the truth or don't. It's your decision to make. But know that you have my support and your aunt's support one hundred percent. You don't have to lie to us. We're your family, and we love you unconditionally."

Addie sniffles again, then launches herself into Elizabeth's arms. When she finishes hugging Elizabeth, she hugs Stella as well.

"I have an idea," Stella says. "Why don't we book your mama and daddy a hotel room down in Anaheim, and tomorrow we'll go down and meet them."

"Meet them for what?"

Stella sighs. "For Disneyland."

"Oh, I don't know about all that," Addie says.

"Well, what can we do with them here? We've gotta get them out and about." Stella says. "Can't have them poking around here!"

"They don't have their clothes or anything," Addie says.

"We'll bring them," Stella says. "We'll go early."

Addie looks at Elizabeth. "Will you come? And Josh?"

"Oh, honey," Elizabeth says. "You're so sweet to ask. No, absolutely not."

Addie and Stella drive Thom and Joyce to the airport for their return flight. They're too exhausted to speak for nearly the entire ride back. Addie is hiding under her hoodie. Stella hasn't washed her hair since Disneyland, and now she just wants to sleep.

But she has an expert witness case to prep for, which means she's going downtown first thing in the morning to meet with the lawyers. They're preparing for arbitration, and if that doesn't go well, they'll go to trial. And at the end of the week, she's meeting with the sheriff's department to help revamp training procedures.

Even though it's been a difficult week, Stella is happier knowing about Addie's secret, and Addie seems more at ease too. In fact, she's talking about quitting the restaurant now that the secret's out. Stella asked why she kept it up so long, and Addie explained that it was easier to live the cover story than lie outright. Plus, when she first came out to LA, she hadn't been making nearly as much.

Stella misses Elizabeth. She hasn't seen her since Sunday. Just as she's thinking about how much she wants to see her, Elizabeth's call rings through on the car's Bluetooth.

Addie pushes the answer button. "Hi, Elizabeth."

"Hi, honey. Is your aunt there?"

"I'm here," Stella says. "You're on speaker."

"You two survive?"

"Seems like," Stella says.

"We're so tired," Addie adds.

"I bet." Elizabeth hesitates like she has something else to say but changes her mind. "Okay. Well, I just wanted to check in. I'll call later, okay? After work?"

"Sounds good," Stella says. "Bye now."

Addie taps the screen to end the call. They lapse into silence again until Addie says, "When are you going to tell her how you feel?"

"When are you going to tell your mama that you do your makeup on the internet for three hundred and twenty-four thousand strangers?"

"Touché."

Stella preps for her case for two days, then Elizabeth picks up a case, so it's hard to find time to get together. Stella's case is a civil suit between a former police officer and the family of a man who was sent to jail wrongfully. It's an important enough case, but not as interesting as a murder case. When she meets with the attorneys, they argue over the semantics of the criminal code. Stella can reel off police code better than most cops—unless, of course, the cop is Elizabeth Murphy. Before Elizabeth made captain and took over Homicide, she was more of a bureaucrat. Stella is tempted to tell the lawyers she knows the woman who wrote the code, or at least did the last major revision, and would they like Stella to call her and ask what she meant back then?

But she holds her tongue. After all, she bills by the hour now.

Addie thinks about quitting the restaurant, but her bosses beg her to stay, so she drops her shifts down to three a week. It's nice to come home and see her there, nicer still to see her cooking dinner.

"I thought maybe Elizabeth could eat with us tonight," Addie says, "but she has to work late."

"That's a shame."

"I told her to come for dessert even if it's late, but she wouldn't make any promises."

"I have to get up early anyway," Stella says. "What are you doing tomorrow?"

"I have to edit a review I filmed of a new fall launch." Addie closes her eyes to show Stella the eyeshadow.

"Looks beautiful," Stella says. "I still can't believe you let me buy makeup when you're drowning in free PR."

"Gotta live the lie, you know that."

Stella isn't holding a grudge. Addie lets her have all the makeup she wants now, and her vanity is better stocked than any drugstore. And now that Addie isn't hiding the product she gets, there's makeup *everywhere.* She was giving it away to work friends or donating it to shelters as fast as she could review it, but now she keeps it around longer simply because she can.

After dinner, Addie packs up the leftovers. Stella loads the dishwasher, then excuses herself. She's tired, and she has a long day tomorrow. After the arbitration hearing, she'll go directly to the sheriff's department.

By nine thirty, she can barely keep her eyes open and turns off the lamp. Two days of work in a row, and she's exhausted. What's she going to do if she ever goes back to a forty-hour workweek? Or if Mallory starts giving her a regular workload? Is she going to be exhausted every day of her life?

When there's a knock on her door, she wakes up, disoriented. Addie usually just barges in, after nine months of living together like half mother and daughter, half best girlfriends. Stella looks at the clock. It's 11:37. When Addie doesn't open the door, Stella gets up, stumbles to her door, and opens it.

She squints in the semi-darkness. It isn't Addie at all. It's Elizabeth. She's still wearing her work clothes: a silk blouse and slacks and heels. Her glasses are pushed up onto her head. Stella is barefoot and wearing nothing but her pajamas, and she has to look up to see Elizabeth's face.

Elizabeth opens her mouth to speak, but Stella reaches up, curls her arms around Elizabeth's neck, and tugs, pulling Elizabeth into the bedroom. Pulls until she can kick the door closed behind her, until they are wrapped up together in darkness, snug and cozy and alone.

CHAPTER 16

Perhaps it's because she was so deeply asleep that everything feels so dreamlike. Her bedroom is just dark enough. Elizabeth smells exactly how Elizabeth should smell, her scent magnified by a whole day of living, amplified up by how close they are. Stella's nose is in Elizabeth's neck, at the bottom of her hair line, behind her ear.

Elizabeth's breath hitches and then hitches again. Her arms tighten around Stella's waist.

"I think," Stella whispers, "I was just dreaming about you."

The details are fleeting—she can't quite catch them in her mind—but she knows it was her.

Elizabeth makes a small noise.

Stella stretches up until her lips are against Elizabeth's ear and whispers, "Did you come to spend the night, or did you just come for dessert?"

It's a legitimate question, despite the double entendre. Addie promised to save Elizabeth something sweet if she came over.

Elizabeth says "Stella" in an agonized voice. She pushes away and takes a step back to put space between them. She's breathing a little heavily. "What are we doing?"

"Doing?"

"There's something about me you need to know," Elizabeth says.

The dreamlike bubble bursts.

"I want to be the friend you need, but I'm afraid." Elizabeth pulls at the collar of her blouse as if to allow her room to breathe. "I'm afraid that one of us is going to get hurt."

Stella can feel the blood rushing to her head, in her ears as loud as sirens. Stella already knows what Elizabeth is going to say. How she's Catholic. How she prefers men because she's straight. And isn't Stella straight too?

She doesn't know anymore. She doesn't think so.

"I'm sorry, I shouldn't have—"

"You don't have to apologize. I started this," Elizabeth says.

They're standing a foot apart, both whispering. Maybe Stella should have turned the lamp on, but she'd rather not face rejection fully lit.

"I asked for something that I shouldn't have," Elizabeth continues, "because I wanted it. But that wasn't fair to you."

Stella shakes her head, unsure what Elizabeth means.

"You just lost your husband. It's not fair to expect..."

Stella realizes that Elizabeth is crying.

"To expect what?" Stella asks.

"I've never done anything like this before." Elizabeth covers her face with her hands. Stella's not sure what to say to a weepy Elizabeth, who can't seem to communicate what she's crying about.

Maybe she should get Addie. She always seems to know what's going on.

But this feels like something Stella should be able to figure out for herself. She was once a human lie detector. While she doesn't think Elizabeth is lying, there does seem to be some truth that needs to be uncovered.

She reaches out, touches Elizabeth's shoulder. "Come on. Let's sit down." She guides her to the mattress. "Now. Let's start again."

Elizabeth smiles through her tears, wet mascara gathering at the bottom of Elizabeth's eyes. "We did," Elizabeth says. "We started again. And now we're friends."

"I rely on you too much. I know that." Whatever is happening here, Stella wants to be the one to shoulder the blame so Elizabeth can stop crying.

Elizabeth shakes her head. "That goes both ways."

"We can take a step back if that's what you need. No more sleepovers."

"I worry that we're not coming from the same place," Elizabeth says.

"I made you uncomfortable. I'm sorry."

"I'm the one who should be sorry, Stella. I took advantage of your kindness."

This is the first time anyone has accused Stella of being kind. And how exactly did Elizabeth take advantage? "I don't…I don't really know what we're talking about."

"I know."

"Why did you come over tonight?" Stella asks.

"To see you. And Addie."

"I thought maybe you wanted some, you know, contact therapy."

"Yes, but it's not fair to ask that of you." Elizabeth's voice cracks on a new sob. "It's cruel."

"Cruel?"

"To you. To myself, maybe. God, I don't know."

"Hey, I know you have a lot of reasons to—there's the whole Catholic thing. I know that. I'd never expect you to—shit, what am I trying to say? I'd never expect you to involve yourself in something that goes against your religion. And if this is going too far for you—"

"For me?" Elizabeth says, cutting her off.

"I know some women are okay with a more physical friendship," Stella says. "And some women aren't."

"Are you?" Elizabeth asks. "Okay with it?"

Stella nods. "I'm okay with it as long as it's you."

"Oh." Her voice is steady now. She wipes her face with her hands again.

"Are you okay with it?" Stella asks.

"I don't want to do anything if it feels wrong to you. I don't want to take it too far."

Stella suspects her "too far" is a few miles past Elizabeth's.

"What's too far for you? Have we already passed that? Is that why you stopped me?"

"I don't know what's too far," Elizabeth whispers. "I've never done this before."

"Me either," Stella reminds her. She reaches up to pull the glasses from Elizabeth's head. Sets them on the nightstand. Puts her hand on Elizabeth's knee. "Is this too far?"

Elizabeth shakes her head.

Stella touches along the collar of Elizabeth's blouse, her finger grazing her skin. "Too much?"

"No," Elizabeth breathes.

Stella slips her fingers into Elizabeth's hair, resting her palm against the back of her head. She squeezes her fingers together until she holds a handful of Elizabeth's hair, forcing her to lean her head back a little.

"How about now?" Stella asks.

"No," Elizabeth says. "It's good."

Stella leans in, presses her face against Elizabeth's neck. A flush of heat moves through her body. "Too far?"

Elizabeth breathes out raggedly. "No."

Stella presses her lips to Elizabeth's neck, then catches her earlobe lightly between her teeth.

Elizabeth whines softly and tilts her head to give Stella more access.

She bites down a little harder, and then, releasing, whispers into her ear, "Have I crossed the line?"

"No," Elizabeth manages.

And then Stella understands. It's as if she just forced a confession, tangled a murderer up in their web of lies. All that remains is the truth falling into place. She flashes on Addie saying, "You're on the same page," and "She's coming around," and "Hers and hers, I guess."

Stella strokes the satin skin of Elizabeth's neck with her tongue, wet and purposeful.

"Oh *God*," Elizabeth says, the words seeming to escape without permission.

Stella turns and swings her leg over Elizabeth's lap, straddling her completely. "I'm starting to think that there's no such thing as too far," she says, and then leans in. She takes Elizabeth's face in her hands and, just like in her fantasy, slants their mouths together. Stella parts her lips, and Elizabeth's tongue meets hers. Elizabeth pulls her closer. No hesitation.

It's been over a year since Stella kissed anyone, and she can't remember the last time she had a kiss like this. Desperate and hot. The last person she had sex with was Ron, and their sex had become routine, their kisses perfunctory. A more satisfying chore than laundry or dishes, but a chore all the same.

When Elizabeth finally breaks away to take in a ragged breath, Stella kisses her cheek, her temple, and then returns to her mouth.

Elizabeth slips her hand under Stella's pajama top, slides it up her back, then wraps it around her waist until it's under her breasts. Stella whimpers.

Stella finds the top button of Elizabeth's blouse, flicks it open. Undoes the second and third buttons. Pulls the fabric apart and touches the swell of her breasts over the lacy top of her bra. She kisses Elizabeth's jaw, whispers into her ear, "Touch me."

Isn't that how all this started? Elizabeth braiding her hair, Stella sitting between her knees. The hugs. The nighttime cuddles. All leading to this moment. Stella's tongue in Elizabeth's ear, Elizabeth's hands on her breasts.

Stella thinks back to the first time she saw Captain Murphy. She had imagined her as boring and dowdy and, well, old. The captain of Homicide, the ice-cold bitch, the rule-obsessed bureaucrat who cared more about following the letter of the law than about winning cases and sending criminals to prison.

It was like a lightning strike to finally meet her face-to-face. Elizabeth was then, as she is now, a beautiful woman with long red hair, wearing a tailored suit and heels. She was focused in a way that rubbed Stella wrong because it was a little too close to her own demeanor. Stella tried to gain the upper hand by affecting warmth, and it backfired. Elizabeth was smarter than that and offended at the ruse. As a result, it took them years to be comfortable working together.

But now Elizabeth's hands, her lips, her breath are all hot on Stella's skin. And Stella is melting into her.

"I didn't know," Elizabeth says. "I thought it was just me."

"I know," Stella moans. "Honey, I know."

Elizabeth is trembling now. Stella slides off her lap and pulls her down to the bed.

Elizabeth pushes her heels off, and Stella wraps herself around a shivering Elizabeth, the spooning coming easy after so much practice.

"I'm sorry," Elizabeth says. "I'm sorry."

"No, no. None of that."

Stella has a thousand things she wants to say, like how Elizabeth is the most beautiful woman she's ever seen, how she actually wants to live her life, how that's a feeling that she never thought would come back, how she's in love. How she's so sure she's in love. But she says nothing, simply strokes Elizabeth's hair until her breathing is steady again.

Then Elizabeth rolls over to face Stella.

"I can't stay the whole night," she says regretfully. "We both have to be up early."

"I know."

Elizabeth smiles at Stella, then leans in and kisses her gently.

"Maybe I'll see you Friday night?" Stella asks. It's their usual routine, after all.

"Definitely."

Stella watches from the bed as Elizabeth finds her shoes, buttons her blouse, hunts down her glasses. She runs her hand through her hair to tame it, but it's beyond hope.

Elizabeth looks back at Stella. "Friday, then."

"Friday," Stella confirms.

Elizabeth steps out of the room and closes the door behind her, but not before Stella sees a light on in the kitchen. Addie must be editing; apparently that's what takes up most of her time.

After she leaves, Stella is restless, keyed up. Her heart is still pounding, and there's moisture between her legs. The gusset of her underwear is uncomfortably wet. She pulls off her pajama bottoms and underwear and throws them tangled on the floor.

She'll never sleep all revved up like this. She's got to do something. So she thinks about kissing Elizabeth, about Elizabeth's hands all over her, and within a few minutes, she's shuddering into the mattress.

She rolls over, gripping her pillow. Her eyes fill with tears. Dr. Barrett warned her that the first time she had sex she might feel emotional, and Stella thinks that tonight falls under that umbrella, even though they stopped at heavy petting and she'd finished alone. She realizes now that she spent most of this year in such a deep depression that her body wouldn't have responded to sexual stimulus anyway. It's good to feel alive again, to want something. Someone.

Maybe she should go back to see Dr. Barrett again, after all.

Stella's alarm goes off at five thirty, and when she stumbles out to the kitchen, Addie is still sitting at the table.

"Addie!" Stella scolds. "You haven't slept at all."

"I'm almost done." She looks up at Stella, dark circles under her eyes. She has the hood from her sweatshirt pulled on, but her legs are mostly bare in a pair of boxer shorts she uses for pajamas.

"Get some sleep." Stella pats her bare knee as she makes her way to the coffee maker.

"Saw Elizabeth leaving pretty late," Addie says. "Y'all were in there a while."

Stella tries to stifle the smile that creeps onto her face. "Don't you worry about that," she says.

"Did you guys…?" Addie asks.

"We, uh, kissed a little bit," Stella says. "Turns out we may be on the same page about some things after all, Addison."

"Halle-fucking-lujah!" Addie cries.

"You could have told me"—Stella scoops coffee into the filter basket—"saved us all some time."

"You can't just go outing people! You didn't even want to be her friend at first."

"Yeah, because I was attracted to her!"

"Amazing," Addie says fondly. "What a journey you took me on. I loved watching y'all fall in love, but damn! You were stupid about it the whole time."

Stella starts the coffee, then she sits across from Addie.

"I think she's a little freaked out, actually," Stella admits. "She got really overwhelmed."

"Yeah, dude, she's been straight up throwing herself at you, and you were, like, the queen of mixed signals. She was very confused." Addie looks back at her screen. "Oh, thank the Lord. It finally uploaded," and she slams her computer shut. "I gotta get some sleep."

"Wait, now? I need to talk about this!" Stella says. "You can't go now."

"I'm so tired!" Addie whines.

"Just wait a minute! I wasn't sending mixed signals. I was trying to respect her preferences!"

"You couldn't respect her preferences because you didn't know what her preferences were. You never asked," Addie says. "It was infuriating."

"That is not true!"

"Why did you quit therapy?" Addie demands. "You had one more free session, and you were doing well. I think the doctor asked you something you weren't ready to answer, and you freaked out and hoofed it."

Stella stares, slack-jawed. "She wanted to talk about Elizabeth. I think she knew."

Addie grabs a banana from the fruit basket and points it at her. "I think you should go back and apologize to that shrink. Ask her to keep treating you." She tucks the banana into her hoodie pocket. "I'm going to bed."

The coffee maker beeps. Stella pours herself a cup, takes it into the shower with her.

She moves through the rest of the morning in a fog.

The arbitration fails, so there will be a trial. The legal team will have to regroup, so she's off the hook for a while. She goes to the sheriff's department next for a meeting about training. Stella thinks it's more of a screening than a consulting appointment. They asked for Mallory, after all, and Mallory had offered Stella in her stead, so they probably want to meet her, make sure she knows her stuff.

The appointment isn't for an hour and a half. Not enough time to go home, too much time to hang around downtown. She thinks about dropping in at the police administration building to see what Elizabeth's doing. She hasn't been there since Ron died. But she's not about to show up unannounced and uninvited now just because she and Elizabeth kissed.

She thinks about what Addie said this morning. What Addie was saying for months, what she and Elizabeth were both saying about therapy.

She could drive to Dr. Barrett's office. It's only ten minutes away. She doesn't have to go inside. She can sit in her car in the parking lot. Then again, maybe it would be nice to see Dr. Barrett, not because she was right about Elizabeth but because Stella could show her how well she's doing. Maybe Stella wasn't the best patient, but she absorbed what she could over seven or so sessions, used the tools she learned from Dr. Barrett to the best of her ability.

Compared to the first time she sat in this parking lot, there's no question that she's better. Now she's wearing a dress and matching blazer instead of her niece's clothes. She has work and money coming in. She's still sad some of the time, but she's not so depressed, and she hasn't had a panic attack in a long time.

And she's learned some things about herself that she might never have examined otherwise. She would have stayed married to Ron because she hates change more than she hates a not-quite-right relationship. He would have stayed too, she thinks, because he hated failure.

Maybe she'll just pop inside.

The receptionist is not the same one as before. It's a much younger woman with long strawberry-blonde hair, and she smiles when Stella comes up to the window.

"Hi. Did you have an appointment?"

"No, but I'm a patient here. Or I was for a little while." She hesitates, momentarily unsure of herself.

The receptionist waits for her to continue.

"I couldn't make my last appointment because of…reasons," Stella finishes lamely. "But I'd like to reschedule."

"Sure. We can do that," the receptionist says. "Do you have your insurance info and a photo ID?"

Stella gets her wallet and slides her insurance card and driver's license through the window. The woman types something into her computer. "Oh!"

"Something wrong?"

"There's a note in your file records. It says you had one more session on the books, and if you came back, Dr. Barrett ordered that three more be comped."

"Comped? Why?" Stella asks.

The woman shrugs. "Doctor's orders. What date and time are good for you?"

She's about to say anytime, but that's not true anymore. She has things scheduled now. She pulls out her phone and pulls up her calendar app. "What's the next date available?"

"It looks like there's a slot next Monday at eleven. Does that work?"

Stella looks at her schedule. "Yes, that works. I will try not to cancel."

In fact, she did not cancel last time. She blew it off, if she remembers correctly.

"If you need to cancel, give us forty-eight-hours' notice, please," the receptionist says. "Do you want an email or text reminder?"

"Text, I guess."

"Great! You're all set for October 7 at eleven. I'm Lana, by the way."

"Nice to meet you."

"See you then!"

It's much easier this time around. She almost can't remember why she struggled so much last time, even to the point of not being able to get out of the car. She really couldn't do much of anything until Addie and Elizabeth helped her up and out of her grief.

God, she loves them both so much.

She heads to her next appointment, determined not to cry. She can be sappy about her life later, and anyway, she's tired of crying.

Addie still works Friday nights at the restaurant, so by the time Elizabeth gets there, Stella's been home alone for a couple of hours. She has spent most of the day anxious and feeling underprepared to see Elizabeth.

Before Addie left, they sat at the table in the backyard and went through some things.

"Let's Venn-diagram our way through this," Addie said, holding up both hands, making circles with her index fingers and thumbs, then overlapping them slightly. "When the gay and the straight circles overlap, we get this oval called bisexual. I think this is where you and Elizabeth live."

"But I don't think either of us have ever actually—"

"*Actually* doesn't matter, Aunt Stella. What matters is how you feel. Who you're attracted to, whether or not you've ever acted on it."

"I mean, I can admire a beautiful woman, but I've never actually wanted to act on that until Elizabeth."

"Then that's something called demisexual," Addie said. "You don't get attracted to them unless you have an emotional connection."

"But I was attracted to her before I ever really knew her," Stella said.

"Yeah, I think that's bisexual, then," Addie concluded. "That doesn't mean you're fifty-fifty down the middle. You can like men ninety-nine percent of the time and women one percent and still be bisexual."

Stella rolls the conversation over in her mind as she paces the house, waiting for Elizabeth. Maybe in her case it's more like ten percent women. Twenty, max. Really, it's her work she's always been interested in. Men managed to find their way into what little space Stella allowed outside of work. If they were persistent, they made themselves fit. If a beautiful woman did the same thing earlier in her life, would she be having this specific midlife crisis right now?

Perhaps not.

Anyway, her concerns are more about the physical aspect. What if she's just not good at having sex with women? What if she fumbles around and Elizabeth gets impatient? What if they try it and it doesn't go well? What if, after all this, they don't even like it?

Or what if Elizabeth decides that she doesn't like it, and Stella must shove her feelings back into the friendship box? She'd figure out how to do that because she'd rather have Elizabeth as a friend than not at all, but she can't imagine it's easy to unring this particular bell.

Elizabeth texted Stella to let her know she's picking up dinner, so Stella knows she's out of the office. Stella worried that she'd catch a case, but Elizabeth said the day had been mostly administrative.

She's as wound up as a cooped-up tiger. She looks for ways to burn up energy. She zeroes in on a pile of blushes that Addie was photographing and sweeps them into the junk drawer. She empties the drying rack, puts dirty spoons and cups into the dishwasher, straightens the chairs around the table.

She goes around the house, lighting all the half-burned candles. Most of them are scentless. Addie usually buys only one fragrant one because she doesn't like conflicting scents. Now that it's October, it doesn't feel out of place to have candles lit.

After a while, Stella is reduced to picking things up and setting them down again, not actually tidying. When she hears Elizabeth's courtesy knock before she opens the door, she's standing in the laundry room, a box of unopened dryer sheets in her hand. She tosses them back onto the shelf above the dryer.

"I brought Oleego," Elizabeth calls out. "Hope you don't mind!" Oleego is Korean food, and the restaurant is close to Elizabeth's office.

"Sounds lovely," she says, emerging into the kitchen. "Thank you."

It feels a little awkward. Stella imagined they might hug or even kiss, but Elizabeth has her purse on her shoulder, she's holding bags of food, and the moment for greeting gets lost in the shuffle of food and plates.

"I'm starving," Elizabeth says.

"Well, Addie's working, so let's dig in."

Elizabeth carries their plates to the coffee table, their usual eating place when it's just the two of them. Stella brings out a bottle of wine.

"Did you skip lunch?" Stella asks, because Elizabeth has already started eating by the time she finds the wine opener, and it's unlike her not to wait.

"I didn't skip it. It just happened without me."

Stella snorts, then fills their glasses. She turns the TV on. "What should we watch? I promised Addie we wouldn't watch her videos without her."

"What? Why?"

"She's being so weird about the whole thing. I think it would be worse to watch them with us, but her preference is that we don't watch them at all."

"That's not going to happen."

"Because you've already been watching them?"

Elizabeth grins. "The singing ones are adorable."

Stella takes a few bites of her food, picks up the remote again. "Whatever you want to watch."

"There's always *Jeopardy*. There are episodes on Netflix now of the championships."

"I was banned from watching that by my family long ago." Stella says. "Apparently I'm a know-it-all and a teensy bit competitive."

"Mm. Perhaps another time, then."

Stella switches to cable and scrolls through, landing on some home renovation show. It doesn't take much brain power, and it gets them through the meal and half the bottle of wine. By the time they clean up,

Stella feels much more relaxed. It's just Elizabeth, after all. Spending time together is what they do.

"Were you planning on, uh, staying the night?" Stella asks lightly.

"I was, if that's okay with you. That's why I brought my big purse." She gestures to where she dropped it. "Change of clothes."

"It's okay by me."

It's not even nine. Too early to go to bed. But there's nothing that Stella wants to do more than get Elizabeth into her bedroom.

They sit on the couch, looking at each other.

"How are you feeling about things?" Elizabeth asks when the silence stretches on a little too long. "About the other night?"

"I feel good," Stella says. "A little confused."

"Confused?"

"Oh, not about you," Stella reassures her. "Just about, mm, logistics."

"Oh." Elizabeth nods. "Yes, I'm a little nervous about that as well." She flashes a quick smile.

"I think it's one of those things we're going to have to practice." Stella says, not looking at Elizabeth.

When her words are met with silence, she glances up to see Elizabeth looking at her. Elizabeth's usually porcelain skin looks flushed.

"I guess so," Elizabeth says.

"Listen, I know that it's not late, but do you wanna just, I don't know, start now?" Stella asks. She looks at Elizabeth's mouth and then drags her gaze back up to her eyes.

Elizabeth nods.

CHAPTER 17

THEY TAKE TURNS WASHING UP in the bathroom, Elizabeth first, then they rendezvous in the bedroom. Stella shuts the door behind her and begins to chatter nervously about everything that was unsaid for so long.

"We don't have to rush into anything. We don't have to do anything at all. We can stop anytime. Tell me if you don't like something because I just want us to have a nice time, and I worry that—"

"Stella, shut up. Kiss me right now."

She laughs nervously. "I'm just trying to make sure you're comfortable."

"I appreciate that, but please consider me all in." Elizabeth reaches out and pulls her close.

And still Stella chatters on. "You made it real clear that you've never done this before, and I need to reiterate that I haven't either."

"I know," Elizabeth says.

"And I just—"

But then Elizabeth's lips are on hers. They kiss softly until Elizabeth, sensing Stella's hesitation, pulls back. "You just what?"

"I just don't want you to be disappointed."

"That seems unlikely. But if *you* aren't ready, we don't have to—"

"I'm ready!" Stella blurts out.

"So that's settled, then." Elizabeth smiles. "We're both ready to go." She steps back and unbuttons her blouse, yanks it up and out of the skirt, and drops it on the floor. Then she reaches behind to unzip her skirt and steps out of it. She shimmies out of her pantyhose. Her skin is creamy and pale against her black cotton bra and underwear. And she's unbelievably sexy.

She is brave, so brave, Stella thinks, and decides she can be brave too. She whips off her own shirt so fast that Elizabeth laughs, then jams down her bottoms. All she wants now is to get into bed and see where this night will take them.

They sit on the edge of the rumpled bed, kissing slowly, then lie down, pressing up against each another. They quickly find their bearings, and it doesn't take long before slow and gentle are quite a ways behind them.

The feel of Elizabeth's skin against hers is intoxicating, like no drug she's ever tried. Everything about Elizabeth is smooth and silky soft. Everywhere Elizabeth touches makes Stella gasp and moan. They must look ridiculous, squirming so desperately against one another, but Stella is in too deep to care.

Stella's hands are moving too. For years, she lusted after Elizabeth's auburn locks, and now she's getting her fill. With one hand buried in her hair, the other moves down Elizabeth's back and down one leg. She tucks a hand under her knee and hitches it up over her hip. Elizabeth moans.

As she strokes the back of Elizabeth's thigh, she feels Elizabeth undo her bra and push it up so that Stella's breasts are exposed. She pushes the bra off Stella's shoulders, then dips her head until one of Stella's nipples is in her mouth. Stella whimpers as the sensation shoots down between her legs. Elizabeth gently takes her nipple between her teeth, and Stella gasps.

Stella runs her hand up Elizabeth's thigh until it's right between her legs. Her underwear is wet to the touch. Elizabeth's breath hitches, so Stella drags her finger with a little more pressure, then leans in to kiss Elizabeth's neck.

She strokes again, pushing in a little harder, and Elizabeth squirms, dislodging Stella from her neck. "Off," she pants. "Take everything off."

Elizabeth sits up, takes her own bra off. Her breasts are smaller than Stella's and not as saggy. Her ivory skin is creamy and smooth. She looks like a Pre-Raphaelite painting with her pink cheeks and a rosy flush spreading across the tops of her breasts and her thighs.

The room is warming up, so Stella gets up to flip the switch on the overhead fan. Elizabeth is gathering up her hair and holding it up off her neck. She smiles when she sees Stella looking. She drops her hair and, lying back, stretches her hand out to her. "Come back."

Stella has never been overly fond of fumbling through foreplay, more interested in the main event. She's always liked sex. In fact, her best sex has always been either with people she just met or people she didn't like very much. Ron was a good example of both. When they'd started dating, he'd been far more interested than she was. She'd found him cocky, a little arrogant, and too aware of just how handsome he was. She'd started sleeping with him long before she'd grown to like him, let alone love him. The sex had been good enough to stick around for, and for Stella, sex was often about penetration; she wanted the high, she wanted the orgasm, she wanted the deed done and over with. She was always more likely to find her pleasure with someone else inside of her and her own hands keeping busy than some man fumbling around, looking for what shouldn't ever be that hard to find.

It's interesting now, however, because that's not really what they're rushing toward here. If there's no singular main event, then everything becomes the main event. Every touch, every instance of flesh between teeth. One could argue that orgasm becomes the main goal, but with two people perfectly capable of more than one, does that really qualify?

Stella slips out of her underwear and returns to the bed. She slips her hand under the waistband of Elizabeth's underwear and pushes down. Elizabeth lifts her hips, and Stella pulls the panties all the way off and drops them on the floor.

Now they're pressed together, flesh on flesh. They kiss for a long time, their breasts together, their legs tangled, their hips moving. Elizabeth strokes her back, running her fingers along Stella's spine.

Part of Stella wants to keep this slow, easy pace, but she's getting impatient and desperate. She tries to hold off, but it's not long before she reaches between Elizabeth's legs again, only this time there's no fabric in her way, this time she penetrates the wetness directly, and the gasp from Elizabeth is intoxicating. She pulls her finger out enough to stroke Elizabeth's folds, alternately adding pressure, then taking it away until she drags her fingers high enough to start stroking her clitoris. Elizabeth shudders, her breath catching in her throat.

Stella glances up to see Elizabeth watching her, and she smiles, her teeth bared.

Encouraged, she again pushes a finger into Elizabeth and holds it still for a moment, marveling at the sensation of being surrounded by that soft, tight heat. Then she begins thrusting, gently at first, then deeper until, pressing hard and upward, she gets the desired result. She keeps her other hand moving, running it up and down Elizabeth's leg and hip.

With a twist of Stella's fingers inside, Elizabeth moans out a sound between a scream and a yelp. That's what Stella has been hoping for. She likes the whining, the low moans, the heavy breathing, but what she wants is for Elizabeth to make a noise that is undignified and involuntary. Maybe to swear a little.

Stella continues thrusting her finger, slowly at first, then gradually increasing her speed. Stella doesn't believe in breaks, only the relentless, determined search for Elizabeth's pleasure, and she won't stop until she finds it.

Elizabeth's eyes are closed, and she's glistening in the lamplight.

"God, you're pretty." It's the first thing she's said in a while, but she feels like Elizabeth should know.

Elizabeth clenches around her fingers, maybe tries to say something, but it just comes out as a loud sigh.

Stella changes tactics when her wrist starts to ache. Keeping her hand between Elizabeth's legs, she moves her body up over her, licks between her breasts, nips at her collarbone, then kisses her, gently nips her neck. Then she moves back down and pushes two fingers deep into Elizabeth's folds. She uses her other hand to start rubbing Elizabeth's clit again.

Elizabeth twitches. "Oh," she says. "I'm—"

She cries out as her hips jerk, and she grips Stella's wrist, holding it hard against her, holding it through the orgasm, grinding against it while her breath comes out in ragged moans.

Stella continues stroking her but is no longer thrusting with the same intensity. Now she slips her fingers in, pulls them out again slowly, and pushes them back in again, feeling the aftershocks fluttering around her.

"Jesus," Elizabeth says at last, opening her eyes.

"Yeah?"

"*Jesus*," Elizabeth says again. She tries to sit up on her elbows but then thinks better of it. "I need a minute."

"We have all night," Stella says and lies down next to her.

Elizabeth turns her head to look at her. "You're very surprising, Stella Anne Carter."

"I am?"

"Mm. I don't usually…that is to say, I generally find it difficult to…"

"Come?" Stella finishes for her when she hesitates.

"No. Well, yes. Not when I'm by myself. Just with—"

"Men," Stella concludes, then smiles and says, "It's my honor to get you off this evening, Captain."

Elizabeth laughs, low and throaty and joyful. "The pleasure was all mine."

It's Stella's turn now, and she's more nervous now than she was before, unsure about being on the other side. She feels like she's going to jump out of her skin. She wants to keep going, wants her own satisfaction. She's horny and desperate and she's more than ready.

But she doesn't want to disappoint Elizabeth—or herself.

They're sitting up now, astride each other. Elizabeth reaches behind Stella to turn the lamp off. The darkness settles over her like relief. How Elizabeth knew to do that, she couldn't say but she certainly feels more herself with the lights out.

She kisses Elizabeth with abandon, runs her hands down Elizabeth's bare back, feels her shiver. Elizabeth's hands are everywhere, and when she reaches between Stella's thighs, Stella doesn't pull away and she doesn't disappear into the blankness of her own mind. She feels it the whole way through.

It's good, how they are. It gives Elizabeth a different kind of leverage than Stella found with Elizabeth on her back. This way, Elizabeth can be a solid foundation and Stella moves against Elizabeth's hand, sliding on and off her fingers, pushing her clitoris against the palm of her hand. Elizabeth pulls Stella's bottom lip between her teeth while twisting her fingers. Stella likes the roughness of it, and she already feels right on the edge of orgasm, feels it welling up behind her eyes, running down her spine, sparking in her fingertips and toes. All the metaphors—the little death, fireworks, coming undone—they are all are happening at once. It's been a long time since she's hovered so long in the moment just before. And isn't the just before as good as the orgasm itself?

Elizabeth moans into Stella's shoulder. They undulate together, their legs wrapped around each other, the fan cooling their backs and blowing through their hair. Stella can feel herself start to tremble, a sure tell that she won't be able to hold off any longer. Elizabeth's palm grinding against her is maddening.

Elizabeth looks up from where she was watching her fingers disappearing in and out of Stella, sees that Stella is looking at Elizabeth. And then Elizabeth's eyes meet hers, and she sees that Stella is wound about as tight as she can go. Elizabeth says softly, "It's okay," as if she *knows* exactly what Stella is feeling, as if she recognizes the pleasure and the pain from the look on Stella's face and gives her permission to let it go.

Stella starts to shake, and when the orgasm takes her, she slumps into Elizabeth's arms, her face on Elizabeth's shoulder, her arms wrapped tightly around Elizabeth, her vaginal muscles clenching on Elizabeth's fingers. Her orgasm comes in waves, and now she's spasming again, each new crest of pleasure radiating from Elizabeth's hand.

When the last wave ebbs, she realizes that the moans, the wails she heard, came from her.

Elizabeth strokes Stella's hair as she lifts her head, which is still buzzing. Elizabeth's other hand is wet on her thigh.

"Fuck," Stella says because that's all she can really say.

"You okay?" Elizabeth asks.

"Better than okay. Thank you."

"That was amazing," Elizabeth says.

Stella is still trying to catch her breath. "I can't believe we did that," she says, although she knows now that they've both imagined it for some time. She licks her upper lip; it's salty with sweat. "How do you feel?"

"I feel like this is the first time in years I haven't had to talk myself into having sex with someone." Elizabeth looks at Stella. "Isn't that embarrassing?"

"No," Stella assures her. "Honey, no."

"I thought I would be more scared. And I was nervous, but it felt good and right."

"I've thought about you and me together like this well before I even liked you," Stella says. "I thought it was just one of those things, one of those wild fantasies that don't have a chance in hell of coming true."

"Really? Even back when you didn't want Addie to talk to me?"

"Well before that. Practically the first time I saw you."

Elizabeth shakes her head. "That can't be true. You were married, and you were awful to me!"

"I would submit to the court that we were awful to each another," Stella says. "What else could I do? Then, after Ron died and we got to be friends, I was fine being attracted to you and not doing anything about it. And anyway, I was sure you were straight."

"Yeah, well, so was I. Guess we were both wrong."

They shower together. Afterward, Elizabeth talks about getting dressed and going home, but it's late now, and she doesn't follow through. They turn the light off and curl up together in bed, still naked.

Stella is drowsy and content. She falls asleep with her hand on Elizabeth's thigh.

Stella wakes up to see Elizabeth pulling on a shirt. Early morning light is coming through the window. Stella sits up, holding the sheet across her chest. "Hey."

Elizabeth looks at her and flashes a smile as she gathers her hair back and secures it with a plastic clip. Her big bag is at her feet with her blouse from the night before crumpled up inside.

"I'm not sneaking out on you." Elizabeth says softly. "I'm sneaking out on Addie." Elizabeth picks up the bag and slings it over her shoulder. "I had a great time."

"I'd love to see you again," Stella says dryly. "Can I have your number?"

"You should tell Addie whatever you want to tell her, not—"

"You don't have to explain."

Elizabeth picks up her glasses from the nightstand and puts them on the top of her head. Stella feels her chest tighten with a feeling she can't identify. Then she realizes that it's something other than the familiar pain. It's what happens when desire and joy get all swirled up, like a candle burning brightly, chasing the darkness away.

Stella meets Mallory at the same Starbucks where they met the first time. The sheriff's department assignment is a big job. They want her to help rewrite the training modules for investigative work as well as teach their staff how to run future trainings.

"Are you sure about this?" Stella asks. "It's probably gonna be over a hundred hours of work."

"This is exactly the sort of job I would have had to turn down before," Mallory says. "A good project worth a lot of money that I couldn't have juggled with my other responsibilities. As long as you're up for it, I say go for it. How many employees does the sheriff's department have? Fifteen thousand?"

"Twenty," Stella says. "Twenty-two, I think."

"That's a great client to have on the books."

"They agreed to work around the trial I have scheduled." Stella should be excited about a project of this magnitude, but this feels like real work. If she takes this assignment, she really will be moving on. Between this and Elizabeth in her bed, she's finally leaving Ron behind.

"If they wanted the job done fast, they would have gone with Citygate or LD Consulting. But they asked for you specifically," Mallory says. "I think your reputation alone is going to get us a lot of work."

Stella doesn't think much of her own reputation. She basically ghosted the DA's office after Ron died. But she's learning that people understand grief because it's universal. They gave her a great deal of grace, and she's thankful for it.

"I can do it," Stella says, scrolling through the calendar on her phone to check the dates again. "Reputation preceding me and all."

"Do you like it?" Mallory sips her coffee. "Consulting?"

"It's nice to have some control over my schedule. And the pay is better, that's for sure."

She gets regular checks from Marco, some rent from Addie (who insists), and a small pension from Los Angeles County, but last year, she paid out more than she brought in and blew through the bulk of the insurance money when she bought the house. It's nice to not constantly worry about money.

“At this rate, I may have to open an office and maybe hire a receptionist,” Mallory says.

“Let’s just see how this goes first.” Stella glances at her wristwatch. “I need to get going. I have another appointment.”

Stella wants to reassure Mallory that she’s serious about staying on, but she can’t make any promises yet. She learned the hard way that no one can see the future.

“Sure,” Mallory says. “Call me if you need anything or have any questions. Anything at all. You’re doing really well. I think this partnership suits us.”

Maybe Stella is doing well. She doesn’t lose days anymore. Doesn’t wake up late in the evening with no memory of how she spent the day before. She almost never cries anymore. She doesn’t look in the mirror and see a stranger, doesn’t feel like she’s floating above herself, like she’s watching herself on TV.

“Thank you,” Stella says.

Lana, the perky new receptionist at Dr. Barrett’s office, has her hair in a ponytail today. She looks up when Stella walks in.

Stella’s hair is pulled back in a barrette, and she feels it tight against her scalp. There was traffic on the drive over, and she worried about being late. Or maybe she’s just nervous in general. She doesn’t usually tuck her tail between her legs and slink back somewhere, but she made an exception for this.

Lana checks her in, and she barely gets to sit down before Dr. Barrett opens the door to her office.

“Come on in, Stella.”

Stella slings her purse over her shoulder and follows her in, feeling like she’s going to the principal’s office. She sits in the same chair, looks at the same art print, listens to the same clock ticking on the wall. Dr. Barrett looks the same too, except her hair is shorter.

“Well,” Stella says.

“Well.” Dr. Barrett smiles, her eyes crinkling. “Welcome back.”

CHAPTER 18

STELLA COMES HOME TO THE kitchen filled with lights, a camera on a tripod, and a couple dozen little orange pumpkins. The camera is focused in front of the oven. Addie is squatting next to it.

"What on earth is going on here?" Stella asks, setting her purse on the table. "And what smells so good?"

"I'm filming a video of baking pumpkin bread." She's wearing a lightweight smock apron with straps that cross in the back. "I already filmed the mixing, and now I'm filming a time lapse of it baking." She looks up at Stella. "Where have you been?"

"I..." Stella runs her finger through a layer of flour on the countertop. "I went back to therapy."

"What?" Addie stands up from her crouch. "Oh, my God! What made you change your mind?"

Stella thinks about lying, but coming fresh out of therapy, it feels wrong.

"Elizabeth and I had sex," Stella says. She feels heat rising to her face. She wasn't going to tell Addie right away, was going to talk about it more with Elizabeth first, but standing here with her niece, she feels compelled.

"*What?*" Addie spins around happily, nearly toppling her tripod and camera in the process. "Are you screwing with me right now?"

"I am not," Stella promises.

Addie squeals and runs a lap around of the house before coming back into the kitchen. "Was it *goddamn amazing?*"

"Calm down," Stella says. "Jesus, the neighbors can hear you."

Addie ignores her. "I gotta call *Liz!*"

"You'd better not!"

"Why not?" Addie looks at Stella while she leans over to catch her breath. "Did she not like it?"

"I just…" Stella crosses her arms. "I mean, we both had a nice time."

"Wait, you had a nice time? That's it? Was it bad?"

"It wasn't bad. It was—I don't want to go into details," Stella says, though she really does.

The timer on the oven beeps.

"Shit," Addie says. She reaches out to turn the camera off and then stretches over the tripod to turn the oven off too. "Don't go anywhere. I want to talk about this more, especially therapy!"

"I'm just gonna go change," Stella says.

She spends more days in real clothing now after spending a year in sweats and oversized T-shirts, and she misses the casual dress of her previous life, though not the fatigue and debilitating sadness.

She puts on a T-shirt and her old black sweatpants and reemerges to see Addie filming the finished loaf of pumpkin bread, the army of tiny pumpkins artfully surrounding it.

Stella waits patiently.

"You can talk," Addie says, reaching up to adjust one of the lights. "I'm going to voice over everything anyway."

"Oh. Okay." Stella says, pretending that she knows what that means.

"So, you went back to therapy." Addie is calmer now, focused on her work.

"I did. I stopped by Dr. Barrett's office a couple of weeks ago and made an appointment."

Addie looks up. "God, I'm so proud of you."

"Well, thank you, sugar."

"Are you going to go back?"

"Yes. I have three more sessions, and then I'll decide if I want to keep going on my own dime." Stella leans against the counter, staying out of Addie's way.

Addie has switched to taking pictures. "Did you talk about Elizabeth? I mean, I know your therapy is none of my business, but—"

"Yes," Stella says. "To both."

"Does Elizabeth know you went back?"

"Not yet. I haven't seen her since…you know."

"Since the sex." Addie grins. She aims her camera at Stella and snaps a picture so quickly she doesn't have time to react.

"Addison!"

"Why don't we invite her over for pumpkin bread?" Addie asks, breezing past the expected scolding.

"It's Monday night. She's probably busy."

"Have you not talked at *all*?"

"We've texted a little, but she caught a case on Saturday," Stella reminds her. They hadn't gone to church, and her thoughts about what they would do after they sat in a pew like very good girls for an hour hadn't quite panned out like she planned.

"I'm just going to invite her." Addie pulls her phone out of her apron pocket. "I promise not to mention anything about therapy or the sex."

Stella drops her face into her hands. "I don't want you to get too excited about this."

"Aunt Stella, you're really making it sound like the sex was bad," Addie says.

"It was not bad. Trust me. It was very enlightening for us both. It's just that we're old, and this whole transition is not easy."

"I think people—especially women—coming out past middle age is pretty common," Addie says, her thumbs moving quickly across her phone.

But Stella is not quite ready to ride the I-came-out-in-middle-age float in the Pride parade. "See, that's what I mean! No one has decided to come out! And what Elizabeth and I do when we're alone shouldn't have any bearing on anything! Just because we, you know…"

"Went to bone town?" Addie suggests.

"Just because we made *love* doesn't mean anything official. Maybe I shouldn't have told you!"

"It's going to be okay. I promise."

"I feel very anxious about it," Stella admits. "Dr. Barrett says any sort of change after a long period of grieving is difficult. And now I'm not only seeing someone new, but I've just had sex with a woman. Just kissing her felt wild enough!"

"Had you ever thought about it?" Addie asks, tucking her phone back into her apron. "Kissing girls?"

"I mean, everyone has probably thought about it, but that doesn't mean they act on it. Do you act on every thought you have?" Stella frowns. "Why are you smiling like that?"

Addie shrugs. "I've never thought about kissing girls."

"Oh."

"I think if you had been born when I was born, you wouldn't have waited until you were in your fifties. And I think if Elizabeth hadn't been raised Catholic, she wouldn't have waited either. You two are a product of your generation, of your upbringings, but I hope those obstacles don't stand in your way because Elizabeth really likes you, and you're completely head over heels for her, Aunt Stella." Addie smiles. "I love you both like you were my own children."

"Frankly, I liked it better when you were hiding something and didn't have time to be this sassy," Stella says, but puts her arms around her niece and hugs her. "Brat."

Addie's phone buzzes, and she lets go of the hug to look at it. "She's coming over."

Stella is both nervous and happy. She wants to see Elizabeth, of course, but she's probably tired from working all weekend. Plus, maybe she's had time to think about what they did and has changed her mind. Although if Elizabeth had even half the good time that Stella did, she'll want to do it again too.

Elizabeth appears twenty minutes later, which is a little surprising. The case must be going well, or they're in that lull where they're waiting for lab work. Addie has added icing to the pumpkin bread and is taking more pictures.

Stella comes into the kitchen and waves at Elizabeth, her hand flapping awkwardly in the air.

"It looks perfect," Elizabeth says, gesturing to the pumpkin bread. "Our little Betty Crocker."

"People like fall videos," Addie replies. "Like fall is even a thing in this state." In fact, the only hint that it's fall is the fact that it isn't over eighty-five degrees right now.

"I didn't know she could bake."

"She can do anything, I think," Stella says fondly.

"Not math!" Addie says cheerfully. She sets her camera on top of the microwave and begins carrying armfuls of little pumpkins into the backyard.

"How's work?" Stella asks Elizabeth.

"It's fine." Elizabeth leans back against the counter and steps out of her high heels. "Did you see Mallory today?"

"Yeah. We decided to take on that sheriff's department project."

"Did you? I'm glad to hear that. They're due for an overhaul. I know the LAPD liaison fairly well, if you want me to introduce you."

"Maybe." It was hard enough to accept her help when they weren't sleeping together. Is it even ethical to do so now?

When Addie comes back in, they're still standing on either side of the room. "Y'all want coffee? Tea? Heroin?"

"I would take a cup of tea." Elizabeth smiles, but her words are sharp. She picks up her shoes and moves them over by the door.

"I can make a pot," Stella offers, happy to have something to do.

Stella moves to pull down the electric kettle from the cupboards where it's stored with the tea. Elizabeth steps aside to give her room. Stella unplugs the microwave so she can plug the kettle in.

Stella realizes now that all the cute, homey touches Addie has added to the house since she moved in aren't just her innate good taste but have been curated for her online life. Stella merely gets to benefit.

Addie takes the rest of the pumpkins outside. Elizabeth reaches out as soon as she's gone and brushes her fingers against Stella's wrist.

"Hi," she whispers.

Stella sucks in her breath, glances at Elizabeth. Her smile reaches her eyes, crinkling them at the corners.

"Hi," Stella says. "I'm glad you came over."

"Me too," Elizabeth looks at her mouth. "I—" She cuts herself off when Addie comes back in.

Stella fills the kettle and plugs it in. "Have you eaten dinner?"

"I ate a late lunch."

"What time did you get to work today?"

"Oh, around six."

"You could have gone home, you know."

Elizabeth shrugs. "I really like pumpkin bread."

Maybe pumpkin bread is a euphemism. Or maybe that's Stella's hopeful heart.

Stella looks at Addie, who is watching them dreamily. When Stella glares at her, she returns to loosening the loaf from the pan with an offset spatula.

They take the bread and the tea to the living room. The loaf is good, moist and spicy. Elizabeth and Stella praise Addie profusely.

"I thought you just did makeup," Elizabeth says.

"I do. But having some variety is good, and lifestyle stuff is always popular. People want to see how you live your life, even if it's a lie. No one actually lives in such a curated way. I wrestle with being authentic and presenting things that are interesting and watchable." She turns to Stella. "Aunt Stella, what did you do today?"

Her warm feelings evaporate. "Addie, what are you doing?"

"Should have kept it to yourself!"

Elizabeth looks between them. "What?"

Stella sighs. "I went back to therapy."

Elizabeth blinks. "Really? That's wonderful."

"I was being hardheaded about it, I guess," Stella says.

"Is that what Dr. Barrett said?" Elizabeth asks.

"No, it's what you two said," Stella says, "and you were right."

"Wow," Elizabeth says.

"Wow," Addie echoes.

"Shut up," Stella says.

"Come home with me," Elizabeth tells Stella, and that's all it takes to convince Stella to agree. And as Elizabeth watches her pack an overnight bag, she says, "Addie knows, doesn't she?"

"Yes," Stella admits.

"Mm. I think that's good."

"I didn't give her details." Stella looks over at Elizabeth to check that she isn't mad at her, then continues. "It felt weird. But she was happy to hear it."

"Is that why you went back to therapy?"

"Yeah," Stella pulls a dress from her closet, something that won't wrinkle in a bag overnight. "I mean, I made the appointment before, so it wasn't because of—"

Elizabeth snorts.

"I quit therapy the first time, if I'm being completely honest, because she kept trying to get me to talk about you. And I knew that if I started talking about you, she'd figure out how I really felt, and I just wasn't ready." Stella zips her bag closed, then looks up. "I'm sorry."

"Why are you sorry?" Elizabeth asks gently.

"Because I think you were ready first."

"Ah," Elizabeth says. "But was I? Did you not tell me that you wanted to hate-fuck me the moment we met?"

Stella gasps, a little scandalized, but more turned on by Elizabeth's language. "We gotta go. Right now. Put your shoes on."

Elizabeth stands up and steps into her heels.

"Wait." Stella closes the door. "I want—"

Just one kiss. Elizabeth obliges. She slips her tongue into Stella's mouth like they've been kissing for hours, kissing for years. It's agony to stop.

"Come home with me," Elizabeth says again softly.

Stella nods.

They take two cars. Stella has her meeting with the sheriff's department at nine a.m. tomorrow, but Elizabeth will have to go in early, might even get called in earlier. Maybe it's for the best. Stella uses the drive to calm herself down. She doesn't want to jump Elizabeth the moment they get inside her condo. She wants to talk to her about her day, make sure she has something to eat besides pumpkin bread, just be a normal person.

She gets in the door without incident. Elizabeth steps out of her heels. Stella leaves her flip-flops next to them. Elizabeth hangs up her purse on a hook by the door, tosses her keys into a ceramic bowl on the narrow table.

Stella is about to take her bag into the bedroom when she realizes Elizabeth has stepped into her personal space, pressing her back against the door. She's kissing her again, just like in her bedroom but hotter, more insistent. Stella feels her intent. Her bag slides out of her hand and thuds to the floor.

They maneuver their way to Elizabeth's bedroom, around a wall, down the hallway, and through a door. Elizabeth loses her blazer somewhere along the way, and Stella's zip-up hoodie has fallen off too.

Elizabeth pushes Stella face down onto the rumpled bed and crawls on top of her, aligning their hips. "I thought about you all weekend," Elizabeth whispers as she pulls Stella's shirt up out of her sweatpants, exposing Stella's lower back. She puts her hands over the bare skin. Stella's will to hold off is nonexistent, and so she squirms enough that she can roll over and wraps her legs around Elizabeth's hips. Stella hums her agreement as she tries to unbutton Elizabeth's blouse without ripping it apart. The top of her breasts pushes up over her bustier, and Stella kisses the freckled skin she has revealed.

Elizabeth shoves her hands down the front of Stella's sweatpants and into her underwear. She groans at the contact, lets her legs fall, and sits up a little to give Elizabeth more space to maneuver. Elizabeth kisses the skin at the vee of her T-shirt while her fingers slide against Stella, spreading the moisture around.

And then she pulls her hand out, pats Stella's hip. "Move," she orders. She gets up off the bed, pats Stella's hip again, a little harder this time. "Roll over. On your knees."

She says the words quietly, but Stella knows an order when she hears one, and she scrambles to comply.

"Don't move," Elizabeth commands. Or is this Captain Murphy?

Elizabeth eases her sweats and underwear down over her hips until they're around her knees and she's completely exposed and vulnerable.

Stella whimpers, bracing herself for whatever comes next. Elizabeth gently strokes her backside, moves to her inner thighs, then to her knees and presses outward. Stella spreads her knees as much as the bunched-up clothes will allow. She's tempted to look over her shoulder, but the command in Elizabeth's voice rings in her ears.

Elizabeth kisses one of Stella's bare cheeks, then drags a finger through Stella's wet lips and slides it in gently, using it to keep spreading the lubrication around. Stella forces herself to be still, as much as she wants to move against Elizabeth's hand. She hangs her head down and closes her eyes.

Now Elizabeth pushes two fingers in, and Stella whimpers with each thrust. With her other hand, she rubs Stella's clit, but it's not quite enough. Stella wants something more, something harder, more pressure because she is just out of reach of her goal.

Maybe that's the point.

She lifts her head and looks over her shoulder. Elizabeth is still wearing her bustier and skirt. Her glasses are pushed up on her head, holding her hair back, and she's concentrating, a small line between her eyes.

Stella clears her throat, and Elizabeth glances up with a stern expression.

"I said don't move." She pulls her fingers out but keeps her thumb moving.

Stella huffs and turns back around. Grabs a pillow and holds it against her. Later, when she thinks about how her bare ass was waving around in the air, she might feel embarrassed, but for now, she wants Elizabeth inside her again.

The next sensation is hot and wet, and she realizes that Elizabeth has her tongue inside her. "Oh God," she moans. "Oh, my God. You don't have to do that."

Elizabeth pulls back, says, "Oh, I do. I really do," and moves her mouth down until she is sucking Stella's clit.

The pillow absorbs Stella yelp.

Elizabeth just continues to surprise her. Stella is the stubborn one, hell-bent on getting her way and bulldozing through any obstacle. She thinks of Elizabeth as being more diplomatic, reserved, traditional, demure. Apparently, however, when it comes to her sex life, she's much bolder than Stella ever imagined.

To Stella's immense benefit and pleasure.

When Elizabeth's tongue penetrates her once more, she shoves her whole face into the pillow so that she doesn't alert the entire building how well she's getting fucked right now. Elizabeth uses both hands to brace herself on Stella's hips, slides her tongue down and laps at Stella's clit.

Elizabeth's poor pillow is going to be covered with Stella's spit from her trying to chew through it. She's got that shaky feeling again, the trembling that happens when she's about to come. She tries to stave it off, tries to think about how her knees are aching, her back hurting from being in this submissive position for so long. How her pants are still around her knees, how she must sound, whimpering like this. Why can't she be quiet during sex ever? How do people do that?

Elizabeth cycles between tonguing her and sucking on Stella's clit, adding so much pressure that the orgasm hits Stella like a freight train, and she mashes her face into the damp pillow. Elizabeth keeps her grasp on Stella's hips, forcing her to stay. She's burning from the inside out. She muffles her scream, lifts her head so she can breathe, then groans again.

Elizabeth keeps sucking and licking until Stella gets hit with another wave, a second orgasm on the heels of the last, and when that one finally subsides, she's sweating, covered in her own spit, and crying a little.

Elizabeth gently eases Stella onto the mattress and rubs her hand along her spine. "You're okay. I've got you." She pulls Stella's sweats all the way off and drops them.

Stella sucks in air. She looks at Elizabeth, still standing in her bustier and skirt, hands on her hips, glasses atop her head. Only her lipstick is a little smeared, and her chin is wet.

"Well," she says, "I'd say that was a success."

It's late, but they can't stop touching each other. They doze a little, but the bare skin is hard to resist, and Stella finds more places to touch or lick or explore.

"We should stop," she whispers as Elizabeth slides her body along her thigh.

"No. Don't stop," Elizabeth says through the haze of pleasure. "Never stop."

Stella reaches out to touch her again when the doorbell rings.

They look at each other, startled, then Elizabeth rolls off the bed.

"What time is it?"

"After two," Stella says, pushing her hair out of her face.

Elizabeth ducks into the bathroom and comes out with her bathrobe on. The doorbell rings again as she ties the sash. She runs her hand through her hair in a vain attempt to freshen it up.

Stella pulls on her sweatpants, then darts out to gather the clothes left in the hall. She puts on her hoodie and zips it up over her breasts but stays in the hallway just out of sight.

She hears Elizabeth open the door, hears a man's voice, though she can't distinguish the words. She inches a little closer.

"It's in my purse. I didn't hear it," Elizabeth says.

"We called three times. I was worried. It's not like you not to answer."

Now Stella recognizes the voice.

"Honestly, I'm fine, Sam. I just didn't hear it. Tell me the update."

"Well, we picked up the guy's brother," Lieutenant Warren says. "We're holding him overnight. We can take a crack at him in the morning."

"Okay. Good work."

"Are you sure you're okay? Your face is all red, and you have a big scratch on your neck."

"I'm fine. It's nothing," Elizabeth says.

"Let me take a look."

"No, Sam, really—"

Stella steps around the corner and says in her sternest attorney voice, "She's fine, Lieutenant."

Elizabeth glances at Stella, then closes her eyes.

Warren looks at her. "Stella?"

"We didn't hear the phone," Stella reiterates. "But as you can see, she's fine."

Warren stares at her slack-jawed, then looks back at Elizabeth in her robe, flushed, scratched up, her hair a mess, and clearly awake at two in the morning. "Oh."

"Good night, Lieutenant," Stella says.

Warren looks back at her. "Okay. So...okay."

"I'll see you tomorrow," Elizabeth says, reaching around him to pull open the door.

"Yeah," he says. "Night, Captain."

"Good night," Elizabeth says, and closes the door behind him.

Elizabeth turns to look at her. "You shouldn't have done that," she says.

"I know," Stella agrees.

Elizabeth rubs her forehead. "Fuck."

Stella flinches when she says it. Flinches again as Elizabeth walks by her and into the bathroom, slamming the door shut.

CHAPTER 19

Stella wonders if she should leave. Elizabeth is clearly upset. When Ron was angry, he always wanted her gone, could hardly stand the sight of her.

But she doesn't want to spend the rest of the night, the whole next day, or any amount of time feeling like she doesn't know where they stand. They were having such a good time.

She waits five minutes and then knocks softly on the bathroom door. "Elizabeth?" Her voice is thin, wobbly. "Please come out and talk to me."

She doesn't expect pleading to work. She had a lot of fights with Ron through closed doors while he hid in the guest room or the bathroom. When he did come out, it was often to leave for an AA meeting, so she sat alone in the house and waited for him to come home. When he did, he was usually still mad. She hated their fights where she slipped up and broke some unspoken rule she didn't know that he had and then had to wait for forgiveness, always slow to come.

But Elizabeth opens the door. She's been crying.

"I'm sorry," Stella says. "I couldn't stand the thought of him touching you."

Elizabeth throws herself into Stella's arms.

"I'm sorry too," she says. "I'm not ashamed of you, Stella. And I'm not ashamed of what we are."

Stella holds her, surprised. It hadn't occurred to her to be ashamed.

"I know that. But I never should have—you're in charge of how you tell your team." She hesitates and then adds, "If you even want to tell them at all."

Elizabeth pulls back to look at Stella. “I hurt Sam very badly because his feelings were much further along than mine. I mean, I liked spending time with him, and I wanted to be in love with him like he was in love with me, but I wasn’t.” Her voice breaks. “Every time Sam touched me, I didn’t feel a thing. I simply wasn’t interested, and that wasn’t fair. It meant that I had to step back, but I couldn’t tell him why.”

Stella reaches up and wipes Elizabeth’s tears with her thumbs. Leans in and kisses her softly. “Sam is a good man.” she says. “He’s not going to tell everyone what he saw.”

Elizabeth nods, still sniffling. “When he got shot, I was so worried. He thought that meant I wanted to try again. But I was already so deep into things with you, Stella, even though I thought nothing would ever happen. I couldn’t think of anyone but you.”

Now Stella wells up. “Only you,” she echoes. “I understand completely.”

Elizabeth hugs her again.

“Let’s get some sleep,” Stella says. “A few hours are better than nothing.”

They crawl back into bed. Elizabeth turns off the light and falls asleep immediately. Stella rolls up against her, lies awake a bit longer, thinking about the agony Elizabeth went through fighting against something her whole life, trying to be something she’s not. Why had she waited so long? And what is it about Stella that made her finally give in?

Whatever it is, Stella’s glad they found each other, glad they’re here now, skin to skin. She watches the light come in the window as the sun starts to rise.

Addie comes home from the post office midmorning on Saturday with two big bags of packages. It’s all products that companies sent her. Stella sits on the couch with her coffee, watching her sort everything into labeled acrylic bins, stopping once in a while to swatch things on her arms, or on Stella’s paler skin when her own arms get full, and post the video or image from her phone.

A few minutes later, her phone starts buzzing. Addie grins. “They want to know who you are.”

“They who?”

"My subscribers." She recently hit a milestone with half a million. "They know that's not my arm. Can I take a picture of you?"

"Oh no. God, no." It's been a long week. She spent some of Tuesday recovering from the near all-nighter with Elizabeth, then doing prep work for the sheriff's project. She spent Wednesday, Thursday, and Friday in meetings. She woke up late this morning, and she's still in her pajamas.

"We'll put a filter on. Come on."

They stand in front of the window and scroll through filter options, choosing one that puts cat ears and whiskers on them. It makes their faces round and smooth, their eyes huge.

After Addie posts it, her phone buzzes until it nearly vibrates off the table. "They like it," she says. "They say we look alike."

"Do they not know you live with me?"

"I mean, they do, but it's turned into this big thing, like, how no one ever has seen you," Addie explains. "I was trying to keep your life private."

"Thanks," Stella says. "Guess that's over now."

"Well, you aren't so sad anymore. You're so much better."

"I guess I am," Stella agrees.

"How are things with Elizabeth?"

Stella confessed what happened and how she made Elizabeth cry. How she knew what the right thing to do was, and how something else took over. How Elizabeth forgave her.

An incident like this in her marriage would have turned dark and rotten, would have festered, and it still feels like the other shoe might drop. But Elizabeth called her every day this week and is coming to pick her up for dinner later today. Right now, she's home, doing the chores that got neglected last weekend, like buying food and doing laundry and paying bills.

"Okay, I think. She said she talked to Sam and that he said he understood."

"It's not you, it's me." Addie cuts through some packaging on a new blush compact. "A classic."

"Sometimes it's just the truth." Stella offered to call Lieutenant Warren herself and try to smooth things over, but Elizabeth had declined, saying it would not be helpful.

Addie snaps another picture with her phone. "Would you ever consider being on my channel?"

"What?" Stella grabs the pile of cardboard that has started sliding down. "Why?"

"Because you're important to me."

"I mean, what would I have to do?"

"I would do your makeup. I'm hoping Elizabeth will let me too."

"Did you ask her?"

"Not yet." Addie moves on to a stack of eyeshadow singles. "I mean, we watch a lot of makeup videos together, right?"

Stella nods.

"Most of my subscribers are in their twenties like me or in their thirties. I think they would value seeing women of other ages, seeing makeup techniques on different generations."

Stella laughs. "That was very diplomatically put. You can just say old skin."

"*Mature* skin is the industry term."

"You know we'd do anything for you," Stella says. "I'll do whatever you want."

Addie looks down at her phone. "What are you doing right now?"

Stella showers and fixes her hair, frets about what to wear. Addie suggested something solid, something in a deep, rich color, but everything Stella owns is either black, white, or pink floral.

She calls Elizabeth.

"Hi," Stella says. "Listen, I agreed to let Addie film me for one of her videos."

Elizabeth snorts. "You did? Why?"

"Because I love her! You can make fun of me later, but I don't know what I should wear! She said no patterns, something in a solid color. I think she's describing your closet, not mine."

"Ah, okay. Wear that blue dress with the little gold buttons. The one that looks sort of nautical."

"Really?" Stella pulls out the dress. "You don't think it's too dark?"

"I think you look lovely in that."

"Okay, I trust you. And by the way, you're next," Stella says. "Can't run from Addie."

"*Ha!* She can try!" Elizabeth says. "See you soon, Stella Anne."

She puts on the dress. She's been avoiding it because it doesn't have a lot of stretch, and she was eating a lot of junk food, but it fits fine. Even zips easily.

Addie is waiting when Stella goes into her bedroom. One half of her room is staged for filming, and the other half looks like the wrong end of a Calabasas estate sale with piles of clothes and makeup and shoes.

"Oh, that's pretty," Addie says when she sees what Stella is wearing, and Stella feels like she passed a test using Elizabeth's class notes.

A TV tray is piled high with makeup, and the lights are blazing. She spends a few minutes instructing Stella about how to look into the lens and not the viewfinder or monitor. Suggests some safe topics in case there's a lull in conversation. Addie shows her a list of questions she wants to ask Stella.

"I promise not to ask about all of the incredibly gay sex you've been having."

Stella rolls her eyes. "Yeah, I'd appreciate that. Thanks."

"I'll let you look at the final video before I upload it, and if there's something you don't like, we can edit it out, okay?"

Stella nods. She's been filmed before in a courtroom, and the trick is to never acknowledge the cameras. She suspects the sensation of being watched, of giving a performance, is the same.

Addie puts Stella at ease immediately, chattering away while talking about the products. She puts a primer on Stella's skin, then mixes two foundations together to create a color that suits her better than anything she's bought herself at the drugstore.

It's relaxing, having Addie dab at her face with a damp sponge. It makes it easier to talk about herself. She answers softball questions about where she grew up, where she went to school, her favorite makeup product, the three most important things in her handbag.

"Gum," she says, "my phone, and an emergency candy bar."

But it's a lot of makeup: primer, foundation, concealer, powder, contour, and blush. It takes an hour just to apply the base.

They take a break so Stella can pee and get something to drink. She washes her hands and inspects herself in the mirror. It feels like she's wearing a mask, but her skin looks smooth and beautiful, especially since the makeup hasn't started settling into the wrinkles around her eyes yet.

Back in front of the camera, Addie asks, "What's the best thing about living with me?"

"I love living with you, actually. The best thing is when we get to spend time together, sitting on the couch watching YouTube, or playing a game, or drinking in the backyard. I just love you. And you've made this house so much more like a home. You're good at the little things, like lighting a candle or arranging things to look pretty or buying fresh flowers now and then."

Addie smiles. "Thank you."

"You're welcome, sugar."

"Okay, what's the worst thing about living with me?"

"Well, since I didn't know about this channel for the first *several* months of you living here, I would say your secrets," Stella says pointedly.

"Oh, you wanna talk about secrets?" Addie asks.

"We're talking about you now!" Stella laughs.

"She's got some secrets, people," Addie says to the camera. "But we'll save that for another video."

Addie applies three different colored eyeshadows but skips eyeliner because Stella's eyes are so deep set that no one will be able to see it once the false eyelashes are on.

After the makeup is done, they film what Addie calls glamour shots, where Stella sits and turns her head coquettishly. It feels incredibly awkward, but afterward, Stella admits she looks beautiful, even if it took over two hours to achieve it.

"How long will it take to edit?" she asks, reaching up to brush her finger against the fake lashes. They feel heavy and strange.

"A few hours. I can start tonight."

"How long will it take to get this stuff off?"

Addie shoots her an alarmed look. "You can't take it off before Elizabeth sees it! I'm going to send her a picture."

"Honey, she's doing chores and stuff. Just let her be."

"Sit here." Addie points at the chair. "I'm just gonna fluff this…" She arranges Stella's hair. "Okay. Now, look down and then look up when I tell you, okay?" She picks up her phone and steps back across the room. "Relax your face."

Stella relaxes her lips, unclenches her teeth.

"Now! Look up!"

She raises one eyebrow and tilts her head a little as she looks up. Addie takes the picture.

"Christ. That's perfect."

"Let me see it before you send it," Stella says, but Addie is already moving her fingers over the screen.

"Too late! You can see it now."

She holds up the phone, but when Stella tries to put on her glasses, they bump up against the false eyelashes. She takes Addie's phone out of her hands and pinches the screen to make the picture bigger.

It's pretty good, actually.

While she's holding the phone, Elizabeth responds. The text comes through from *Aunt Liz* as a banner at the top of the screen, and it's a long line of smiley face emojis with hearts for eyes.

"Why don't you come to dinner with us?" Stella asks. She's standing in front of the refrigerator after exchanging her blue dress for sweatpants and a sweater. There's not much to eat in there. Stella did two loads of laundry and cleaned up the kitchen. Maybe she should have gone to the market too, but Whole Foods on a Saturday is not something she does willingly. Ralph's is farther away and has terrible parking. And she will rot in her grave before she ever steps foot in Trader Joe's again.

"I'm supposed to go to this event at eight," Addie says.

"For what?" Stella asks.

"The new Milani Cosmetics launch."

"Don't you usually work weekends?" Stella shuts the refrigerator door.

"I quit the restaurant a couple of weeks ago."

"You did? Why didn't you tell me?"

"You and Elizabeth were going through your own things. Besides, it didn't matter."

"It matters to me. I want to know what's going on with you," Stella scolds gently. "What made you do it?"

"I had to skip a different event anytime I worked a weekend shift, and I finally decided, why am I skipping what makes me exponentially more money to bring people bad steaks? Then one night, a group of girls recognized me and wanted to take pictures with me at work, and I just decided it was time."

"Oh, my God! You're famous," Stella teases.

"No, they were like fourteen."

"Honey, at the rate things are going for you, you should think seriously about telling your mama and daddy about this job."

"La la la." Addie holds her hands over her ears. "I don't want to talk about that right now."

"Trust me, I put off hard conversations with my parents for most of my life, and things would have gone a lot smoother if I'd come clean instead of waiting for them to blow up in my face!" It's the kind of advice she wouldn't have taken at Addie's age, and it's what Ron told her all the time. And he was probably right.

"I will think long and hard about that. Cross my heart," Addie says.

"Okay, well"—Stella waves her hands in the air—"setting that aside, if your makeup thingy isn't until eight, you can come to dinner with us first."

"No, you guys have your date—"

"We can do date things after. I want you to see Elizabeth, and I know she always wants to see you."

"Okay," Addie says, relenting.

"Who are you going with tonight?"

"No one," Addie says. "I don't really want to stay that long, so I'm just going to go in, get the swag bag, have a drink, and come home."

"You're going alone?" Stella raises her eyebrows. "Is that safe? Where is it?"

"It'll be fine. It's at the Carondelet House off Wilshire and Rampart."

"We can go to Westlake for dinner, which is close to your event. We'll drop you off and pick you up."

"You can drop me off, but I'll take a Lyft home," Addie says. "I gotta go get ready."

Elizabeth arrives early. Stella is still in yoga pants and a sweater. She grins when she sees Stella. "I just wanted to see how pretty you look in person."

"It's like wearing a death mask," Stella says. "I couldn't do it every day."

"Maybe not, but you do look nice."

"Thank you."

"Can I—I mean, I don't want to ruin your lipstick." She waits for permission, her hand hovering over Stella's hip.

"Oh, it's one of those dry-down kinds. It's fine." They kiss briefly and then kiss again, longer and softer.

At last, Elizabeth pulls herself away. "Where do you want to go for dinner?"

"Would you mind if Addie went with us? She has an event at eight and we could drop her off. I know it's not exactly the most romantic—"

"Addie wants to come? Oh good!"

"But I guess it's fine," Stella says dryly. "It's near Westlake."

Elizabeth glances at her watch, then pulls her phone out of her pocket. "Let me call around and see if it's not too late to make a reservation somewhere."

Elizabeth is wearing dark jeans, an ivory blouse, and black heels. She looks like she could settle for takeout just as easily as a fancy restaurant.

Addie comes back into the room. She has slipped on a black, lacy cocktail dress and heels.

"Well, shit," Stella says and slinks off into her bedroom. Elizabeth finds her a few minutes later, scowling into her closet once more. "I got us a reservation at Pacific Dining Car in half an hour, and—what's the matter?"

"You two are so pretty, and I look like a disaster next to you!" Stella says.

"We *just* talked about how pretty you are," Elizabeth says. "I'm wearing jeans."

"I hate all my clothes!"

"That blue dress was fine. Put that back on," Elizabeth says.

Stella frowns. "You don't think it's too stuffy compared to you two?"

"No," Elizabeth says. "Anyway, I can assure you at the very least you'll get laid."

"So," Dr. Barrett says, "how are you feeling?"

Stella shifts in her seat. "Fine. Good."

"Last time," Dr. Barrett says, glancing down at her notes, "we talked about Elizabeth."

"Yes. We finally did, didn't we?"

Dr. Barrett smiles. "How's that going?"

"Really well. Except I think we had a spat."

"You think?"

"No, wait. I messed up is what happened," Stella says. "I stepped out of line, but I apologized and she forgave me."

"Is that surprising to you?" Dr. Barrett asks. "That your apology was accepted?"

"Ron wasn't—I mean, I shouldn't speak ill of the dead, but he wasn't very forgiving. He liked to hold a grudge." Stella shrugs. "And I wasn't easy to be married to."

"In this space, you can say whatever you want about your late husband. I don't think you are speaking ill of him. I think you're speaking honestly."

Stella nods. "Okay."

"And you and I both know that the tough parts of your marriage don't dissolve because you're grieving."

"You're saying I can call him an asshole and still miss him," Stella says.

"Elizabeth isn't prone to grudges?" Dr. Barrett asks.

Stella thinks for a moment. "Elizabeth is very—oh, what's the word—composed, I guess. Even when she's mad, she stays cool. I expected her to freeze me out, but she didn't."

"That's good, don't you think?" Dr. Barrett asks.

"Yes, but it's left me with this vague sense that she's just waiting to throw it back in my face." Stella doesn't really think Elizabeth will do anything of the sort, but she can't stop herself from saying so.

Dr. Barrett writes something down.

"I mean, I don't think she's going to, but I can't shake that sense of impending doom."

"You said last time that Elizabeth was married once too. To a man?"

"Yeah." Stella says. "A man who would make Ron look like a prince, from what she's said."

"What kind of marriage did they have?" Dr. Barrett asks. "From what she's said."

"Well, he was an alcoholic, for one thing. I mean, Ron was too, but he had stopped drinking by the time we met. Elizabeth's husband also gambled and finally walked out on her and their young children."

"It's easy to enter a new relationship with the echoes of the previous ones still ringing in our ears, and most of us have a type that we're drawn to. But every partner is going to be different and expecting Elizabeth to respond like Ron is giving you that sense of dread, I think."

Stella nods. "She's not Ron."

"No."

"I like that about her," Stella says. "Ron was really calm and cool-headed until he wasn't. But he was so cute and charming when we first met that I didn't expect him to have a temper." She glances at Dr. Barrett's hands folded in her in her lap. "You're married, I see."

"I am. For eight years."

"First one?"

Dr. Barrett chuckles. "So far." She looks at Stella kindly. "That's the first personal observation you've made about me."

"Shrinks aren't supposed to talk about themselves, right? You're just supposed to listen?"

"Some people are very interested in their therapists," Dr. Barrett says. "Especially people with skills like yours. People who study human nature. Who read people for a living. I was a little concerned about that, actually. You seemed to have no interest in me or the work we're doing here."

"That's not true! Even after I stopped coming, I used a lot of the tools you gave me. I heard your voice in my head all the time. And I noticed you cut your hair. So there."

"So there," Dr. Barrett repeats with a smirk.

"I just feel like I've been asleep for a long time, and I'm only now waking up and thawing out. I thought I didn't have anything to be awake for, but now I have all these good things in my life, and I'm worried that maybe I don't deserve them." She wipes her eyes. "Because I've done some not so great things in my life and made some stupid choices, and to end up here, now, happy and in love? How is that fair?"

Dr. Barrett leans forward. "Everyone deserves love, Stella. And life isn't fair. Those are two universal truths you can take to the bank."

Stella crosses her arms, sniffles a bit, then says, "You got homework for me or what?"

Dr. Barrett leans back and thinks for a moment. "How about you let Elizabeth decide whether you're worthy of her love? If she wants to give it to you, then you're worthy."

"Remember when my homework was to just go outside?" Stella asks. "That was easy."

"That was homework for the Stella who was still asleep. You're awake now!"

"Yeah," Stella agrees. "I guess I am."

CHAPTER 20

"You know what? I'm just going to send an email," Addie says the Monday before Thanksgiving.

Stella is finally going to court for the wrongful imprisonment case, and she's rushing around to get ready. She only needs to give her professional opinion about how the police interpreted the law, but she absolutely has to be on time.

"Send an email to who?" Stella asks as she looks under the coffee table for her shoes.

"To Mama and Daddy," Addie says. "About my YouTube channel."

Stella whips her head up, slamming it on the bottom of the coffee table. "Ow! Shit!"

Addie rushes over. "Are you okay?"

Stella feels the bump on the back of her head. "I'm not bleeding," she says, straightening up, though it hurts and she'll probably get a headache. "Do you think sending them an email is the best idea?"

"Yes," Addie says, though she doesn't sound confident at all. "Because I'm not going home for Thanksgiving, so they'll have until Christmas to get used to the idea."

"They can get used to the idea if you call them too," Stella says. She flashes on the shoes she's looking for. She left them next to Elizabeth's shoes in her condo. She must have worn flip-flops home. Shit.

"They're already mad I'm not coming home for Thanksgiving! Anyway, I've already started writing it."

Stella goes back to her room to find another pair of shoes. She needs to leave in four minutes.

Addie follows her. "Do you want to hear it?"

"Honey, I have to leave for work," Stella says.

"I don't mean now," Addie mutters.

Stella grabs her shoulders. "Listen, kiddo, I love you, and I want to talk about this, but I have to go. And I suspect you're up at seven thirty because you haven't been to sleep yet. So go to bed, and we can talk about it when I get home."

"Fine."

Stella kisses Addie's cheek, leaving a lipstick print. Addie without makeup looks like a kid again. Stella worries about her. She's doing so well, but she works all the time filming or preparing to film or editing, and now that she isn't working at the restaurant, she doesn't have many friends. Thanksgiving will be good for her. Josh will be in town, at least, and Addie can talk to him. Elizabeth's oldest son, Michael, is coming too, and he's bringing his girlfriend.

As she drives to the courthouse, she thinks about Elizabeth all aflutter with autumn preparations. A wreath on the door made of red and yellow leaves. Little pumpkins scattered about. A welcome mat with a cornucopia on it. A scarecrow figurine in the center of the dining room table. She even switched her bed to rust and orange plaid sheets, a forest green comforter, and a decorative pumpkin pillow.

"Oh my," Stella said when she was over last. "How festive."

"I love the holidays," Elizabeth said dreamily.

That comment gave Stella a jolt of something that she felt when she first started hanging around Captain Murphy's murder room. Stella wasn't sure if she wanted to punch her or screw her. Maybe a little of both.

Stella has never cared for the holidays. She likes Halloween because of the candy, but Thanksgiving and Christmas are obligations she has no interest in filling, especially once she moved across the country. She never once dropped everything to fly back home.

And it's not about Ron either. She's already lived through one holiday season, though she has no earthly idea of what she did for Christmas last year.

Elizabeth talks about Thanksgiving as if it's understood that Stella will come over, but they haven't really discussed what to tell her family or whether anyone besides Sam Warren knows about their relationship.

It shouldn't matter, and it doesn't to Stella, but she knows it matters to Elizabeth. She screwed it up with Sam, and she doesn't want to step in it again.

She worries all the way to the courthouse.

At least she's on time.

Michael is a family name, which is understandable. So is Addison. Family names happen. Michael was Elizabeth's father, who had died only a few years ago. But Stella has a hard time understanding why, of all the nicknames for Michael, they'd gone with Mickey, and why now, fully grown, Elizabeth's son sticks with it.

The Wednesday before Thanksgiving, Elizabeth's phone rings while she's in the shower.

Stella glances at the screen: *Mickey Murphy*.

Stella almost answers it because maybe it's important but decides to let it ring. Maybe Elizabeth mentioned Stella to her son as a friend or former colleague. Maybe she let him know that she invited a friend to the meal. Or maybe Mickey has never heard of Stella. She's not about to out Elizabeth *again* before she's ready.

Elizabeth's phone rings again. This time it's Josh.

Stella picks it up. "Elizabeth's phone, Stella speaking," she says, slipping off the barstool to carry her mug to the sink.

"You two screening calls?" Josh asks. It sounds like he's in a car, which means Mickey and his girlfriend have already picked him up.

"She's in the shower, and I don't know him, so I didn't want to answer." Stella says. She's not sure if Josh knows about their relationship. Surely, he at least suspects.

"We're leaving Santa Cruz now, and we should be there around three," Josh says.

"We're excited to see y'all," Stella says. "Drive safe, okay?"

"See you soon." Josh hangs up.

Stella walks through the bedroom, knocks lightly on the bathroom door, then pokes her head in. "The boys called. They'll be here at three."

"Good!"

Stella watches Elizabeth's silhouette through the frosted sliding glass doors. Elizabeth slides the door open just enough to look at Stella. Her hair is slicked back. "What's wrong?"

"What do you want me to be for this dinner?" Stella asks.

Elizabeth tilts her head a little, and she blinks. "What do you mean?"

"I mean, do you want me to be your friend? Do you want—do your children know about us? I don't want to screw this up for you."

"Ah, yes," Elizabeth says. "I thought maybe we could tell them together."

Stella stares at her in surprise. "Together? Why do I have to—my kid already knows!"

Elizabeth studies her. "It would be helpful for us to be a united front, Stella Anne."

"Don't do that thing with my name. That's evil!"

Elizabeth smiles. "Do you want to come in here with me?"

Stella huffs, then sighs. "Yes."

Stella takes off her clothes, pulls her hair into a high bun, and steps into the steamy shower. Elizabeth puts her arms around her, pulling her close. Stella relaxes into the warm embrace.

"I can't do it without you," Elizabeth murmurs into Stella's ear. "I can't face them alone."

Stella *knows* she's being manipulated, and the words may be true, but the delivery is as devious as can be. "Ooh, I hate you!" she says, though there is no real venom in the words.

"I love you too," Elizabeth says, turning them around so the warm spray hits Stella's back instead of hers.

Stella pulls back to look at her. "Do you? Love me?"

"Oh, honey. Yes, I do. I love you." She kisses Stella's cheek, then her other cheek, then her lips. "Is that okay?"

Stella nods, her lip trembling. A sob escapes her, and she brings her hands up to hide her face. Elizabeth holds her tight, the water still raining down on her back.

Ron probably loved her in his own way, but their marriage was rocky and even dangerous. They treated one another like competition, not partners. When he died suddenly, she knew she would be alone from then on. To be loved now by Elizabeth Murphy—her nemesis, her tenuous ally, her friend, her lover—seems like a miracle.

She tries to say it back, but the words are lost against Elizabeth's wet skin.

"I know, sweetheart," Elizabeth says. "I know you do."

Stella goes home before the boys arrive. She's full of nervous energy, and Elizabeth is kind of manic, pressing napkins and adjusting the centerpiece and making yet another shopping list, even though she went to the store the day before and her refrigerator is full to bursting.

"Come back for dinner," Elizabeth calls after her.

At home, Addie is making pies for the big meal tomorrow while she photographs the process. All the windows are open because the kitchen is hot from the oven. She's wearing an apron over her pajamas, but her face is fully made up. High glam at odd hours is becoming normal.

"I couldn't sleep," Addie explains, "so I got up, made the dough, then took pictures while I let it chill."

"Honey, you need a vacation."

"Yeah." Addie sighs. "Actually, I got invited to a brand trip, so I guess I could do that."

"What does that mean?"

"The company takes a bunch of us somewhere tropical while they launch something new. In return, we vlog the trip and talk constantly about the product. It's still work, but it's more relaxing. I heard there is one going to Fiji this year."

"Wow. And you just pay airfare?"

"I don't think I have to pay for anything." She lines two pans with pie dough, then looks at Stella carefully. "Have you been crying?"

"No!" Stella lies.

"Yes, you have. Your eyes are red. What happened?"

"Nothing." Stella tries to brush off her concern. "Elizabeth wants us to tell her kids about..."

"Being gay?" Addie offers when Stella peters out.

"Being in love or *whatever*."

"Ha!" Addie says. "I'm not sure Josh will be surprised, but I don't know about her other kids."

"Just the older son and his girlfriend this time. Not the daughter."

"It's weird that she has these other kids we don't know," Addie muses. "She has this whole other life."

"Yeah," Stella says.

"Do you not want them to know?" Addie pours pumpkin filling into the first waiting crust.

"I want whatever Elizabeth wants. I'm just afraid of messing up again." She watches as Addie transfers the pie into the oven. "What do you mean, Josh won't be surprised?"

"Gays know gays. Also, after that dinner with Mama and Daddy, he told me he thought you two looked close, and wouldn't it be cool if you went full *L-Word*."

"He said *what*?"

"You did go full *L-Word*, so what do you want from me?" she asks. "Oh God, do I really want to do a full lattice crust for a cherry pie? Who likes cherry pie? Why would Elizabeth ask for a cherry pie? Does she hate me?"

Addie is just as manic as Elizabeth, so Stella slips out of the kitchen. She takes her laptop into the backyard and sets it up on the table. Addie added a booster, so the Wi-Fi reaches into the yard now.

She needs to work on the last round of edits for the sheriff's department, then she'll get a break from the project before the actual training happens. She has a second visit to the UCLA law school scheduled as well as a class visit to Loyola Marymount before their finals. And then she has several expert witness cases booked, just as Elizabeth predicted.

She prepares her monthly invoices and sends them off to Mallory, who emails right back, admonishing her for working so close to a holiday, then emails her again with a listing for a small office space downtown and asks what Stella thinks.

So Mallory was serious about growing her business. It would be nice to have an office again. It's better for prospective clients to come to a physical space instead of meeting them in coffee shops. She looks at the listing. Two offices, a conference room, and a reception area. Floor-to-ceiling arched windows. An older building with a brick façade. Nothing like the sleek interior of the police administration building or the dated midcentury district attorney's metropolitan office.

Stella can see herself there. She writes back that she likes it.

The moment Stella and Addie walk in, each holding a pie, Mickey's girlfriend says, "Wait a minute. I know you."

"Oh no," Addie says softly.

"You're the girl who did the mermaid thing where you used the fishnets for scales. My little sister watches you," she says, grinning.

Addie smiles awkwardly. "We brought pie."

Elizabeth introduces everyone. "This is Sabrina," she says, indicating Mickey's girlfriend. "This is Stella, and clearly you know Addie." She takes Addie's pie. "And this is Mickey."

Josh and Addie hug, and Josh says, loudly, "Leave her alone, Sabrina!"

Elizabeth's son is tall and handsome and shares his mother's dark hair and high cheekbones. Even their teeth look similar. He shakes Stella's hand politely, but she can read the question in his eyes: *why isn't this pre-Thanksgiving meal just for family?* They should have done this tomorrow, but Elizabeth wanted the air cleared before the actual holiday meal.

Stella sets her pie on the kitchen counter next to the other one. Elizabeth's eyes are wide behind her glasses. Stella wants to lean in and kiss her but doesn't dare.

Dinner is buffet-style barbecue. Mickey barbecued the ribs, and Elizabeth made burgers and a big bowl of potato salad. It's a lot of food for six people.

"She's a nervous cook," Addie whispers to Stella as they settle around the table with their plates.

Josh and Elizabeth sit at the respective heads of the table. Addie sits facing Sabrina and between Stella and Elizabeth.

"So," Stella says when they're all seated, "your mama says you work a lot."

Mickey swallows a mouthful of food before he can answer. "Oh yeah. Yep."

"Tech support," Josh says when Mickey doesn't elaborate.

"At UC–Berkeley," adds his mother proudly, as if he's a professor or the dean.

"Impressive," Stella says. "Do you work at Berkeley as well, Sabrina?"

"I teach preschool."

"Aw," Addie says. "I love little kids."

"Yeah, they're really cute," Sabrina says. "Adorable little petri dishes. They're very generous with their germs."

Stella suspects Sabrina hasn't been dating Elizabeth's son very long. There's something about the way they hold themselves, something about Sabrina's level of discomfort.

"These ribs are amazing," Addie says.

"Thanks," Mickey replies.

They eat awhile in silence. Finally, Sabrina asks, "And, Stella, what do you do?"

"I'm a legal consultant." Stella doesn't elaborate. Elizabeth glares at her, but Stella isn't interested in talking about herself or distracting from the conversation they're dancing around.

"We used to work together," Elizabeth says and then, reaching for her glass of water, nearly tips it. She catches it, smiling nervously.

"Oh," Mickey says. "Right. Stella. You were the lawyer, yes?"

"Once upon a time."

"And now you're friends."

"Yes," Elizabeth says. "Actually, about that."

Stella's leg muscles twitch, and she feels her animal instincts dangerously close to taking over. Every cell in her body is telling her to bolt. Addie reaches under the table and wraps her hand around Stella's forearm so she can't make a break for the door.

Everyone is waiting for Elizabeth to continue, but she's looking at her son like a deer in the headlights.

"What?" Mickey looks at his mother.

Addie squeezes Stella's arm and, when Stella glances at her, nods toward Elizabeth as if to say *help her!*

Elizabeth finds herself again. "I thought maybe now would be a good time to let you know that, uh…that—"

"Oh, my God," Josh says. "No way."

"Shut up, Josh," Addie says softly.

"But—"

Addie glares him into silence. "Let them do it."

"What are we talking about?" Mickey asks.

"I…" Elizabeth begins, but she looks like she swallowed her tongue. Jesus, she's going to make Stella do this after all.

Stella clears her throat. "Your mama and I aren't just friends. We're girlfriends." She glances at Elizabeth, who is as white as a ghost. Then she glares at Mickey like he's a witness facing cross examination. What he says next will determine their relationship moving forward. She hopes for his sake that he chooses correctly.

"Yes," Elizabeth says softly.

"Huh?" Mickey asks.

"Oh, my God, dude. They're gay!" Josh says, snapping his fingers in Mickey's face. "You know, gay? People are gay, Mickey."

"I know what gay is. I'm just…surprised."

"I'm bisexual, actually," Stella says to no one in particular. Everyone turns to look at her. Addie looks kind of proud. It's the first time Stella has said it, after all. "Not that that matters right now, I just… Anyway, your mama wanted you to know. And now we all know."

"Does Dad know?" Mickey asks.

"Your father and I aren't currently on speaking terms," Elizabeth says in a tone that Stella recognizes. Closed off. Cold.

"I know that you don't really know me," Stella says. "And if you and your family want to process this, Addie and I can leave and let you—"

"No," Elizabeth snaps. "No one is leaving in the middle of dinner."

"I thought you said she was Catholic," Sabrina whispers loudly to Mickey.

"Even Catholic people are gay, Sabrina," Josh says disdainfully.

"Mom, I'm happy for you," Mickey says. "And you too, Stella. Melissa and I had written off Mom ever dating anyone again."

"Thank you, Mickey," Stella says.

"I would like to call your sister and tell her myself," Elizabeth says.

Josh winces and holds up his phone. "Sorry, Mom. Shit. I already put it on the sibling group chat."

Elizabeth closes her eyes and says softly, "*Josh.*"

"Sorry! I'm just excited! Like, I know how hard coming out is, and I thought you two were going to dance around it forever!"

"Wait. You knew?" Mickey asks.

"You're gay too?" Sabrina asks.

"I didn't know. I suspected. And yes, Sabrina, I'm gay too. People are gay."

"Okay," Elizabeth says. "Well. All right."

From across the room, Elizabeth's phone rings. She pushes back her chair and goes to the kitchen to take the call. In the ensuing silence, they hear Elizabeth says, "Darling, no one meant to make you feel that way" as she passes them on her way to the bedroom.

"We should leave," Stella says desperately.

"How about Josh and Sabrina and Mickey and I go out," Addie says. "We can get a drink and give you and Elizabeth some time to finish up prep for tomorrow. I know a great bar. We can all have a chat about how tomorrow is going to go for your mother." Her words are menacing.

Josh gets up. "Great idea."

Stella gives Addie the keys to the SUV, and she hustles everyone into jackets and out the door.

"There's a couple twenties in my wallet," Stella offers.

Addie rolls her eyes. "I make more than you. I've been paying your mortgage for like five months, and you haven't even noticed."

And then they're all gone, out the door.

Stella is fine with money but is terrible at looking at her bank account. It's entirely plausible that's exactly what Addie has been doing. Ron is either spinning in his grave or laughing from his cloud, that's for sure.

Stella starts cleaning up the mostly untouched meal, putting food away and putting plates into the dishwasher. She leaves her own food out on the counter to eat later.

Elizabeth comes out while Stella is filling the sink with hot, soapy water.

"Where'd they go?"

"Addie took them out for a drink," Stella says. "Smart girl. How'd that call go?"

"Oh, fine. I would have liked to control the story a little more, but she was very sweet. Mostly upset that I hid it from her."

Stella turns off the water and begins washing cookware. "You hid it from you pretty well too."

"I'm sorry," Elizabeth says. "I thought tonight would go differently."

"Did I overstep? It seemed like you were struggling to get it out."

"I was struggling," Elizabeth admits. "I just froze."

"It's not easy to change directions this late in life."

"You made it look easy," Elizabeth says.

"Did I?" Stella says. "Nothing about this last year has been easy except falling for you."

Elizabeth presses her hands over her heart. "That's so sweet."

"What about tomorrow, Elizabeth? What about Marco? Isn't he coming?"

"Marco knows."

"You told Marco?" Stella asks, surprised.

"Well"—Elizabeth wipes her hands on the kitchen towel and drags Stella's half-eaten dinner across the counter toward her—"he knew something was off with Sam and me. He asked me about it. I brushed him off." She takes a bite of potato salad. "And then he said something like, 'Did Lieutenant Warren find out about your affair with Stella Carter?' I think the look on my face gave it away."

Stella snorts.

"He was just kiddng! He was always teasing me about it because he knows how poorly we got along when we first met and how close we are now." Elizabeth laughs. "He teases me when you call me at work or when I mention that I'm seeing you later, and it's turned into an inside joke between us. But then, suddenly, you and I were very real."

"Marco won't care," Stella says. She dries her hands on a dishcloth and goes to sit next to Elizabeth.

"No, he doesn't. He was very kind. He likes you."

"What about the rest of the division?"

"I'm not going to make an announcement. I wouldn't announce it if I were dating a man."

"But would you hide him?" Stella asks. "Ban him from your office?"

"Ban him? Stella, you aren't banned from the squad room. I thought you were avoiding it, that it was difficult for you to even come back into the building."

"It is."

Elizabeth rolls her eyes. "You know you're welcome there. The team would love to see you."

"There's a new prosecutor now. I doubt the squad misses me."

"Oh, I don't know about that," Elizabeth says, picking up a pork rib. "I think you were one of a kind, ADA Carter."

Stella rolls her eyes, but the comment warms her up inside.

Addie takes Mickey and Sabrina back to their hotel and drops Josh off at the condo. Stella has never spent the night with Josh down the hall, and she asks him several times if it's okay.

"Yes, of course," he says. "*Mi casa es su casa.*"

Stella and Elizabeth close the door to the bedroom and get ready for bed, being extra quiet. They crawl into bed and turn off the light. Elizabeth sets her alarm for five a.m. so she can get the turkey in the oven.

But somehow Elizabeth climbs on top of her, her tongue in her mouth. They kiss until Stella feels dizzy with it, until she can't keep her hands still anymore, and she reaches under the covers and pulls up Elizabeth's long T-shirt. She has nothing on underneath.

Elizabeth breaks the kiss and whispers, "Oh, we shouldn't."

"Should've thought about that before!" Stella whispers back.

Elizabeth relents immediately, sits up, still straddling Stella, and pulls her T-shirt off completely, exposing her naked body. Stella slides her hands up and caresses both breasts.

Elizabeth is hot and wet against her skin. Stella tweaks one nipple, then runs her hands back down to stroke Elizabeth's hips. "Slide on up here," Stella says.

"What?"

"You heard me."

"We're supposed to be quiet, and you want me to sit on your face?" she whispers louder than she needs to.

"Sh-h-h," Stella says, pulling Elizabeth's hips toward her. "You can do it."

Elizabeth carefully moves up, pushing up on her knees a little so Stella can shimmy down. She holds onto the headboard for support.

Stella navigates a hand free and touches Elizabeth first, warms her up a little, makes sure she's wet enough. She moves her thumb against her clit for a little while until Elizabeth lets out a long, soft sigh.

Stella tilts her head up, cranes her neck. Drags her tongue through Elizabeth's swollen wetness. Elizabeth moans softly and lowers herself down, crossing her arms over the top of the headboard and resting her forehead on her arms. It muffles the noise and directs it toward Stella. Now she can hear any noise she makes, and she dearly loves to hear Elizabeth come undone.

As always, Elizabeth is much braver in the bedroom than Stella expected her to be. She is usually the first to jump in and try things and is never embarrassed about the things they do and share and feel. Stella understands. They're too old to act like shy, virginal schoolgirls. While there are things they've never tried before, nothing about sex is brand new, and they both know it's better when you leave all embarrassment at the door and just embrace whatever makes you feel good. But for Elizabeth, Stella suspects there's also an element of having waited so long for something she'd wanted so desperately.

"Oh," Elizabeth says when Stella pushes a finger into her.

She flicks her tongue against Elizabeth's clit, hoping to get her off fast and hard.

"Yeah," Elizabeth breathes. "That's so good. Fuck."

Stella laps at her for a while like a cat with a bowl of cream. Elizabeth's hips thrust against her mouth, and Stella flattens her tongue to give Elizabeth more pressure. She withdraws her finger slightly, then pushes it in again with a hard thrust.

"Fuck! Jesus." Elizabeth is no longer trying to keep her voice down.

Stella hums happily against her, slurps loudly once, then twice, because she knows Elizabeth likes that, before catching the underside of her clit against her teeth and giving it a little scrape. She circles it with her tongue again soothingly.

"Oh my God," Elizabeth says. She throws her head back and grinds herself against Stella's mouth. Stella looks up to see Elizabeth holding her own breasts, lost in her pleasure.

Stella sucks Elizabeth's clit into her mouth again and flicks it rapidly with her tongue, intent on finishing her off quickly to keep her quiet.

Elizabeth moves one hand from her breast and clamps it over her mouth. She groans into it, then drops her other hand to the top of Stella's head, tangling her fingers into her hair as she falls forward with the force of her orgasm. Stella feels her muscles clenching, spasming around the finger still inside her. The wetness gushes against her tongue.

She releases Stella's hair and raises a knee over her face, then falls back on the mattress, her head by Stella's feet, panting. Stella sits up to look at her.

"So much for being quiet," she whispers. "Maybe Josh will think we were in here praying to Jesus."

"I think I was," Elizabeth says softly, her voice hoarse.

Stella flips around to lie next to Elizabeth. She kisses the space between her breasts and takes her hand. There's a little scalloped crescent moon where Elizabeth bit herself to keep quiet. Stella kisses that too.

"My thighs are burning."

Stella leans down to kiss Elizabeth's still trembling legs, leaving a glossy smear on her skin. Her face must be soaked. She rolls off the bed.

"Don't go."

"I'm just going to wipe my face off," Stella says, slipping into the bathroom. She digs out a makeup wipe because she's too tired to completely wash her face. Then she stands in the bathroom doorway, looking at Elizabeth still lying on her bed. Elizabeth reaches down to rub at her hip flexors.

Any other night, Stella would crawl over a blissed-out Elizabeth and coax another orgasm from her. Would make her come until she cried out, until her throat was raw, until Elizabeth begged her to stop. Elizabeth deserves all the pleasure she's missed out on for so many years. But not tonight.

"Come on, pretty lady," she says, returning to the bed. "Under the covers."

Elizabeth turns around and crawls under the comforter. Stella pulls it up until she's covered.

"Wait," she says. "We need to keep going for you."

"No, honey, I'm fine," Stella says. "We need to go to sleep."

Stella is turned on, but not enough that she won't be able to fall asleep. Elizabeth is out of it anyway, after such a stressful evening. And she'll be tired and stressed out tomorrow as well.

Stella curls up next to her with a sigh of contentment.

CHAPTER 21

Addie's email to her parents did not go over well. Stella had warned her that even a phone call wouldn't be as good as a face-to-face conversation. So Addie made plans to go to Nashville for Christmas. She begged Stella to come with her, but Stella flatly refused. She has no interest in being a buffer between Addie and her parents, no interest in spending time with Thom or Brick or any of their extended family.

She told Addie she doesn't have to go to Nashville either, if she doesn't want to. No one's forcing her. She could spend the holidays with Stella and Elizabeth instead, but Addie refused, even though she's dreading the time with her parents.

They're silent on the drive to the airport, and Addie is still sullen when they arrive. She slams the SUV door and throws her suitcase onto the sidewalk. "See you later," she says and starts to walk away.

"Hey!" Stella yells after her. "Come here!" After a year of Addie taking care of her, it's time for Stella to step up and be the adult.

Addie turns around.

"I love you." She catches up to Addie and pulls her into a hug. "Fly safe."

"Love you," Addie mutters.

When Stella gets home, she tosses her keys into the bowl by the door and sets her purse down. The lights on the Christmas tree that Addie put up the day after Thanksgiving glow gently from the living room, giving the house a cozy feeling.

As soon as Addie put up the tree, she started filming videos in front of it. She banned Stella from the house because she was too noisy—grinding coffee or opening the squeaky slider to the back yard or answering her phone—and ruined Addie's shots.

"Go stay with Elizabeth," Addie said. "I'll tell you when you can come home."

At some point, it started feeling like Stella lives in Addie's house and not the other way around. Addie pays the lion's share of the bills, including Stella's mortgage, saying that any downtown apartment she rented would be double what she pays to live in Stella's little house. But Addie's YouTube channel is their third roommate, and it takes up so much space that Stella is starting to think their arrangement is no longer sustainable.

She voiced her concern to Elizabeth, who shrugged and said, "So move in here. Let her have it."

If she moved in with Elizabeth, Addie could turn one of the bedrooms into a filming room. And as much as Stella loves having the newest makeup and best skincare at her disposal, there's always so much *product* in the house.

Moving in with Elizabeth might be a good solution, but Stella worries that she'll be moving in because it's easier and not because she wants to. She moved in with Ron because he wore her down about how much money they'd save and how he never saw her, and how at least if they shared a house he'd get some attention now and again. She finally conceded, trying to be the partner he needed, but she always fell short anyway, and neither of them were happy in the long run.

Elizabeth is not trying to wear her down. She merely suggested it, and Stella reminds herself that Elizabeth isn't Ron.

For tonight, it's nice to have the house to herself for once. She turns on the television to the evening news, starts a load of laundry, then hauls a basket of clean clothes out to the living room to sort and fold. When the news is over, she shuts off the television and signs into Addie's Spotify account. A while back, Addie created a special playlist for her with every song that Stella ever mentioned liking, and Stella plays it now.

Then she goes to the refrigerator to find something to eat. There's some old leftover Chinese food, some raw chicken that needs to be cooked, and milk and butter. She tosses the Chinese food, sticks the chicken in the oven to bake for later in the week, and makes macaroni and cheese for her dinner.

She eats at the table while scrolling through her phone, then takes out the kitchen trash so the house won't smell like rotting Chinese food in the morning.

Now it's not even eight o'clock and she's bored with TV, bored with chores, bored with the music, bored with herself.

She calls Elizabeth. "You wanna come over?" Stella asks, holding her cell phone against her shoulder while she folds clothes. "You wanna sleep here?"

Elizabeth arrives in jeans and a green plaid flannel button-down that accentuates her eyes and sets off her already luxurious auburn hair. "I was wrapping presents," Elizabeth says when she gets there, "but that can wait."

Stella had fretted over what to get Elizabeth for Christmas, but she'd finally gone to a jewelry store and picked out a necklace. An emerald on a delicate chain, something that would sit prettily at the base of her throat and sparkle. Maybe it's too much. She'll find out soon enough; Christmas is only a handful of days away. One of Stella's least favorite holidays, something she hasn't looked forward to in years and years. But now she finds herself excited.

Stella makes cocoa, and they sit at the table with their hands wrapped around their mugs.

"Well," Elizabeth says, "Mickey and Sabrina broke up."

"Good."

Elizabeth snorts. "I was very sympathetic on the phone."

"You're a good mother," Stella says. "Does that mean Mickey's coming for Christmas?"

"It does!" Elizabeth beams. "All three of my children will be with me at Christmas. It's not something I get very often."

"Who did the dumping?"

"She did, but he said he was relieved."

"You don't think— I mean, they won't feel like I'm intruding by joining y'all, will they?" Stella asks. She expects Elizabeth to jump down her throat, but Dr. Barrett told her to push past her fears and express her feelings to Elizabeth. That not voicing her fears gives them more power. That the way to remember that Elizabeth won't respond like Ron did is to prove it to herself over and over.

"I don't think so, no," Elizabeth says after a moment of thought. "But either way, they need to get used to it."

Stella sips her cocoa, lets the sweetness sit on her tongue for a moment. "Elizabeth?"

"Mm?"

"Were you serious about us moving in together?" she asks.

"I think we should talk about it. But, yes, I meant it."

"Because I've been thinking that Addie could use the space here. If I moved in with you, we wouldn't have to haul our stuff back and forth all the time."

"I see." Elizabeth wipes a drip off the side of her mug. "You want what's best for Addie."

"No! I didn't mean it like that. I just want to make sure I don't leave her behind."

"Josh says it's a lesbian stereotype to move in together right away." Elizabeth's eyes twinkle. "He'll make fun of us."

"I think women are different. I really had to talk myself into living with a man: his smell, his mess, the hair in the sink. His ugly furniture. That was a real commitment. You and I already know we'd live together pretty well, don't you think?"

Elizabeth grins. "We have so far, though I worry about Addie living alone," she says.

"Oh, so now *you* want what's best for Addie!" Stella says. "*J'accuse*!"

"Shush. I meant I worry that she'll work all the time and never have any fun, and she won't have you to pull her up to the surface. What's the point of having a beautiful life online if it's all for show and no one is living with you?"

"She said she's going on a brand trip in January with people like her. Maybe she'll make some friends. It's a big deal that she agreed to go at all, I think."

"Okay. But what about your house? I know it was important for you to get back into this neighborhood. Are you sure you're ready to leave it?"

"I do like it," Stella concedes. "But I think it was more about trying to get back to the life I had before Ron. Like I could just undo all that pain. Which seems silly now."

Elizabeth nods.

"Anyway, I'm not selling the house. And if Addie ever decides to move, we can rent it or sell it then."

"And maybe buy that dream house we always talk about."

"Maybe," Stella agrees.

Mallory signs a lease at the beginning of the year, and they move in midmonth. Then they go back and forth about hiring a receptionist. They could easily forward calls to their phones, but if they want to use the office space to host clients, it's better to have someone greet them.

Stella tries to weasel out of helping Mallory with the hire, but Elizabeth points out that Mallory could hire someone annoying, and Stella would have no ground to complain because she didn't help.

So she weeds through résumés, Mallory narrows down the pool of candidates further, and Stella blocks off two days for interviews.

"I hate interviews," she tells Mallory when she arrives at the office.

"Didn't you used to essentially interview people for a living?" Mallory asks, amused.

"This is *not* the same," Stella says. "It's hard to know who someone really is. They're all on their best behavior. They could be lying through their teeth. I won't know, and the few questions I could ask to find out are illegal!"

"It's a part-time receptionist job," Mallory says. "It's probably going to be mostly college students."

College students and a few single mothers. Plus two men, who spend most of the interview trying to negotiate to forty hours, even though the listing clearly stated twenty.

Stella takes great pleasure in tossing their files into the proverbial trash.

They hire Angie, a single mother in her forties with two kids. It would be a second job for her, and sometimes her schedule will get a little crazy, but she is the most composed, has a lot of experience, and seems smart.

The office move has pushed aside her personal move. Elizabeth and Stella have agreed that she will move into the condo, but there's no hard and fast date, and she hasn't even started seriously packing. But once they hire Angie and the office is set up and running, Stella's work life becomes easier. More streamlined. Angie assesses prospective clients, keeps their calendars, takes messages, even makes coffee in the morning.

One day Stella comes home after work and finds Addie in the living room with several other tanned and beautiful girls. And she realizes it's time to move.

"Don't take off your shoes," Elizabeth says the moment Stella walks in the door one evening. This is peculiar because Elizabeth has absolutely trained her to remove her shoes first thing.

She freezes. "What's wrong?"

"I want to show you something," Elizabeth says. "Put your purse down, bring your keys."

They go to the elevator, and Elizabeth presses the button for the fourteenth floor. "We're going up to look at a unit," she says. "The people living there have somewhere to go, so we need to make it quick. You were later than I thought you were going to be."

"There was an accident, I think. Traffic was awful. Why are we looking at a unit in a building we already live in?"

"Because," Elizabeth says, ushering her out of the elevator, "there's a bigger unit for sale on the top floor. They don't come up for sale very often."

"You want to move up three floors?"

"I want to look at the unit. That's all." She knocks on the door, and a woman opens it. "Thank you for waiting."

"Not a problem," the woman says. "Larry and I have to run, so shut the door behind you when you leave."

"Thank you, Aimee," Elizabeth says. "Thanks for letting us take a look."

They step aside as the couple leaves the apartment and then shuffle in.

"How do you know them?" Stella asks. She's not surprised. Elizabeth seems to know everybody worth knowing. She's good at networking, something Stella has never excelled at. And because she's bad at it, she has never thought it important. Elizabeth is slowly convincing her otherwise.

"Well, we're neighbors now," Elizabeth says. "But Larry used to work with my ex at the same law firm about fifteen years ago."

The condo is bigger and nicer, though not wildly different. There are the same fixtures, same cabinets, same wood floor. There's a small third bedroom and a more spacious guest bathroom. But the kitchen is much larger, boasting an island as well as a breakfast nook.

They walk around in silence until they're back at the front door. "Can we even afford this?" Stella asks.

Elizabeth tilts her head. "Maybe. I think so. The condo is worth more now than when I bought it. You have some money saved, thanks to Addie and your new job. We could do it."

They head back downstairs.

"Is the extra space worth the hassle of moving?"

Elizabeth shrugs. "We have four kids between us. It would make holidays easier."

"We've always talked about an actual house," Stella points out.

"That's true," Elizabeth agrees. "I'm not saying pack your things again. I just wanted to show you an option."

"Maybe we should think about it."

Elizabeth nods. "I agree. Let's sleep on it."

But then Elizabeth starts sending her other listings. A four-bedroom house with a pool in Sherman Oaks. A three-bedroom townhouse in Culver City. A house in Stella's neighborhood with an extra bedroom and a separate in-law unit in the back. Every listing makes Stella more anxious. The idea of a dream house is no longer something comforting; it's now something that looms.

She doesn't see Dr. Barrett regularly anymore but knows she can make an appointment any time she feels like she needs a check in. So she makes an appointment and brings her up to date on her life—Addie living on her own in the house and Stella living with Elizabeth.

"I'm happy," Stella says. "I don't feel like I'm going back to a dark place, but the idea of moving makes me feel… I can't figure out exactly what I'm scared of."

"It's a lot of change for anyone," Dr. Barrett agrees.

Her advice is the same. To communicate with Elizabeth about her feelings. To let Elizabeth know that she's afraid.

She brings it up that evening.

Elizabeth is sitting up against the headboard with a case file on her lap. She closes it to talk to Stella, looking at her over the top of her glasses. "I thought you might feel better if we started living fresh in a new place together instead of the condo belonging to me and you just live here," she explains.

"Maybe someday," Stella says. "But I don't think I'm ready yet."

"Okay. Let's give it a year, see how things are going." Elizabeth leans over to kiss her. "After all, a lot can change in a year."

Her smile makes Stella want to laugh and cry at the same time. Instead, she pulls the case file off Elizabeth's lap and crawls on top of her.

Elizabeth insists that Stella come up to her office, say hello to everyone in the squad room. It's the dinner hour, so most people are off the floor, but Maria's clearing off the whiteboard they use to track their current cases and Lieutenant Esposito is still at his desk, squinting at something in the light of his desk lamp.

She rings the buzzer to be let in. Esposito turns and grins when he sees her, then hurries over to open the door.

"You're a sight for sore eyes, ADA Carter."

"I don't work for the district attorney anymore, Lieutenant," she says and hugs him. He's shorter than she remembers, and she feels like he's lost weight too. "It's good to see you."

"You don't have to be a stranger, you know."

"Oh, well," she says, tucking her hair behind her ear, "it's always strange to—I don't know. I don't want to make anyone feel weird."

"I don't think anyone here feels *weird*," Esposito says.

Elizabeth emerges from her office, slipping into her blazer. The emerald necklace Stella bought her for Christmas hangs at the base of her throat.

"Thank you for picking me up," she says graciously, even though she demanded it. And she leans in and gives Stella a peck on the lips.

It's not a secret that Stella moved in with Elizabeth, but Elizabeth never talks about her personal life, never involves her staff in things that don't concern them. It's a big step for her to acknowledge openly that Stella is her partner, even if only in front of Maria Castillo and Tony Esposito, who surely already knew.

"Good to see you, Carter," Esposito says as they leave. She could swear his eyes twinkle, but it might just be a trick of the light.

At mass on Sunday, the priest announces the passing of Dorothy Northcott, and Stella feels empty and bereft. Elizabeth asks if Stella had ever even met Dot Northcott.

"I did!" Stella says. "Once. It was the first time I came to church with you. I met her while you were taking communion. She knew before we did that we were more than just friends."

Elizabeth looks baffled. "She did?"

"I want to go to her service."

"Okay," Elizabeth says.

She really didn't know the woman, but anyone who made Stella feel something other than sadness at that time in her life deserves to be paid a final respect.

Stella realizes she may not be entirely rational when it comes to thinking about death. It seems like the moment she finishes grieving the passing of someone she loves—her mama, her daddy, her husband—someone else is right behind them. And someday Elizabeth will die.

Isn't that what really scares her?

Elizabeth is past sixty, and as beautiful as she is, Stella can already see time marching across in her gray roots, in her failing eyesight, in the crepey skin of her inner arm. No amount of Addie's fancy serums can stop time.

Plus, Elizabeth is still out in the field, still dealing with murderers and other criminals. How many times did someone take a swing or a shot at Stella for prosecuting their case? Or show up at her house armed and angry?

Now she understands Ron's constant fretting about the dangers of her job better than she ever did when he was alive. She understands that he really loved her, even though they never were a perfect match. As tempting as it is to harp on Elizabeth to retire, to offload the most dangerous stuff to her team, to stay home every once in a while, she doesn't because she knows how important the job is to Elizabeth.

On the day of Dorothy's service, Elizabeth zips up the back of Stella's black dress, runs her hand down her spine. Lifts her hair and kisses the nape of her neck.

There's more to life than death. There's Addie, showing up at just the right time to pull her up and out of the pit that Stella was sinking into. There's Mallory and their new venture together. If Stella glanced over her shoulder, she'd see grief, depression, and loss. But when she looks forward, there's Elizabeth. The bees under Stella's skin, her bones, and her heart start to buzz and hum. She's alive now and actually living.

Maybe that feeling was simply hope, and it was fluttering inside her all along.

OTHER BOOKS FROM YLVA PUBLISHING

www.ylva-publishing.com

COMING HOME

(*The Calgary Chronicles – Book 1*)

Lois Claorec Hart

ISBN: 978-3-95533-064-4
Length: 371 pages (104,000 words)

Rob, a charismatic ex-fighter pilot severely disabled with MS, has been steadfastly cared for by his wife, Jan, for many years. Quite by accident one day, Terry, a young writer/postal carrier, enters their lives and turns it upside down.

A triangle with a twist, *Coming Home* is the story of three good people caught up in an impossible situation.

HOOKED ON YOU

Jenn Matthews

ISBN: 978-3-96324-133-8
Length: 281 pages (98,000 words)

Anna has it all – great kids, boyfriend, good teaching job. Except she's so bored. Perhaps a new hobby's in order? Something…crafty?

Divorced mother and veteran Ollie has been through the wars. To relax, she runs a quirky crochet class in her English craft shop. Enter one attractive, feisty new student. A shame she's straight.

A quirky lesbian romance about love never being quite where you expect.

BARRING COMPLICATIONS

(*The Love and Law Series – Book 1*)

Blythe Rippon

ISBN: 978-3-95533-191-7
Length: 374 pages (77,000 words)

When a gay marriage case arrives at the US Supreme Court, two women find themselves at the center of the fight for marriage equality. Closeted Justice Victoria Willoughby must sway a conservative colleague, and attorney Genevieve Fornier must craft compelling arguments to win five votes. Complicating matters, despite their shared history, the law forbids the two from talking to each other.

MAJOR SURGERY

Lola Keeley

ISBN: 978-3-96324-145-1
Length: 198 pages (69,000 words)

Surgeon and department head Veronica has life perfectly ordered… until the arrival of a new Head of Trauma. Cassie is a brash ex-army surgeon, all action and sharp edges, not interested in rules or playing nice with icy Veronica. However when they're forced to work together to uncover a scandal, things get a little heated in surprising ways.

A lesbian romance about cutting to the heart of matters.

ABOUT EMILY WATERS

Emily Waters is a Children's Librarian who loves reading picture books and middle grade fiction and doing storytime for little ones. A citizen of the internet, Emily is a fan of all things fandom and pop culture. Her other interests include reading, binge watching old television shows, drinking coffee, and saying "Gasp! A dog!" anytime she sees a dog.

Emily currently resides in Northern California with her family.

CONNECT WITH EMILY

Website:www.emilyraywaters.com

Facebook: www.facebook.com/emilyraywaters

Twitter: twitter.com/emilyraywaters

E-Mail: emilyraywaters@gmail.com

Honey in the Marrow

ISBN: 978-3-96324-724-8

Available in e-book and paperback formats.

Published by Ylva Publishing, legal entity of Ylva Verlag, e.Kfr.

Ylva Verlag, e.Kfr.
Owner: Astrid Ohletz
Am Kirschgarten 2
65830 Kriftel
Germany

www.ylva-publishing.com

First edition: 2022

This is a work of fiction. Names, characters, places, and incidents either are a product of the author's imagination or are used fictitiously, and any resemblance to locales, events, business establishments, or actual persons—living or dead—is entirely coincidental.

Credits
Edited by Alissa McGowan and Julie Klein
Cover Design by Maria Klokow
Print Layout by Streetlight Graphics

www.ingramcontent.com/pod-product-compliance
Ingram Content Group UK Ltd.
Pitfield, Milton Keynes, MK11 3LW, UK
UKHW041636190726
13854UKWH00006B/2527

9 783963 247248